FORSAKEN SOULS

A Bailey Flynn FBI Mystery Thriller,
Book Six

Melinda Woodhall

Melinda Woodhall

Melinda Woodhall
Visit my website at www.melindawoodhall.com
Printed in the United States of America
First Printing: March 2025
Creative Magnolia

CHAPTER ONE

A strong gust of wind ruffled Lorraine Holbrook's dark hair as she dug a set of keys out of her enormous handbag and unlocked the door to the coffee shop. Glancing up at the angry clouds gathering overhead, she wondered if the tropical storm that was churning toward Miami would strengthen into a hurricane.

Like I don't have enough to worry about already with–

Before the gloomy voice in her head could finish the thought, a cheerful voice called out behind her.

Lorraine turned to see Morgan Tate hurrying down Salacia Street toward her. The new barista was holding a Holbrook Coffee Company cap to her head with one hand to stop it from flying away. She lifted the other hand as she broke into a jog.

"Wait for me!"

Moving gracefully despite the sturdy black work shoes and oversized green apron she wore, Morgan slipped into the shop behind Lorainne, bringing a gust of warm air with her.

"I almost got blown away out there," the young woman said as she straightened her black-framed glasses and smoothed down her hair, which had started to come free from the thick braid that fell over a slim shoulder.

"Hopefully, this is the worst of it," Lorraine said as she locked the door behind the barista and made sure the CLOSED sign was still turned outward. "The storm isn't expected to hit Miami, so we should be in the clear."

She turned on the lights and looked around the cozy room, half-expecting to see her mother standing behind the counter or her father restocking the shelves.

A sharp pang of regret knifed through her as she hurried across the silent, empty room, willing herself to focus on the task at hand. It was almost time to open the shop. She didn't have time to feel sorry for herself.

I can't think of Mom and Dad now. I can't think about what they'd say if they were alive to see what I've done.

Lorraine felt sick to her stomach at the thought.

Her hard-working, law-abiding parents had spent decades of their lives building up the Holbrook Coffee Company. She was almost relieved they were both dead.

At least now they'll never have to find out what I let happen to the business they loved. They can rest in peace.

Circling behind the counter, she turned on the espresso machine and grinder before brewing a batch of fresh coffee.

As she worked, Morgan Tate readied the barista station for the busy morning ahead, making sure it was fully stocked with the necessary milk, syrups, and coffee beans.

They both jumped when they heard the loud, high-pitched buzz coming from the call button by the back door.

Lorraine hurried into the storeroom, opened the door leading out to the alley behind the shop, and collected the fresh pastries that were delivered each morning by the local bakery service.

Carrying the brimming box to the front of the shop, she handed it to Morgan, who inhaled the sweet aroma with obvious relish before turning to expertly sort and arrange the pastries behind the display window as Lorraine watched the younger woman with approval.

The new barista had only been working at the shop for a few weeks but she had already proven herself to be a quick learner who was up for any task.

Best of all, she always maintained a positive attitude, even with the most difficult customers.

No amount of grumbling, complaining, or stony silence from the customers seemed to bother Morgan.

In fact, it seemed to Lorraine as if the younger woman didn't notice when someone was being rude.

Or perhaps she just chooses to ignore it. Maybe I should try that.

Feeling a gentle vibration against her hip, Lorraine dug her phone out of her pocket. As she squinted down at the notification, her mouth tightened into a hard line.

A new DM from SirGrendel88 was waiting in her inbox.

She was tempted to simply delete the latest message from the internet troll without reading it, but her finger moved as if it had a will of its own and tapped on the screen.

The message opened to display a single sentence.

Are you ready to die?

Dread settled over her as she stared down at the words.

Before she could delete the hateful message, a knuckle rapped on the front door, making her jump and almost drop the phone. She suppressed a grimace when she saw the muscular man in mirrored sunglasses standing outside.

Ignoring the CLOSED sign, she unlocked the door and stepped back to allow Claude Kessler to enter the shop.

As usual, the investor appeared to be jumpy and impatient. His dark eyes scanned the room, stopping on Morgan, who was refilling the napkin dispenser next to the cash register.

He gave an unhappy nod in the barista's direction.

"I thought you'd be alone," he said in a voice so low only Lorraine could hear him. "And the courier should be here shortly. Is the package ready to go?"

"It's in the back," she said stiffly, motioning toward the hallway that led to the storeroom.

Sucking in a deep breath, she called across the shop, trying her best to sound normal, even though she wasn't sure she knew what normal was anymore.

"Morgan, you can go ahead and open up as usual. I'll be in the back if you need me."

She didn't wait for the barista's response as she turned to follow Kessler down the short hallway, her resentful eyes studying his dark, wavy hair before dropping to his broad shoulders, which strained against the thin white linen of his expertly tailored shirt.

She knew other women might find the man attractive but she knew too much about him to fall for his artificial charm.

Now that she knew Tombstone Imports wasn't a legitimate company and that Kessler was part of a dangerous criminal enterprise, she was repulsed by his nice guy routine.

She just wished it hadn't taken her so long to figure out his true intentions.

But when he'd first walked through the shop's door, Lorraine had been facing imminent bankruptcy, despite her best effort to keep the Holbrook Coffee Company going after both her parents had died within months of each other.

And Kessler had arrived like a blessing sent out of the blue. Like a slick-talking guardian angel sent to rescue her from the humiliation of bankruptcy and ruin.

He had presented himself as an angel investor, assuring her that he could help her save the struggling coffee shop, luring her with the offer to keep the business afloat and save her parents' legacy.

Lorraine had instantly taken the bait, falling for his shameless scheme hook, line, and sinker.

Her cheeks burned with embarrassment.

What an idiot I was to think that a man like Claude Kessler could be a gift from heaven instead of a demon straight out of hell.

She had failed to see who and what he really was and once the initial investment from Tombstone Imports had been deposited into the shop's bank account, it had been too late.

Kessler had started making strange demands, and Lorraine had naïvely complied, assuring herself that he was a successful businessman and that he must know how to run the company better than she did.

After arranging for the coffee shop to switch to a new supplier who shipped coffee to the store directly from Colombia, Kessler started running large cash transactions through the till and opened several new bank accounts, which he insisted on managing himself.

It was only after she'd caught a glimpse inside a bag she

hadn't been supposed to see that Lorraine allowed herself to acknowledge what was really going on.

But by then, the damage had been done.

Her signature was already on all the deposit slips and order forms and Kessler's dirty money was already being laundered in an account under her name.

And even if she hadn't been scared of getting arrested for drug trafficking and money laundering, Lorraine would have been terrified of the men working with Kessler.

He called the men couriers, but Lorraine thought they looked more like predators. They had hard faces and angry eyes, and they showed up in the alley behind the store at all hours, carrying away heavy bags containing something much more addictive than coffee.

It hadn't been hard for Kessler to convince her that cooperating with the organization he represented was her only option.

"It's not up to me," he'd said more than once in response to her repeated requests to end their arrangement. "But I can assure you that my boss would never allow it. He's not the type of man who takes no for an answer. It's safer for you to keep things as they are."

So she had capitulated, partially out of fear and partially out of the lingering hope she could save the business.

But now the threat of bankruptcy seemed like the least of her worries compared to the very real possibility that she could spend years in prison serving out a sentence for a drug trafficking conviction.

It was time to draw the line, even if it meant she'd have to face the wrath of Kessler's boss.

"I can't do this anymore," Lorraine said as soon as she and Kessler were in the back room alone.

She motioned to the big burlap bags piled along the wall, each one weighing over a hundred pounds.

They were supposed to be filled with fresh Arabica coffee beans but Lorraine knew that select bags contained a much more valuable product. One that was worth millions of dollars on the street.

"I know what you're doing and I'm scared I'm going to get in trouble," she said. "It has to stop."

"Like I told you before, my boss won't like to hear that," Kessler said, turning to face her, his dark eyes unreadable. "He may do something we'll all regret. Why don't we just-"

His words were cut short by a sudden pounding on the back door.

"That'll be the courier," he said, glancing up at the clock on the wall. "He's early."

Striding past Lorraine before she could protest that they were in the middle of a conversation, he threw open the door.

A man in a gray hoodie stood outside.

"Come in," Kessler invited as if welcoming the man into his own home. "You're early today."

As the courier stepped into the storeroom, Lorraine realized that she'd seen the man before.

He was the same angry-looking man who had picked up a delivery earlier in the week.

"The package is over there," Kessler said.

Turning toward a heavy, stainless steel worktop freezer,

he pointed to the big burlap bag lying on top.

The courier frowned and stuck a hand into the pocket of his hoodie, making no effort to move toward the bag.

"We have a problem," he said. "Mr. Stone's worried."

Kessler's face instantly clouded over.

"What are you talking about? Worried about what?" he demanded. "And why are *you* telling me this if Stone is the one who's worried?"

"Because he thinks you're playing him," the courier said, taking a menacing step closer. "He thinks you're working with the feds to try and trap him."

The statement earned an incredulous snort from Kessler.

"That's crazy. Why the hell would Stone think that?"

"Because I told him you were."

A flash of silver caught Lorraine's eye as the courier pulled his hand from his pocket, producing a gun with a stainless steel finish that gleamed under the LED lights overhead.

Jumping back with a startled scream, she watched in horror as Claude Kessler bolted for the open door to the alley.

A gunshot rang out before he made it through.

Lorraine screamed again as Kessler was slammed against the wall by the force of the bullet in his back.

She watched as he fell heavily to the floor, staring in numb disbelief at the blood stain that was spreading over his expertly tailored white linen shirt.

"You...you shot him," she stammered, unable to tear her eyes away from the man dying at her feet. "We...we need to call an...an ambulance. He needs help."

But the courier wasn't listening to her.

He was standing motionless with his head cocked to one side as if he was trying to hear something inside the shop.

Just then Lorraine heard light footsteps coming down the hall. And was that the sound of a low, urgent voice?

Before she could open her mouth and call for help, the courier was behind her, one arm wrapped around her throat and the other arm holding the gun to her head.

"Don't move or I'll blow your head off."

Sucking in a deep breath, Lorraine tried to keep still as the door swung open and Morgan Tate appeared in the hallway.

The barista's cap and glasses were gone and her green eyes were alert and clear. She held a big black gun in her hand.

"FBI, put your weapon down!" the young woman yelled as she held out the gun.

The courier responded with a nasty laugh as he gripped Lorraine to him, using her as a shield.

"Oh, I don't think so," he snarled. "I saw through your disguise right away, *Agent Flynn*."

"Agent Flynn?" Lorraine gasped out.

Tightening his hold on her neck, the courier began to slowly inch toward the back door, pulling her with him.

"Didn't she tell you?" he asked, sounding almost amused. "She's not a barista and her name's not Morgan Tate. She's Special Agent Bailey Flynn and she's with the FBI."

His voice hardened.

"She and Kessler have been playing you for a fool all this time. They've been trying to trap all of us into incriminating ourselves and Mr. Stone."

Lorraine tried to make sense of what he was saying.

She had heard about Mr. Stone.

Kessler had mentioned him several times before, making it clear that Stone was the man behind Tombstone Imports. He was the one calling the shots and giving orders to the thugs who worked for the shady organization.

Stone was the boss she'd been too scared to cross.

If Kessler was dead, Stone must have ordered the hit.

Locking eyes with the woman she now knew was an undercover agent, Lorraine silently pleaded with her.

Please don't shoot. Please don't shoot. I don't want to die.

Pointing the gun straight ahead, Bailey Flynn flicked her eyes back to the courier and took another step into the room.

"Drop your weapon and back away," she said. "We can talk about this. No one else has to get hurt."

"That's where you're wrong, Agent Flynn," the courier said. "Someone else does have to get hurt. You see, Mr. Stone wasn't happy to find out you were running an undercover operation on him. When I told him you'd managed to turn Kessler and Lorraine, he put out a hit on both of them."

He jammed the gun into Lorraine's head as if to emphasize his words, causing her to shift, momentarily revealing his face to the agent, whose eyes widened with recognition.

"You?" she gasped. "But, why would you-"

"Stone ordered it," he snapped. "That's why I killed Kessler. And why I have to kill Lorraine."

"But Lorraine isn't working for the FBI," Bailey protested, taking another step closer. "And Kessler wasn't working for us either. But I think you knew that."

Her eyes narrowed.

"I think you wanted to get Kessler out of the way for some reason. What I can't figure out is why *you* would be working with Stone in the first place."

She was now standing only a few feet away.

"Why are you doing this?" she asked.

"I have my reasons," he said, his voice suddenly filling with suppressed rage. "In fact, I've been dying to get this chance ever since the day you killed my old partner Ronin Godfrey at Summerset Park."

Shock filled Bailey's face, followed by confusion.

"You're upset I shot Ronin Godfrey?" she asked as sirens sounded in the distance. "But why would–"

Her question was cut short by a deafening blast.

The agent slammed back into the stainless steel freezer behind her, prompting Lorraine to let out a hoarse scream.

As blood splattered across the heavy metal appliance, she lifted her right foot and kicked back with all her might.

Her shoe connected with the courier's knee, causing him to grunt in pain and drop his arm, giving her a chance to wrench free and stagger toward the back door.

Jumping over Kessler's dead body, she managed to stay on her feet as she burst into the back alley and started to run toward the sound of the sirens, which were getting closer with every step.

She didn't realize she'd been shot until her cheek hit the pavement with a jarring crash.

Pain spiked through her chest as she tried to move, so she remained perfectly still, listening as footsteps approached and a shadow fell over her.

The courier crouched beside her, holding the gun where she could see it.

"You never answered my DM," he whispered in her ear. "Tell me now...*are you ready to die?*"

Lorraine gasped in sudden understanding.

"You're *SirGrendel88*? You're the troll?"

"That's right," he said, producing a malevolent smile. "I'm Grendel. And I came for you just as I promised."

Aiming the gun at her forehead, he tightened his finger on the trigger. Lorainne squeezed her eyes shut just as the world exploded into darkness.

CHAPTER TWO

Bailey Flynn drifted on a calm sea of darkness, moving ever closer to the single beam of light that glowed on the horizon, beckoning to her with a tantalizing promise of peace and contentment. As she floated toward the light, a shadow fell over her. A leering man in a dirty white t-shirt and jeans loomed above her. She struggled to move, to sit up, but her arms and head were too heavy to lift.

"Is that you, Godfrey?"

The name sent a shiver through Bailey. She tried to look around but couldn't move her head.

"Where's Dolores? What did you do to her?"

Forcing her hand to move, Bailey instinctively reached for her Glock. She frowned as Ronin Godfrey faded away and her fingers settled over cold metal.

"She moved!" an excited voice called out from somewhere above her. "She just grabbed the bedrail! And she frowned!"

Bailey slowly opened her eyes, blinking against the bright sunlight streaming in from the window across the room.

She was lying in a hospital bed. That much she was sure of. And Ronin Godfrey wasn't in the room with her.

It was just another bad dream.

As the quick *thud, thud, thud* of her heartbeat started to slow, Bailey closed her eyes again and exhaled in relief.

She'd somehow managed to pull herself out of her recurring nightmare about Ronin Godfrey, the predator she'd killed three years earlier, and was back in the waking world.

I'm going to be okay.

The reassuring thought was followed by another, less comforting observation.

But I am in the hospital...so maybe I'm not okay after all.

A soft hand fell on her arm.

"Bailey? Can you hear me?"

Turning her head toward the familiar voice, Bailey opened her eyes to see her mother's anxious face.

Jackie Flynn stood beside the hospital bed, staring down at Bailey with worried green eyes.

"Oh, thank God, you're awake," she said, grabbing Bailey's hand and squeezing it tightly. "You've put me and your father through hell and back these last ten days."

"I'm sorry," Bailey croaked softly, although she wasn't sure what she had done to cause her mother's distress.

She wasn't even sure where she was.

"Ten days?" she asked, trying to make sense of it all. "Where am I? What's happened?"

Jackie sighed as she ran a hand through her short, silver hair and straightened her suit jacket. Considering her mother's claims that she'd been through hell, Bailey thought she looked surprisingly pulled together.

She couldn't say the same for her sister, who was suddenly standing at her bedside holding a small cup of water as she nudged Jackie out of the way.

"You're in the Summerset County Medical Center," Cate Flynn said, holding the cup to Bailey's dry lips. "You've been in an induced coma for ten days."

Her auburn hair hung limply around her pale face and her green eyes looked puffy and tired. The blue blouse she was wearing, which was one of her favorites, was wrinkled and missing a button.

"You were badly hurt," Cate said. "Do you remember what happened?"

Bailey stared up at her sister, trying hard to concentrate.

She remembered getting ready for work in the apartment she'd rented as Morgan Tate. A storm had been brewing that morning and she'd gone back for her umbrella so she had been running late.

After that, all she could remember was the dream about Ronin Godfrey. And then she had woken up in the hospital.

"I can't remember," Bailey finally admitted, giving a slight shake of her head, which was starting to ache.

"There was an incident at a coffee shop just south of Miami Beach," Cate said, speaking slowly. "Several people were shot at the Holbrook Coffee Company on Salacia Street."

She helped Bailey take another sip of water.

"You were there," she said. "You were shot in the chest, but you were wearing a bullet proof vest under your clothes at the time. The vest deflected the bullet but the force of it slammed you backward."

Staring up at her sister in surprise, Bailey tried to grasp what she was being told as Cate continued.

"You hit your head on the corner of a freezer pretty hard," she explained. "The doctors said it was hard enough to cause a traumatic brain injury. When you developed a subdural hematoma, they decided to put you in an induced coma."

"And I've been out for ten days?" Bailey asked.

She looked toward the window and saw that the sky outside was a calm blue. The tropical storm that had been threatening the city must have moved on.

"That's right," Cate said. "I've stayed with you practically the whole time. And Mom and Dad have been–"

"Oh, I'd better go get your father and tell him you're awake!" Jackie suddenly said with a start. "I talked him into going home and getting some sleep, but he'll want to be here. The poor man has been worried sick."

Once she'd disappeared into the hall, Bailey looked up at her sister with a worried frown.

"What about Ludwig?' she asked. "Is he okay?"

Her heart squeezed in her chest at the thought of the German shepherd. She'd had to leave the search and rescue dog with his former handler and retired FBI agent, Sid Morley, before going deep undercover.

"Ludwig's with Morley," Cate assured her. "He's safe."

As Bailey started to ask about Dalton, the door swung open and a slim Black woman in a white lab coat came into the room. Picking up the clipboard hanging on the end of the bed, she smiled at Bailey.

"I was surprised to hear you were already awake," she said, crossing to the bed. "It usually takes longer than this once we stop the medication."

Her smile widened.

"I'm Dr. Pendergrast, by the way. I've been guiding your medical care since you arrived. It's good to finally meet you. And I imagine you have a few questions for me."

Bailey nodded and tried to clear her throat.

"Am I going to be alright?" she asked. "I mean, if I was in a coma for ten days, that must mean I was in bad shape. What's my prognosis? Will there be permanent damage?"

"You suffered what we call a traumatic brain injury, or a TBI, which can cause the brain to swell," the doctor said. "The swelling can restrict the flow of blood and oxygen, which in some cases can lead to damage of the brain tissue."

She smiled reassuringly.

"In your case, the coma helped alleviate the swelling. It gave your brain the necessary time to rest."

Looking down at the clipboard, she flipped through several pages and nodded with satisfaction.

"It seems your vital signs are doing well," she said. "Now, let me just check on your wound and see how that's healing."

As she spoke, she bent over to examine Bailey's dark blonde hair, focusing her attention on the back of her scalp where the skin around a reddish laceration had been stapled together in a neat line."

"The cut is healing nicely," she said. "Luckily, with surgical staples, we didn't need to shave the area around the wound. And they can be removed before you leave."

Bailey lifted her hand and gently felt the back of her head, which was starting to throb.

"When exactly can I leave?" she asked.

Dr. Pendergrast laughed.

"If you're eager to leave, that's a good sign," she said. "But first we'll need to perform a neurological exam. That will allow us to assess motor and sensory functions and-"

"What about memory loss?" Bailey interjected, suddenly worried. "If I can't remember getting hurt, does that mean I have brain damage?"

The doctor hesitated before answering.

"I think the term *brain damage* may be too strong. If you're struggling to recall the events surrounding your accident, it's likely due to retrograde post-traumatic amnesia.

"This kind of memory loss normally diminishes over time. In many cases, the memories gradually return."

Once Dr. Pendergrast had finished the exam and left the room, Cate cleared her throat.

"What's the last thing you remember?" she asked. "And why were you at the Holbrook Coffee Company on Salacia Street anyway?"

Bailey wasn't sure how to answer. She couldn't tell her sister about her undercover assignment in Miami Beach.

Not until she figured out what had happened.

And not until she found out if the undercover operation had been compromised or if it was still ongoing.

As if reading her mind, Cate waved away the question.

"We can talk about all that later," she said. "I'll just go and see where Dad is. Oh, and you have a visitor who's impatient to see you. I'll let him know you're awake."

As Cate slipped out of the room, Bailey hoped her sister had been referring to Dalton West.

She hadn't seen the private investigator since she'd gone deep undercover in early September as part of Operation Tombstone, which had been tasked with identifying the man who'd taken control of Chuck Ashworth's trafficking cartel.

The cartel boss had operated with near impunity for decades under the name Mr. Tumba, but he was dead now.

He had been taken out by a traitor within his own organization. A traitor who had somehow managed to forge an alliance with Emil Lazar, a corrupt agent within the FBI who had died while trying to carry out their plan.

The traitor had destroyed the Tumba Cartel from the inside out, killing its leader, stealing its assets, and recruiting its former members into a new organization that now operated under the name Tombstone Imports.

Convinced that billionaire Jordan Stone was the traitorous man running the cartel, Bailey had been forced to make a difficult decision.

She knew from personal experience how dangerous Stone was. She couldn't just leave South Florida while he was still free to terrorize her hometown.

So she'd made the decision to accept an assignment to the undercover operation led by Special Agent Will Griffin instead of going back to Washington D.C. to rejoin the special crimes task force to which she'd previously been assigned.

Once the decision had been made, Bailey had been eager to expose Jordan Stone and his criminal operation, which had been smuggling drugs into the country using legitimate coffee shipments to hide their activities.

And when an informant told them that the Holbrook

Coffee Company was being used as a delivery location and money laundering operation for Tombstone Imports, Bailey had volunteered to go in deep undercover as a barista to see what she could find out.

It hadn't taken long for her to notice Claude Kessler's frequent presence in the coffee shop or to ascertain that Lorraine Holbrook was in business with the trafficking gang.

But she'd needed evidence linking Kessler to Jordan Stone.

And the last memory she had was of her walking down Salacia Street toward the coffee shop thinking of the crypto billionaire.

Sometime after that, a gun had been fired at her chest.

Luckily for her, as the leader of the undercover operation, Will Griffin had demanded she wear a bullet-proof vest under her uniform. He had seen the armed couriers who visited the coffee shop on a regular basis and hadn't wanted to take any unnecessary chances.

The shop uniform's collared polo shirt and bulky apron had concealed the slim-fitting vest, and Bailey had taken to carrying her Glock in a hidden compartment in the bottom of a weathered backpack, although she'd been sure that no one suspected her of being anything more than a carefree barista. Sure that her cover was totally secure.

So, who figured it out? Who shot me?

The questions circled her aching head as she tried to think.

Had it been Lorraine or Kessler?

Or maybe Jordan Stone himself?

Had she somehow revealed herself? Or had one of them been tipped off about the operation?

The answers still hadn't revealed themselves by the time the door swung open and Cate reappeared.

Bailey's heart jumped as she caught a glimpse of fair hair in the doorway behind her sister, and then it fell back into place when she realized her visitor wasn't Dalton West.

"Look who's here to see you, Bailey," Cate said with forced cheerfulness. "It's Griff."

Stepping aside to reveal a tall, handsome man with fair hair and blue eyes, her sister allowed Special Agent Will Griffin to slip past her into the room.

"I'll just give you a few minutes to talk," Cate said, letting the door swing closed, leaving them alone.

An awkward silence fell over the room as Griff sank into a chair beside Bailey's hospital bed.

"I'm really glad you're alright," he said. "I've been calling and checking on you and...well, I'm relieved."

His voice held none of the cocky confidence she was used to hearing from him.

"How much do you remember?"

"Nothing about the shooting in the store," she admitted. "Dr. Pendergrast told me I probably have something called retrograde post-traumatic amnesia."

Griff lifted an eyebrow.

"That doesn't sound good."

"She said it's actually pretty common for people who have a traumatic brain injury. You lose your memories of the events right before the injury but over time they gradually return. Of course, it's frustrating not to know who shot me."

Trying to ignore the growing pain in her head, she turned

her eyes to him with interest.

"I need you to tell me everything you know about the shooting," she said. "What happened at the coffee shop?"

Griff shifted uncomfortably in the chair as if he'd known the question was coming and had been dreading it.

"Well, it all happened so fast, at least from my perspective. One minute I was in my car driving to work and the next you were calling me saying you heard a gunshot and needed urgent backup."

His face tightened at the memory.

"I immediately called for back-up, and I sped down to Miami Beach as fast as I could. But by the time I got there, they'd already found you in the back room, unconscious."

He swallowed hard.

"You'd hit your head against one of those heavy, stainless steel freezers. There was blood on the floor and they recovered a spent 9mm bullet on the ground, so at first they thought you'd been shot in the head.

"Then they realized the bullet hit you in the chest and that you were wearing a vest. The vest stopped the bullet but the force knocked you down. You hit your head pretty hard.

"We found Claude Kessler on the floor beside you and Lorraine Holbrook in the alley. They'd both been shot dead."

Wincing at the thought of the shop owner lying dead on the dirty asphalt, Bailey wondered why Lorraine had been involved with Kessler and Tombstone Imports in the first place. Perhaps the woman had been duped.

Whatever her reason, the decision to work with the cartel had led to her violent death.

"It looks as if the same gun was used on all three victims, so we're thinking there was a single shooter," Griff continued. "And the evidence we heard backs up that theory."

Bailey frowned as she rubbed her head.

"Evidence you *heard*? What evidence is that?"

The question prompted an involuntary grimace from Griff.

"The agents who responded to the scene of the shooting took your phone into evidence and checked it before returning it to your family," he said. "It turns out you somehow managed to record a conversation between you and the shooter. When you're feeling better, I'll play it for you."

Forgetting about her headache, Bailey reached out and grabbed Griff's arm.

"Play it for me now," she said. "I need to hear it."

With a reluctant sigh, Griff reached into his pocket and pulled out his phone. He tapped several times on the little screen and then held it out between them.

Instantly, Bailey heard footsteps and then her own urgent whisper on the recording.

"I just heard a scream and a gunshot in the storeroom. I'm heading toward the back and I need urgent backup."

There were more footsteps followed by a loud gasp that sounded like Lorraine.

Then Bailey heard her own voice yelling out.

"FBI, put your weapon down!"

A man's deep, gravelly voice responded.

"Oh, I don't think so. I saw through your disguise right away, Agent Flynn."

As the man on the recording gritted out her name, Bailey glanced up at Griff with wide green eyes. He motioned for her to keep listening.

"Agent Flynn?"

Hearing the confusion in Lorainne's voice, Bailey remained silent, wanting to hear what the shooter said next.

"Didn't she tell you? She's not a barista and her name's not Morgan Tate. She's Special Agent Bailey Flynn and she's with the FBI. She and Kessler have been playing you for a fool all this time. They've been trying to trap all of us into incriminating ourselves and Mr. Stone."

The man's bitter words confirmed what Bailey had feared. The operation had been compromised. But how?

She tensed as she heard her own voice again.

"Drop your weapon and back away. We can talk about this. No one else has to get hurt."

The man was quick to reply.

"That's where you're wrong, Agent Flynn. Someone else does have to get hurt. You see, Mr. Stone wasn't happy to find out you were running an undercover operation on him. When I told him you'd managed to turn Kessler and Lorraine, he put out a hit on both of them."

Bailey heard herself gasp.

"You? But, why would you-"

The stunned words sounded like an accusation to Bailey. Could she have known the man?

Listening more closely, she strained to recognize his voice.

"Stone ordered it. That's why I killed Kessler. And why I have to kill Lorraine."

Bailey tensed as she realized what was about to happen.

"But Lorraine isn't working for the FBI. And Kessler wasn't working for us either. But I think you know that. I think you wanted to get Kessler out of the way for some reason. What I can't figure out is why you would be working with Stone in the first place. Why are you doing this?"

She sounded genuinely puzzled.

"I have my reasons."

Rage had taken over his voice.

"In fact, I've been dying to get this chance ever since the day you killed my old partner Ronin Godfrey at Summerset Park."

Bailey's eyes widened at his mention of the killer.

"You're upset I shot Godfrey?"

Her question was accompanied by the faint sound of sirens in the distance.

"But why would-"

Bailey jumped at the sound of a deafening blast from the phone, followed by a hoarse scream from Lorraine. Then a door crashed open and running footsteps could be heard.

The shooter was obviously giving chase.

Bailey winced as another gunshot sounded from further away. Voices and footsteps approached and sirens sounded.

"The shooter must have chased Lorraine outside and then heard sirens and fled instead of coming back to finish you off," Griff said. "You're lucky, I guess."

He cocked his head.

"In the recording, the shooter said he recognized you. And it sounds as if you knew him, too."

Bailey nodded.

"And he mentioned Ronin Godfrey," she murmured, her head pounding. "He called him *my old partner Godfrey* as if he had known him well. Maybe even worked with him. If only I could remember..."

Frustration made her clench her fists and a machine next to her began to beep.

Griff stared at the flashing lights in concern but Bailey ignored the machine.

"This means we've got Stone, right?" she asked, her face now creased in pain. "I mean, we just heard the shooter say that Stone ordered the hit. Surely that's enough to justify bringing him in for questioning?"

While Bailey had long suspected Jordan Stone of working with Mr. Tumba and the cartel, the recording was all the proof she needed to be sure he was now running the criminal enterprise. She knew without a doubt that Stone had been the one who put a hit out on her, as well as Kessler and Lorraine.

"We've got a warrant and we've been looking for Stone," Griff admitted. "Trouble is, we can't find him."

Bailey shook her head in disbelief.

"So, no shooter and no Stone," she said, trying to sit up. "And I can't offer any help. Not while I'm in here."

She felt her head begin to spin.

"What has the investigation turned up so far?" she asked. "Any evidence...any leads yet?"

Griff cleared his throat.

"Actually, ballistics uncovered a connection to another possible crime in the area," he said, his eyes flicking to the beeping machine. "But I'm not sure now is the time to get into that."

Before he could continue, the door opened and a nurse rushed in to look at the machine, followed by Cate, who had been waiting just outside.

"Is she okay?" Cate demanded. "What's happening?"

"We need to clear the room," the nurse said as she ushered Cate and Griff into the corridor. "You can wait outside."

CHAPTER THREE

C ate Flynn watched helplessly as the nurse closed the door behind her. She had been worried sick for the last ten days, spending most of her time sitting at her sister's bedside and pacing the hospital corridors, not knowing if Bailey would live or die.

The uncertainty and emotional stress had been unbearable, prompting Cate to end her campaign for a seat on the Summerset County judicial bench only days before the scheduled primary.

How could she attend promotional events and participate in campaigning activities while Bailey lay in a coma?

The possibility that sleazy defense attorney Tony Brunner might be elected as a county judge had suddenly seemed less of a catastrophe than it had before.

She supposed the fear of losing her sister had put everything into perspective. Although, now that Bailey was awake and alert, Cate suspected her sister may not agree.

She was sure to start asking questions soon. And she wouldn't be pleased to hear that Cate had quit the judicial race before the primary had even taken place.

Hopefully, Bailey would be mollified by the fact that

Marilyn "Mimi" Harper, the only other candidate in the race, had received enough votes to force a runoff against Brunner.

Both Cate and Bailey knew the woman well based on her long-standing friendship with their mother.

Mimi was a seasoned attorney and popular law school professor who'd grown up in Belle Harbor. She was the perfect alternative to a man like Tony Brunner, who'd made a lucrative career representing wealthy criminals.

The fact that the defense attorney associated with his disreputable clients outside of the courtroom, and perhaps even took part in some of their questionable business dealings, made him unsuitable for the bench in Cate's eyes.

"I'd better get going."

Cate spun around as Will Griffin spoke behind her.

Her eyes narrowed as she studied his handsome face, which appeared drawn and grim under his outdoorsman tan.

He'd been in her sister's room when Bailey's monitor had summoned the nurse. Had he said something to upset her?

"So, you're just going to leave?" she asked. "You don't want to go back in?"

"I need to go," he repeated, glancing at his watch. "And I've pretty much said all I came to say in any case. Tell Bailey I'll be back to check on her soon."

Something about the way he avoided making eye contact told Cate she shouldn't hold her breath.

"Okay, I'll let her know you've gone."

With a distracted nod of his head, Griff turned and made his way to the elevator at the end of the hall.

Moments after the elevator doors closed behind him, they

slid open again to reveal a solidly built man in a dark suit.

Cate summoned a wan smile as Detective Jimmy Fraser stepped off the elevator and walked toward her.

"How's she doing?" he asked in a faint Jamaican accent. "Any change since they stopped the medication?"

"You have perfect timing," Cate said. "She woke up about an hour ago. The doctor's already been in to see her. And there's a nurse in there now checking her out."

Fraser nodded with approval.

"That's great news," he said. "I'm happy to hear it. And if she's up for it, I'd like to ask her a few questions. She may be able to help with a homicide case I'm investigating."

The door to Bailey's room swung open before Cate could reply. She turned as the nurse stepped into the corridor.

"Is she alright? Can we go back in?" Cate asked.

The nurse nodded.

"But I've given her some pain medication, so she might be sleepy," she cautioned. "Try not to upset her."

As she hurried away, Cate stepped into the room.

"Are you up for another visitor?" she called out softly.

"Is it Dalton?" Bailey asked.

Her voice was hopeful.

"Sorry, but it's just me," Fraser said with a rueful grin. "I heard you were awake. I wanted to see how you're doing."

As the detective moved into the room to stand at the foot of the bed, Bailey managed to hide whatever disappointment she felt at not seeing Dalton.

"That's very nice of you," she said, raising a sarcastic eyebrow. "I didn't know you cared so much."

Fraser produced a guilty grin.

"Well, I also have a little business to conduct," he admitted. "You see, there's been an interesting development in a case I'm working."

His grin slowly slipped away.

"Actually, it's something I think you need to know."

Bailey cocked her head in interest and then winced in pain, prompting Cate to speak up in protest.

"I don't think my sister's in any condition to-"

"No, I want to hear this," Bailey interrupted. "What is it, Fraser? What do I need to know?"

Running a hand over his dark, close-cropped hair, Fraser glanced warily at Cate before he continued.

"The last thing I came here to do is upset you," he said. "But I found out yesterday that a bullet we entered in NIBIN had a hit. When I heard they were stopping the medication and that you may be coming around, I thought-"

"What does any of this have to do with Bailey?" Cate cut in, although she had a terrible feeling she already knew.

The database managed by the National Integrated Ballistic Information Network contained digital images of spent bullets and cartridge cases. It was used by law enforcement agencies across all jurisdictions to link crimes.

She could only imagine that if Fraser was at Bailey's hospital bedside, the bullet he was referring to must be linked to her sister's shooting.

Moving up to stand beside the bed, Cate took Bailey's hand, both seeking comfort and wanting to give it to her sister as she braced herself for Fraser's revelation.

"The Belle Harbor PD collected and submitted a bullet to NIBIN a few months back hoping to get a lead," Fraser explained. "The bullet was embedded in a skull discovered at the old Summerset Railroad Depot.

"The place hasn't been in use for over fifty years, but some teenagers were following the track, probably looking for a place to smoke weed, and they stumbled onto the skull."

Bailey's hand tightened around Cate's as he spoke.

"I heard about that skull," she said. "Eloise Spellman has been working with the medical examiner's office to try to figure out who it belongs to, right?"

"That's right," Fraser said. "Unfortunately, we haven't been able to identify the victim, yet. All we know at this point is that the skull belonged to a young man."

He cleared his throat.

"And thanks to the hit in NIBIN we got yesterday, we also know that markings on the bullet found in the skull matched markings on a bullet found on the floor of the Holbrook Coffee Company in Miami Beach ten days ago."

Shock filled Bailey's face.

"It appears the gun used to shoot you was also used to kill the owner of the skull at the railroad depot."

Fraser's voice was grim as he continued.

"We're conducting an expanded search of the depot later today. If we can find the gun or the rest of the remains, we may be able to identify our victim...and perhaps your shooter."

Glancing down at Bailey, Fraser lifted an eyebrow.

"So, if you're up for it, I'm hoping you'll tell me

everything you know about the perp who shot you."

"I don't remember anything that happened that morning," she admitted in a strained voice. "I can't tell you much, but if you want to sit down, I'll tell you what I know."

* * *

After leaving Bailey and Fraser alone in the hospital room to continue their conversation, Cate rode down in the elevator feeling considerably lighter.

It was as if a terrible weight had been lifted from her shoulders. She could finally leave the hospital without feeling that if she left, she might never see her sister alive again.

Walking out to the parking garage, Cate was filled with a sudden rush of gratitude and relief.

Bailey isn't going to die!

Although her sister had lost her memory of the shooting, Cate was confident she had suffered no serious or lasting brain damage, and that she would make a full recovery.

Finally, after ten excruciating days, the immediate crisis had passed. Now they could all turn their focus on finding the shooter before he could kill anyone else.

Climbing into her white Lexus, Cate checked her watch and started the engine. Her fiancé, Summerset County medical examiner Mason Knox, should be in the office now.

If he wasn't busy in the autopsy suite, she could surprise him with the good news that Bailey had woken from her coma. She could also ask him about the skull he and forensic anthropologist Eloise Spellman had been trying to identify.

When she arrived at the medical examiner's office twenty minutes later, she found Mason sitting in his office working his way through a thick stack of files on his desk.

Pleased to see that her fiancé's dark hair and handsome face weren't covered by the protective gear she usually found him wearing at the office, Cate impulsively bent over the desk to give him a lingering kiss.

"Bailey's awake," she said as soon as their lips parted. "She regained consciousness this morning."

"That's wonderful news."

Getting to his feet, Mason circled the desk.

"How is she?" he asked, taking both her hands in his.

"She's alive and alert, although she doesn't even remember what happened to her," Cate said, blinking back sudden tears. "They still need to run some neurological tests, but the doctor said that with time and rest, she should make a full recovery. She may even regain her memory."

Mason pulled her in for a hug.

"I'm really glad to hear it," he said. "How did she take the news about you ending your campaign?"

Cate's happiness dimmed at the question.

"I didn't get around to telling her yet," she admitted as she pulled back to look up into his face. "Everything just seemed to happen so fast. One minute Bailey was in a coma and the next she was looking around the hospital room, telling us that she couldn't remember anything."

"Then Agent Griffin stopped by the hospital and Detective Fraser and...well, there wasn't time to talk about the campaign once he'd told her about the bullet in the skull."

Suddenly remembering what she'd wanted to ask Mason, Cate looked up at him with a frown.

"You do know about the bullet markings, don't you?"

Mason nodded.

"Yes, Fraser called me this morning. He said ballistics had come back suggesting the bullet lodged in the skull found at the Summerset Railroad Depot was fired from the same gun used to shoot Bailey at a coffee shop in Miami Beach."

"What can you tell me about the skull?" Cate asked. "I know you and Eloise Spellman have been examining it and running tests and...well, what have you found out? Do you know who it belongs to? Or how long it was at the depot?"

She stared up at him hopefully.

"We don't know a lot, unfortunately. We believe the skull belonged to a young man. And we think it was likely dumped at the depot about ten years ago.

"Up until this point, we've treated the skull as if it's part of a ten-year-old cold case. But now that we know the gun is still in circulation, and that it was used in another shooting just ten *days* ago, I'd say the case is extremely hot."

Cate's green eyes narrowed.

"Somehow, I doubt the shooter shot our John Doe at the railroad depot and then stuck the gun in a drawer for ten years until he committed the shooting at the coffee shop," she said. "I bet it's been used since. And it could be used again if we don't find its owner."

Gesturing toward the hall, Mason lifted an eyebrow.

"Would you like to see the skull? It's in the cooler room."

Surprised by the offer, Cate hesitated and then nodded.

She followed him down the hall and through the autopsy suite to the cooler room, instinctively holding her breath as the acrid odor of formaldehyde, decay, and disinfectant surrounded her.

Passing a row of stainless-steel drawers against the wall, Mason stopped in front of a drawer near the end.

"This is where we've been storing the skull while we're working to identify the owner," he said as he pulled the drawer open.

Cate cautiously glanced inside.

The skull stared up at her with its empty eye sockets. The bone had darkened during its years in the soil as had the remaining teeth embedded in the jaw bone.

"Detective Fraser said that he was planning to search the depot for more evidence this afternoon," Cate said softly as she studied a small chip in the skull's front tooth. "I just hope he finds something to tell us who this man was and why he was killed."

CHAPTER FOUR

Detective Jimmy Fraser rubbed at the smooth skin of his jaw and sat back in the red vinyl hospital chair, unsettled by Bailey's account of the events that had taken place at the Holbrook Coffee Company the morning she'd been shot. Although she had lost all memory of the shooting itself, she managed to capture an audio recording that revealed a name Fraser had hoped never to hear again.

"You want a drink?" he asked, gesturing to the pitcher of water on the bedside table. "Because I certainly need one."

Bailey smiled and shook her head.

"No thanks. But help yourself."

Picking up the pitcher, Fraser poured water into a small Styrofoam cup, gulped it down, and then poured some more.

As he set down the cup, he studied Bailey's pale face, relieved to see a determined spark in her green eyes.

"So, you have no idea who the guy was?" he asked. "Even though you recognized him at the time?"

"That's right," Bailey said patiently. "That's what memory loss means. It means you can't remember what happened, who you saw, or what you did."

Her eyes met his and she sighed.

"I'm sorry, I know it's frustrating, but if I knew who the shooter was, I would tell you."

Fraser wasn't totally convinced.

While Bailey had admitted that she'd been at the coffee shop as part of an undercover operation, she'd also told him that she couldn't share some of the details while the operation was still ongoing.

He couldn't be sure she wasn't holding back the shooter's identity to protect the undercover agents working with her.

"So, the shooter said he knew Ronin Godfrey?" Fraser asked. "You think that's why he shot you?"

Bailey hesitated as if unsure how to answer the question.

"Well, I *was* the one who killed Godfrey," she said. "And if the shooter was Godfrey's partner as he claimed, he may have wanted revenge."

Leaning forward, Fraser cocked his head.

"What do you think he meant by *partner*? You think he was Godfrey's business partner, or maybe a romantic partner? Or did he just mean they were friends?"

"I'd say they were partners in crime if I had to guess," Bailey said. "I don't think Godfrey had many friends."

Fraser couldn't argue. From what he could remember, the child killer had often been described as an anti-social loner.

In fact, most of the people Fraser had interviewed during the follow-up investigation into his death had called Godfrey off-putting or strange.

And those had been the nice ones.

Those who'd known Godfrey since childhood claimed he'd been a bad seed. An evil psychopath from the start. They said they'd known he was dangerous long before he had abducted and killed Dolores Santos.

They claimed the system had failed the little girl, who hadn't been much older than Fraser's own daughters when she'd been abducted from the sidewalk in front of her house.

Fraser's curiosity about Godfrey's relationship with the shooter suddenly flared into anger at the possibility the man might be carrying on Godfrey's evil legacy.

Before he could share his suspicions with Bailey, he saw her stifle a yawn and noticed that her eyes were beginning to droop closed with fatigue.

I guess my theory about the shooter's motives will have to wait.

Checking his watch, Fraser got to his feet.

"I'd better get going," he said. "When I leave here, I'm going to meet Gallagher at the old railroad depot. He and Officer Boswell are bringing Brutus and Caesar to search for the remains that go along with the skull."

Bailey nodded sleepily at the mention of the Doberman pinschers who'd once belonged to Mr. Tumba, but who now worked as search and rescue dogs for the Belle Harbor PD.

"You should ask Sid Morley to join in," she said in a drowsy voice. "He can bring Amadeus and Ludwig to..."

Her voice trailed away as her eyes blinked closed.

"I'll let you rest," Fraser said, backing toward the door.

But Bailey didn't hear him.

She had already drifted off to sleep.

* * *

Fraser sped south along Memorial Parkway toward the old train depot with all four windows in his black Interceptor rolled down. Warm wind whipped through the vehicle as moody gray clouds hovered overhead.

Scrolling through his music app, Fraser selected a soft rock playlist that Linette and his daughters never let him listen to when they were with him.

He forwarded past a dozen songs before he found the one that had been stuck in his head all morning.

As the melancholy intro to *Runaway Train* by Soul Asylum flooded through the vehicle, he switched lanes, looking for the turnoff to the old depot.

He recalled from his last trip out to the site that the entrance to the abandoned train station was overgrown and hidden from the road by a scraggly forest of pine trees and saw palmettos.

When he passed the sign for All Souls Cemetery, he knew he was getting close and slowed, prepared to make the turn.

Steering the Interceptor down the rough gravel road, Fraser saw Detective Geoffrey Gallagher standing in front of a dilapidated wooden building up ahead.

His partner's large, bear-like figure overshadowed the shorter Officer Boswell, who stood beside him holding a leash in each hand. At the end of each leash was a sleek black Doberman pinscher.

The newly trained search and rescue dogs had previously been owned by Chuck Ashworth, the big boss of the Tumba Cartel, who had named them Brutus and Caesar, likely hoping the animals would prove to be ruthless warriors.

However, the twin Dobermans had turned out to be agreeable animals who seemed to enjoy participating in missing person searches with the Belle Harbor PD.

They'd been trained by retired FBI agent Sid Morley, who had immediately agreed to join in the search at the depot after Fraser had called to tell him about the skull, the matching bullets, and the connection to Bailey Flynn.

As Fraser parked the Interceptor, he saw that Morley had beaten him to the site.

The older man was making his way toward him, his prosthetic leg giving him a slightly unsteady gait as he called to a large black German shepherd.

"Amadeus! Come here, boy!"

The former agent smiled as a smaller tan and black German shepherd appeared, pulling a tall, leanly muscled man with blonde hair and a worried expression after him.

"Hold on, Ludwig!" Dalton West called out as he approached Fraser. "We're here to join the search party. Morley said you might need some help."

Fraser nodded.

"We'll take all the help we can get," he said as he looked around in dismay, noting the trash and debris strewn around the old wooden building, which had been defaced with graffiti.

A faded sign was affixed to the wall beside the front door. It appeared to have been hung decades earlier, back when there'd been talk of turning the depot into a historic site that would attract tourists and history buffs.

While the talk had soon faded away, the sign remained,

informing Fraser that Summerset Railroad Depot had opened in 1899 as a key stop on one of Florida's first cross-state railroads, which had connected Belle Harbor to Willow Bay, a small city all the way across the state on Florida's Gulf Coast.

According to the sign, coal-burning trains had once sped along the now-dilapidated tracks to deliver passengers and cargo to eight stations along the line all the way up until the 1960s, when the entire line had been discontinued.

Stepping inside the building, Fraser looked around with interest at what remained of the office where passengers had once bought tickets and sent telegrams to far-off locations.

Next to the office, he surveyed the freight room and loading dock before stepping back outside where a row of derelict train cars and boxcars sat alongside the old train tracks.

The exterior of the train cars were all badly worn, rusted, and defaced with graffiti, and he saw that the windows had all been broken out, leaving the barren ground scattered with shattered glass.

Sticking his head into one of the boxcars, he saw that the inner walls were also covered with graffiti. The entire place had been vandalized, making a search for forensic evidence difficult and even dangerous.

"Okay, I guess we'd better get started," Fraser called out. "This could take a while and the wind's picking up."

As Boswell and Morley snapped leashes onto the dogs' collars, Gallagher pointed back toward the road.

"You really must be confident if you already called in the CSI team," he said as a van came trundling toward them.

"Are you sure we're going to need Madeline?"

Fraser nodded.

"We'll need her if we want to find what we came here looking for," he said.

Turning on his heel, he walked over to the CSI van, which had parked next to his Interceptor.

He waited as the door opened and the CSI team leader stepped out. Madeline Mercer's dark bob blew around her face as she held up an evidence bag.

"What's that?" Dalton asked.

"The skull was wrapped in an old bandana when it was found. Some teenagers were probably thinking of using the place as a hangout," Fraser explained as Madeline opened the bag. "I figured the dogs will need something to scent if we hope to find the rest of the remains."

Madeline bent over and held the bag out.

"Get the scent, boys," Morley called out.

All four dogs eagerly nosed and sniffed at the torn fabric, their tails wagging frantically behind them as the handler urged them to pick up the scent.

When Morley gave the signal, Madeline closed the bag and stepped back, giving the dogs room to run as Boswell and Morley held on to their leashes.

Sticking his furry snout in the air, Amadeus sniffed at the wind while Ludwig dropped his nose to the ground and began to walk in small circles.

The German shepherds were still searching for the scent when Brutus led out an excited bark and took off down the train tracks with Caesar following closely behind his twin.

As Officer Boswell and Gallagher hurried after the Doberman pinschers, Morley waited patiently for Amadeus and Ludwig, who had both begun to move slowly but steadily toward the boxcars.

Fraser stood beside Dalton West, watching as Morley limped along behind the dogs, following them from one boxcar to the next.

"How many cars do you think there are?" Dalton asked after a few minutes, straining to see the end of the line.

"Looks to be a dozen or more to me," Fraser said.

Surveying the area around the boxcars and rusty track, he noticed a break in the fence bordering the property to the east, which he assumed must belong to All Souls Cemetery.

Before he could explore further, one of the dogs let loose with a raucous bark.

"Come on," Dalton called. "Let's see what they've found."

Jogging along the row of cars, they soon came to the last car on the line, a faded red caboose.

Through the broken window, they could see that both Ludwig and Amadeus were inside, barking with excitement as Morley held them back.

Fraser went to the door of the caboose, half expecting to find that the dogs had cornered a raccoon or other scavenger.

But the dogs were scratching and barking over the rusted base of what had once been a bunk bed for the overnight train crew. They were frantically signaling that the scent they were looking for was within.

As Morley called the dogs off and pulled back on their leashes, Fraser crossed the battered wooden floor and stared down at the thin metal bunk.

"You want me to call Madeline over here before you open it?" Morley asked from behind him. "She should really-"

A high-pitched screech cut off his words as Fraser wrenched up the rusty metal and peered inside the base.

He frowned down at the remnants of a pair of jeans and a white t-shirt. A coil of red and blue rope had been twisted around the clothes.

Looking more closely, he could see several grayish bones peeking out from beneath the tattered cloth.

"I think you were right," he said, looking over at Morley and Dalton. "We need to call Madeline over here."

He stood and took a step back.

"This is a crime scene."

As Dalton left the boxcar in search of Madeline, Fraser sucked in a deep breath.

His eyes fell on the wall behind the bunk.

"Looks as if someone went to a lot of effort to leave their tag over those bones," Morley said, nodding at the graffiti spraypainted on the wall.

Fraser turned to him, confused.

"Their tag?"

Morley nodded.

"Graffiti artists usually choose a unique name or logo. They call it a tag," he explained. "The more tags they leave the more street cred they have."

He gestured to the wall where the tag *SirGrendel88* had been spraypainted in red and black letters. On the opposite wall, the tag *RonnieG* had been spray-painted in blue.

47

"You think whoever tagged the wall could have left these bones here?" Fraser asked as he took several more photos. "Sort of like a signature?"

"It's a long shot," Morley said. "But if the graffiti artist didn't put the victim here, they may have seen who did."

Footsteps sounded outside and then Madeline was there. Her dark eyes scanned the interior, taking in every detail of the scene as she crossed to the bunk and looked inside.

"You'll need to call the medical examiner," she said as Fraser came up behind her. "These are human remains. They'll need to be treated as such. Besides, they could be a match to the skull in the M.E.'s cooler."

"That's right," Fraser said. "Which is what I was hoping when we came out here. I told Bailey this morning that–"

"You spoke to Bailey?" Dalton cut in. "This morning? She's awake?"

"No one told you?" Fraser asked. "I thought you knew."

But Dalton had already turned and was gone.

CHAPTER FIVE

Bailey shifted on the hospital bed, trying to find a position that didn't aggravate the terrible throbbing in her head. No matter which way she turned, she couldn't get comfortable. And she was beginning to question her decision to turn down the intravenous dose of fentanyl Dr. Pendergrast had offered her earlier. Perhaps she'd overestimated her pain threshold.

No, I can do this. I've just got to tough it out.

She was determined to be discharged as soon as possible. Which meant showing the doctor she could function without relying on mind-altering pain medication.

Closing her eyes, Bailey willed herself to fall back into the deep sleep that had shielded her from the pain over the last ten days. But her mind churned with questions and worries, refusing to rest.

She jumped at the sound of a man's voice at the door.

"Bailey?"

For one terrible moment, she imagined the shooter from the coffee shop had come to finish the job Jordan Stone had hired him to carry out.

Then she recognized the familiar tone and warm timbre of

the man's voice and saw Dalton West step into the room.

"Are you awake?"

Forgetting about the pain in her head, she smiled as he approached the bed, holding a bouquet of red roses, his blue eyes anxiously searching her face as if he was looking for the answer to a very important question.

"Finally," she said, reaching for the button to raise the back of the bed. "I thought you'd forgotten all about me."

"I must have stopped by a dozen times in the last ten days," he protested. "Then this morning, Morley told me that the bullet they found at the scene of your shooting had a hit in NIBIN. A matching bullet had been found in a human skull dumped at the old Summerset Railroad Depot. I went over to help with the search for the rest of the remains."

Bailey looked up at him in surprise.

"You were there with Fraser and Morley?" she asked. "Did they find anything?"

"They found more bones," he confirmed. "And some old clothes. Ludwig sniffed them out in an abandoned caboose."

Upon hearing the dog's name, Bailey tried to sit up but the wires from the machine beside her held her down.

"How is Ludwig?" she asked. "I miss him."

"He's good," Dalton assured her. "Last I saw, he was in a train caboose with Amadeus. They were both excited to have found the bones. I left straight after that. When Fraser told me he'd spoken to you earlier, I couldn't believe it. I drove straight over."

Setting the roses on the bedside table, he reached for her hand, holding it gently in his as if he feared it might break.

"How are you? What did the doctor say?"

Bailey inhaled the familiar scent of his cologne, enjoying the warmth of his hand in hers after so many weeks apart.

"Dr. Pendergrast said I suffered a traumatic brain injury which caused me to develop a subdural hematoma."

She kept her voice light, not wanting to worry him.

"And it seems I now have retrograde post-traumatic amnesia, which basically means I have no memory of the events leading up to my brain injury."

"Is the amnesia permanent?" he asked, gripping her hand more tightly. "Will you get your memory back?"

It was the same question Bailey had been asking herself.

"I'm not sure," she admitted. "Although, the doctor said with this sort of injury, the memories often come back. But it can take time, and it's usually a gradual process."

She released a heavy sigh.

"I just wish I could remember everything now, but I can't remember anything. Nothing at all."

"You just need some time," Dalton said in a soothing voice. "And you need to rest. Your body and mind need time to recuperate."

Bailey knew he was probably right but she couldn't stand just lying around while the shooter was free to kill again.

"What I need to do is get out of this hospital bed as soon as possible," she countered. "I've got to find out who shot me before he tries anything else."

"You think he'll try something else?" Dalton asked, instantly concerned. "Are you still in danger? Do you know something about the shooter? What were you doing in that coffee shop anyway?"

Not sure where she should start or how much she should tell him, Bailey hesitated.

"I was in the coffee shop on an undercover assignment," she admitted. "I had been working there for a few weeks."

"You were in Miami Beach the whole time?" Dalton asked. "If I'd known you had stayed so close to home, I'm not sure I'd have been able to stay away."

Bailey's eyes watered as she thought about the lonely nights she'd spent in the little walk-up apartment she'd rented as Morgan Tate.

She blinked away the tears and looked down at the hospital bracelet, glad to see her own name printed on the white strip of plastic around her wrist as she continued.

"The operation was related to a drug smuggling and laundering operation we suspected Jordan Stone of running. Somehow, my cover was blown and I was compromised. The shooter took out two other people."

An image of Lorraine Holbrook's round, friendly face flashed through her mind, followed by the echoes of the shop owner's screams on the audio recording.

Closing her eyes, she shook her head, trying to clear it.

"Are you okay?" Dalton asked. "Should I call the nurse?"

"No, I'm fine."

Bailey managed a smile.

"I just have a headache and it helps to rest my eyes," she said. "Now, where was I? Oh yes, I was going to tell you about the visit I got from Will Griffin."

"He's already been to see you?" Dalton asked. "That was

quick. What did he have to say?"

His tone was cool, making it clear he held no affection for the man who had talked Bailey into taking on the dangerous undercover assignment.

"Griff told me that I called him during the shooting, asking for back-up. He let me listen to the audio recording I managed to capture on my phone.

"So, even though I can't remember anything about that morning, I was able to hear myself talking to the shooter."

She suppressed a shudder as she replayed the gunshots she'd heard on the recording in her mind.

First, there had been the blast that had sent her careening into the freezer and then the one that had likely ended Lorraine Holbrook's life.

"It was surreal to hear the shooter's voice," Bailey said. "It was clear from the recording that I knew him."

She held up a hand to cut Dalton off before he could ask the obvious question.

"No, I can't remember what he looked like or who he was, and I didn't recognize his voice in the recording," she said. "But he did mention something that I keep thinking about."

Sucking in a deep breath, she frowned up at him.

"The shooter said he knew Ronin Godfrey."

Dalton raised both eyebrows in surprise.

"He called Godfrey his *old partner* and said he had wanted to kill me ever since I shot Godfrey at Summerset Park," Bailey continued. "And now, every time I go to sleep, I dream about Godfrey...and about Dolores."

Bitterness filled her voice.

"The shooter also said that Jordan Stone had ordered the hit on me and the two other victims he killed."

She shook her head in disgust.

"Of course, I had suspected Stone was Chuck Ashworth's silent partner but now I'm one hundred percent sure. There's no doubt he's taken over the cartel and is now running things. And no doubt he ordered the hit on me."

Looking up, she saw that her anger at Stone was reflected in Dalton's eyes, which were bright and hard.

"If Stone's responsible for you being in that hospital bed, what's the Bureau doing about it?" he asked.

Bailey shrugged.

"There's a warrant for his arrest and they've put out a BOLO on him. So, if he's still in the States, he should be picked up eventually. Other than that, I'm not really sure they're doing anything. Griff left before he could give me any real details. But I assume he's investigating."

Her words didn't appear to reassure Dalton.

"If no one knows where Stone is, that means you're still in danger," he said.

"Maybe the better way to look at it is that I'm still here," Bailey replied. "And I'm still alive."

Dalton looked down at her hand in his and nodded.

"You're right," he said with a deep exhale. "You're still alive. And I'm going to do everything in my power to find Stone and his hired shooter so that it stays that way."

"I appreciate the sentiment," she said. "But as soon as I'm out of here, I'll be going after Stone myself."

She tried to sit up again, struggling against the wires and

sensors that worked to hold her down.

"First things first," Dalton admonished. "You shouldn't be going after anyone until you recuperate fully."

"Now that the swelling in my brain has subsided and the bruises on my chest are starting to fade, there's nothing wrong with me," she protested. "I just need a few days to get my energy back. Then I'll be back at work."

Raising an eyebrow, Dalton cleared his throat.

"And where is work now?" he asked softly. "Now that your cover's been blown, does that mean..."

He left the question hanging but Bailey knew what he'd been about to say.

"I don't know where I'll be working," she admitted. "I don't even know if I've still got a job. All I know is that I've got to get out of here."

Before he could respond, a woman spoke from the doorway. Bailey turned to see that Dr. Pendergrast had entered the room.

"So, you're eager to get out of here, Agent Flynn?"

The doctor spoke in a stern voice that elicited an affirmative nod from Bailey.

"Then you must be willing to follow my orders. And the first order is to listen to your handsome visitor here and get some rest."

"I guess that's my cue to leave," Dalton said, reluctantly letting go of Bailey's hand. "But I'll be back soon. In the meantime, there's someone I need to find."

CHAPTER SIX

Dalton left the Summerset County Medical Center with the same uneasy feeling that had plagued him ever since Bailey had turned down the opportunity to rejoin a prestigious special crimes unit in the FBI's Washington D.C. field office, opting instead to volunteer for a newly formed undercover unit in Miami.

When she'd abruptly left Belle Harbor several months earlier, Bailey had been unable to share any details of her new assignment with her family and friends.

Her sudden absence had been difficult for Dalton.

Especially the part about not knowing where Bailey had gone or when he would get to see her again.

And when he'd gotten the call from Cate Flynn informing him that her sister was in the hospital fighting for her life, he had feared he might actually lose Bailey for good.

So now, as Dalton climbed into his black Dodge pickup, he knew he should be elated that she was back in Summerset County and expected to make a full recovery.

The problem was, as he backed the truck out of the parking space and headed toward home, he couldn't stop wondering if their reunion was destined to be short-lived.

Of course, he had known from the first time they met that her return to South Florida was temporary.

Bailey had made it clear that she'd come back to Belle Harbor with the sole intention of finding Detective Emma Walsh, her ex-partner who had gone missing.

But then Bailey's stay in the area had been extended after Emma had turned up dead and her murder had been linked to an old burial ground full of new bodies.

Leading a joint task force in the effort to identify the victims in the burial ground and bring their killer to justice, Bailey had managed to take down Chuck Ashworth, a serial killer who had trafficked in drugs, weapons, and humans for decades as Mr. Tumba, the boss of the ruthless Tumba Cartel.

The operation had also uncovered a traitor within the FBI when Bailey discovered that Special Agent Emil Lazar had been working with a high-level member of the cartel, an associate Lazar had referred to as his silent partner.

While she'd suspected Jordan Stone had been Lazar's silent partner, there had been no hard evidence linking him to the trafficking operations, no evidence proving the billionaire had used his vast fortune and considerable influence to form a new criminal enterprise. At least, no evidence that would hold up in court.

So Bailey's task force had been disbanded and she'd been given the choice to go back to D.C. or to join a new undercover unit led by Will Griffin out of the Miami field office.

As he merged onto the highway, Dalton couldn't say he'd been surprised to find out Bailey's undercover assignment involved a plan to take down Jordan Stone.

In fact, it may have been the only assignment that could have persuaded her to give up her coveted role in the D.C. special crimes unit and stay in South Florida.

Considering everything that had happened in the last year, she'd likely been too emotionally invested to go back to D.C. and allow Stone and his thugs to carry on with the trafficking of humans, weapons, and drugs which had destroyed so many lives in her hometown.

And Dalton couldn't blame her.

Jordan Stone had already managed to bribe his way out of the previous felony racketeering charges that had been brought against him. There was no telling what he would try next if someone didn't stop him.

While Bailey had nearly taken a bullet in her latest effort to bring Stone to justice, the billionaire had still managed to evade capture after the planned hit at the coffee shop had been revealed.

Shuddering at the thought of how close he'd come to losing Bailey for good, Dalton decided there was only one way he could make sure Stone wouldn't come after her again.

I'll have to catch the bastard myself.

There was little doubt in his mind he was up for the task.

After all, Dalton had been a bounty hunter before he'd moved to South Florida and founded West Security Services, which currently specialized in missing person cases.

Before that, he'd served eight years as an Army Ranger in the 75th regiment, deploying on risky search and rescue missions more times than he cared to remember.

He was as ready and able as anyone else to track down

Jordan Stone, wherever he might be hiding.

Turning the Dodge into the Armory Apartments, he parked in the empty space next to his sister's news van, glad to see she was home so that he could share the news about Bailey.

When he knocked on Sabrina's door, she flung it open, holding her cellphone to her ear.

She gestured impatiently for him to follow her inside and then turned back into the apartment, leaving the door open for him as she paced back and forth.

"Stupid voicemail," she muttered under her breath as he stepped into the living room.

Dropping the phone on the coffee table without leaving a message, she turned to him and sighed.

"What's up, big brother?" she asked, absently running her fingers through her blonde, chin-length bob. "You look like you've got news to share."

"I do have news," Dalton confirmed. "And for once it's good news. Bailey is awake and the doctors expect her to make a full recovery."

Sabrina stared at him for a startled beat and then smiled.

"That is good news. In fact, it's great news."

She sounded genuinely pleased.

"Now I can stop by the hospital and ask her to give me an interview for the new true crime book I'm planning to write about Chuck Ashworth."

Not sure he'd heard correctly, Dalton frowned.

"You're writing a true-crime book, too?"

His comment stopped Sabrina in her tracks.

"What do you mean by *too*?" she demanded, spinning

around to face him. "Are you writing a–"

"No, of course, I'm not," Dalton cut in. "But I saw Madeline Mercer yesterday at the Summerset Café and she introduced me to the man she was with. She said he was interviewing her for a book he was writing.

"Apparently, the guy's a pretty popular true crime author and he's writing a book centered around the recent murders in Summerset County. I think he called it *Slaughter in Summerset County*, or something like that."

Sabrina frowned.

"Did you catch the guy's name?"

"I think it was Gabe," he said and then hesitated. "No, it was Garth. His name was Garth Hamilton."

His sister's eyes widened in dismay.

"*Garth Hamilton* is here and he's writing a book about Summerset County?"

She shook her head in frustration.

"Just my luck," Sabrina moaned. "His last book was on the bestseller list for months. He sold like a billion copies. And he's got an army of followers online. How can I compete with that? No one will even notice my stupid book."

Crossing the room, she stopped in front of Dalton.

"What was Madeline telling him?" she demanded. "Were they talking about Chuck Ashworth?"

Dalton shrugged his shoulders.

"I didn't stick around to listen," he admitted. "But I have a feeling she might have been telling him about the skull they found at the Summerset Railroad Depot a few months back. It had a bullet lodged in it."

"Do they know who it belonged to?" Sabrina asked, suddenly back in her usual roaming reporter mode. "Is the skull linked to some sort of creepy cold case? Or better yet, a serial killer?"

Dalton hesitated, deciding he'd better not share what he'd learned about the ballistics on the bullet in the skull matching the one found beside Bailey's unconscious body at the coffee shop.

His sister could be ruthless when it came to scooping a big story, so he considered his next words carefully, suspecting the BHPD and the FBI wouldn't want Channel 3 News reporting on the connection between the two shootings during their evening broadcast.

"I helped the Belle Harbor PD search the old depot earlier today and spoke to the investigators working the case. They claim that whoever put a bullet in that skull is still out there, and there's no telling what the shooter will do next. So I'd say the case isn't cold. Not by a longshot."

CHAPTER SEVEN

G rendel crossed the room to his old wooden desk, summoned by the familiar *ding* that announced the delivery of a new message. Looking down at his laptop, he saw that he was still logged in under the username *SirGrendel88*, which he used online whenever he wanted to remain anonymous.

He'd started using the name during his freshman year in high school to troll his fellow classmates and he had stuck with it ever since, even adopting a shortened version as his graffiti tag and street name once he'd dropped out of school and ended up in the Summerset Juvenile Detention Center.

After all, what better name could he use to torment those who incited his hatred than that of Grendel, the malicious troll in the thousand-year-old poem *Beowulf*, which as far as he knew was still required reading for the unfortunate majority of high school students.

Opening the new message, he read it twice and then picked up his phone and tapped out the number listed within.

Jordan Stone answered his phone on the first ring.

"You screwed up, *Grendel*."

Stone's voice was cold with fury.

"Bailey Flynn's awake. And she's expected to make a full recovery. You said I could count on you to take care of her. I thought you were a professional."

The rebuke caused Grendel's face to twist into an angry grimace. He didn't like being scolded.

Especially not by a cocky billionaire who was too squeamish to get blood on his own hands and too weak to take care of his own problems.

"How the hell was I supposed to know she'd be wearing a vest?" Grendel protested. "And her back-up arrived before I could go back inside and finish her off. Is that my fault?"

"Actually, it is," Stone replied. "You should have waited until she was alone. You should have aimed for the head."

His voice hardened.

"Turns out you were also wrong about Kessler," he gritted out. "I've been through all his communications and can find nothing implying that he was working with the feds."

Grendel's grimace morphed into a nasty grin at the words.

"Really?" he asked, trying to sound surprised. "That's weird. He was spending so much time at that coffee shop. And I saw him laughing and talking with Lorraine and-"

"Lorraine Holbrook was working for us, you idiot."

The gloves were off now and Stone made no attempt to hide his anger and contempt.

"Kessler worked hard to bring her onboard and she was helping import lots of product," he continued. "Neither one of them had been turned by Bailey Flynn. They likely had no idea she was working an undercover operation."

"If that's the case, then I'd say *they* were the idiots,"

Grendel shot back. "And you should be thanking me for disrupting the operation before they got to you. You might be sitting in jail if it wasn't for-"

"It's your fault I'm a wanted man," Stone interjected. "The feds put out an arrest warrant and a nationwide BOLO for me after your little shooting spree. The only explanation is that you must have done something to point them in my direction."

Thinking back to the events that had taken place in the coffee shop and the bloody mess he'd left behind, Grendel frowned.

There was only one way they could know that Jordan Stone had ordered the hit.

"Bailey Flynn must have been wearing a wire," he said aloud before he could stop himself. "They must have heard everything I said. That must be why her backup arrived so quickly."

Stone was silent on the other end of the connection.

"I can fix this," Grendel quickly added, sensing that he'd made a fatal mistake. "I can find Bailey Flynn and-"

"The damage is already done," Stone said with a frightening tone of finality. "They must have heard you mention my name. It was enough for a warrant. Enough to bring me in. Now I've got to figure out how to fix it. *We* need to figure it out. We need to meet."

The statement sent a shiver of alarm through Grendel.

"I'll send you directions on when and where we will meet in the next few days," Stone said. "Be prepared to travel."

Holding the phone against his ear, Grendel started to

protest before realizing Stone had already ended the call.

He dropped the phone back on the desk and crossed to the window, staring out at the dark night beyond with a new sense of dread. There was no doubt in his mind that he was in serious danger. No doubt that Stone was out there somewhere making plans.

He doesn't just want to meet up with me. He wants to kill me.

After all, Claude Kessler and Lorraine Holbrook were dead, and if Grendel wasn't alive to testify, there would be no one left to bear witness against him in court.

Stone might once again beat any charges the feds or the local police brought against him due to lack of evidence.

Watching as raindrops began to patter softly against the window, running down the glass like tears, Grendel found the sight strangely comforting.

What's the saying? No use crying over spilled milk?

And it wasn't all bad news. After all, he'd made a tidy sum of money for the hit he'd carried out.

And Stone doesn't even know I'd have shot Bailey Flynn for free.

The thought brought a malevolent smile to his face.

He'd been hoping for a chance to take out the FBI agent for years now. Ever since that day in Summerset Park.

Looking down at his hands, he balled them into fists and allowed himself to remember.

Grendel pushed through the crowd, disoriented by the wailing sirens and frantic barking of dogs as he tried to make his way to the far side of the murky pond.

Suddenly, he was pushed out of the way as the police forcibly parted the growing group of onlookers, and paramedics rushed past him, transporting a man on a gurney.

As they wheeled the injured man past, Grendel saw a dark patch of blood seeping through the white gauzy bandage wrapped around his leg.

Taking advantage of the diversion, he hurried on, following the path alongside the hazy water.

He stopped when he saw the woman with dark blonde hair standing in front of a pine tree. She was pacing back and forth beside a man who was sprawled motionless on the ground.

"She shot him," a wide-eyed woman in the crowd said to her companion. "I think she's with the FBI."

Grendel stared at the dead man's face and the grisly red bullet hole between his eyes, careful not to react.

He couldn't let anyone know that he knew the man. That at one time Ronin Godfrey had been his closest confidant. The person who had known all his darkest secrets.

"The girl he took is just past that tree," the woman in the crowd continued. "You can see her foot there on the ground. See her pink tennis shoe? I guess the feds got here too late."

Grendel turned back to see where the woman was pointing.

His eyes moved past Godfrey's dead body to the pink tennis shoe and then returned to the blonde FBI agent's slim figure, taking in every detail as he stepped forward and ducked under the crime scene tape.

"Agent Flynn?"

He waited for her to turn around.

"They said I should ask for you…"

His voice faltered as he looked into Bailey Flynn's green eyes.

As she began to speak, he decided that one day, when they were alone, he would kill her. He'd make her pay for what she'd done.

Grendel recoiled as a tree branch scratched angrily against the window pane. Just then, a flash of lightening illuminated the sky, revealing the storm that now surrounded the house with fierce wind and torrential rain.

He moved back to his desk, driven by the need for a distraction. He needed to take his mind off Jordan Stone and Bailey Flynn. He would deal with them both later.

For now, he would have a little fun.

Sinking into the chair in front of his computer, Grendel typed in a message to his latest target, a local woman named Krystal Devine who considered herself an internet influencer.

Grendel had seen her speaking at Summerset Park several months before. She'd been yelling into a bullhorn, trying to get attention, asking passersby to sign some sort of petition.

Well, she certainly managed to get my attention, whether she wanted it or not.

Ever since that day, he had been trolling her, planting online rumors, and seeding various hate campaigns against her, all the while sending her a barrage of threatening DMs.

Once she'd finally deactivated all of her social media accounts, he'd managed to find both her personal and work email addresses as well as her mobile phone number.

Lately, whenever he drove by her house, Krystal's shades were drawn and her car was parked inside the garage.

It was almost time to take the final step.

Almost time to shut her up once and for all.

Just like he'd done with the others.

He smiled as he realized that no one, not even Special Agent Bailey Flynn, had a clue who he was or what he had done.

CHAPTER EIGHT

Bailey Flynn stood at the hospital window, staring out at the swaying fronds of the palm trees outside with impatient eyes. She could sense Cate hovering behind her, staying close enough to stop her from falling and banging her head again in the event she suddenly collapsed.

"I'm going to be alright, you know?" Bailey said, keeping her eyes trained on the parking lot below. "You don't have to babysit me anymore. I'm sure you have things to do."

"Is that your way of saying you're getting sick of me?" her sister teased. "Because I've only been staying here to get out of going to work and facing Judge Nelson in the courtroom. The guy's insufferable. I guess I shouldn't be surprised considering Mayor Sutherland personally called the governor and recommended him for the appointment."

Before Bailey could respond, Dr. Pendergrast appeared in the doorway, wearing her usual white lab coat.

"Good morning, ladies," she said, flashing them a smile.

Picking up the clipboard hanging on the end of the bed, she scanned the first page and then flipped to the next.

"I have to say I'm amazed at the progress you've made in the last twenty-four hours, Agent Flynn."

She glanced up, looking pleased.

"The neurological tests all came back as normal and your vital signs are stable," she said. "I'd say you'll be able to go home in the next few days."

"I was sort of hoping I could go home tomorrow," Bailey admitted. "I'm starting to go stir crazy cooped up in here."

Dr. Pendergrast's smile slipped away.

"Well, I can't force you to stay," she said. "But I must urge you to carefully consider the consequences of going home too soon. Your brain has suffered a serious injury, and while you're doing well now, you're not out of danger yet."

The ominous words unsettled Bailey, reminding her just how right the doctor was.

I'm not out of danger. Not as long as Jordan Stone's a free man.

After the doctor had conducted a brief examination, she agreed to remove the staples from the laceration on the back of Bailey's head the next day.

As she left the hospital room, Dr. Pendergrast wore a look of worried disapproval.

"I think she wants you to stay a little longer," Cate said. "And I have to agree. You were in a coma for ten days and–"

"And that means that I've had plenty of time to rest," Bailey finished for her. "And every day that I spend in here will make it that much harder for me to track down Jordan Stone once I'm out there."

Expecting her sister to object, Bailey was surprised when she didn't reply. She looked over to see that Cate was staring off into space as if deep in thought.

"Cate?"

Still not getting an answer, Bailey reached out and laid a hand on Cate's arm.

"Hey, are you okay?" she asked. "You've been distracted all morning. And it isn't about me getting discharged tomorrow, is it?"

She narrowed her eyes.

"There's something else, isn't there? Something you're not telling me?"

Cate hesitated and then nodded.

"Actually, there *is* something I've been meaning to tell you. I just wanted to wait until you were feeling better."

Sensing she wasn't going to like whatever her sister had been keeping from her, Bailey sighed.

"Tell me," she said, raising a wary eyebrow.

Before Cate could comply, they heard the *click, click, click* of high heels outside in the corridor.

Seconds later, the door swung open and Jackie Flynn stepped into the room, looking ready for court in a tailored pantsuit and designer pumps.

"Shouldn't you be lying down?" she asked, looking startled to find Bailey out of bed.

But Bailey wasn't listening. She was too busy looking at the campaign pin on Jackie's lapel.

Mimi Harper for Summerset County Judge!

She frowned as she read the words, wondering if her brain injury was messing with her head.

Glancing up, she saw her mother wince and turn to Cate.

"I see you didn't tell her," Jackie said. "I thought you would have found a chance to broach the subject by now."

"What was she supposed to tell me?" Bailey demanded. "That her own mother isn't supporting her campaign?"

Her head began to ache as she glared at Jackie, waiting for an explanation.

"There is no campaign," Cate said quietly. "Not anymore. I dropped out of the race before the primary."

"But...why?" Bailey asked, trying hard to swallow back her disappointment. "Was it because of me? Because of this?"

She gestured around the hospital room.

"When they called and told us that you'd sustained a life-threatening head injury, the primary was less than a week away," Cate said. "I didn't know what was going to happen."

Her voice wavered.

"I didn't know if you were going to live or die. And I didn't know what condition you might be in if you did make it. There was no way I was going to be able to keep on campaigning while you were in here fighting for your life."

Meeting Bailey's eyes, Cate shrugged.

"There will be other years," she said. "Other campaigns. The important thing is that you're okay."

A guilty lump rose in Bailey's throat and for a minute she couldn't speak.

"I'm sorry," she finally said, biting her lip. "I know how much the campaign meant to you. And now I've ruined it."

"It didn't mean as much as I thought it did," Cate assured her. "When I saw you in that hospital bed, I realized what really mattered. You mean more to me than any election. Besides, it wasn't your fault you were in here. I blame the man who shot you."

Hearing Jackie sniffling behind her, Bailey turned to see her mother dabbing at her eyes with a tissue.

"No need to get all mushy about it," Bailey said, blinking away the shine of tears in her own eyes. "Even if Cate's got to wait awhile to get her seat on the bench, we still have a chance to keep Brunner off it."

She gestured toward Jackie's campaign pin.

"How did Mimi Harper do in the primary?" she asked, not sure she really wanted to know the answer. "Did she beat Brunner?"

"It was too close to call," Cate admitted. "An election runoff between Mimi and Brunner will be held in November."

Bailey shuddered inwardly at the thought of Tony Brunner winning a seat on the Summerset County judicial bench.

She imagined the sleazy lawyer sitting behind the raised wooden bench in judicial robes as he presided over the courtroom, his rulings up for sale to the highest bidder.

The possibility made her head ache.

Or maybe it's my bruised brain telling me to lie down.

Making her way back to her bed, Bailey climbed back in, adjusting the bed into a sitting position as she stewed over Brunner's shady history, disturbed by the realization that Jordan Stone's former lawyer and longtime crony could possibly sit in judgment of the corrupt billionaire if a future case was brought against him.

Mimi has to win that election and Stone has to be found soon.

The anxious thoughts circled through her aching head, which had started to throb again.

"I'm going to go now and let you rest," Cate said as she

took in Bailey's pale face. "I promised I'd go see Mason and talk wedding plans."

Lifting her left hand, she gazed at the sparkling engagement ring on her finger.

"My campaign might be over but the wedding is still on," she proclaimed. "And now that you're officially out of danger, I no longer have an excuse to procrastinate."

"That's right," Bailey said, trying to sound enthusiastic about Cate and Mason's upcoming nuptials. "You go see Mason. And once you're done making wedding plans, you can give your fiancé a message from me."

She met and held her sister's curious gaze.

"Tell Mason I'll be coming by to see him as soon as I get out of the hospital," she said. "I need to talk to him about the skull he and Eloise have been examining. The one found at the Summerset Railroad Depot. And I need to find out everything he knows about the bullet that was in it."

Her mind returned to the man in the coffee shop.

"That bullet could lead us straight to our shooter."

CHAPTER NINE

Mason Knox crossed the autopsy suite and stopped next to Eloise Spellman and Madeline Mercer, who were both staring down at the collection of bones laid out on the metal dissecting table. He watched as Eloise used gloved hands to arrange the proximal, intermediate, and distal phalanges of the fingers into their correct positions above the metacarpal bones, constructing the outline of a hand.

"Is this everything they found at the Summerset Railroad Depot yesterday?" the forensic anthropologist asked. "I thought Gallagher told me they'd found some rope with the remains in the boxcar, as well."

"Actually, it was a caboose, not a boxcar," Madeline said.

Mason raised a dark eyebrow.

"What's the difference?'

"The caboose carries the crew while a boxcar carries the cargo," Madeline explained. "And a caboose has a little platform at the back and is always at the end of the train."

Eloise looked at the crime scene team leader with interest.

"I've never seen the old depot," she said as she began to construct the second hand. "Was it as creepy as it sounds?"

A wispy wheat-colored curl had escaped from her protective cap and rested on the pale skin of her forehead.

Madeline shrugged.

"The place is pretty rundown," she said. "No one's done any repairs over the years. I'm surprised it's not been knocked down by a storm yet. And it's been vandalized by teenagers. There's graffiti on the walls and even inside the caboose."

"The rope is in the cooler room," Mason said, not sure how they'd gotten onto the topic of train cars. "I've asked Finola to bring it in. For now, let's get back to the bones."

They all looked down at the remains in front of them.

"You think you'll be able to identify who the bones belong to?" Madeline asked. "Can you determine if they are a match to the skull?"

Holding up what looked to Mason to be a scaphoid bone that belonged in the wrist, Eloise nodded.

"We'll be sending one of the bones to the lab so they can cut off a section and grind it into a fine powder," she said. "The lab will then attempt to extract mitochondrial DNA from the bone powder."

She carefully placed the scaphoid bone alongside the lunate and triquetrum bones on the table as she spoke.

"Once they've extracted the DNA and have a profile, they should be able to confirm if the DNA from the bones matches the DNA from the skull."

"So, you've already extracted DNA from the skull?" Madeline asked. "You've already got a profile?"

Eloise hesitated.

"We have a profile of the mitochondrial DNA from the skull," she confirmed. "Unfortunately, with skeletonized bones, we can't get an autosomal DNA profile, which would give us a lot more information."

Her voice took on an instructive tone.

"Remember that a mitochondrial DNA profile only provides us with information about the subject's maternal line. Anyone in the same direct maternal line will have an identical profile to other subjects in the line.

"For example, the mitochondrial DNA profile for both your mother and your son would be identical to your own."

She pointed to a long bone near the edge of the pile.

"The femur bone is one of the best bones to use to extract mitochondrial DNA, but teeth are also a good choice.

"Luckily, when the skull was found, the jawbone was still attached, so we were able to use the teeth to extract DNA, which allowed us to run the profile through CODIS."

Staring down at the pile of bones, Madeline frowned.

"And was there a match in CODIS?" she asked.

"Unfortunately not," Eloise said. "But we plan to run the DNA profile through some of the other publicly available databases next. And we may even end up resorting to forensic genealogy to track down who the DNA belongs to, but that takes time."

"You wanted the rope?"

Mason turned to see Finola Lawson standing behind him. The assistant medical examiner wore dark green scrubs and her long, coppery hair was covered by a matching cap.

She held a brown paper evidence collection bag, which she

placed on the table before opening it.

Using a gloved hand, she pulled out the length of braided rope, laying it on the metal dissecting table in front of Eloise and Madeline.

Both women bent to stare at the intertwining red and blue strands with interest. The colors had faded somewhat but other than that, the rope appeared to be intact.

"The material is definitely polypropylene," Madeline said. "It's synthetic and works well around water since it doesn't tend to rot or attract mildew."

She straightened and looked over at Mason.

"It's still in good shape but it may look a lot newer than it really is," she said. "And it's been cut right under the knot."

Mason looked down at the knot, which he recognized from his scouting days as a clove hitch.

"I'd expect to find this rope and this knot on a boat's cleat, not a railroad car," Madeline said. "This is the kind of knot I use when I go waterskiing. It makes it easier to quickly adjust the length of the rope."

Finola spoke up behind her.

"That looks like the rope Rachel Cho used to hang herself."

All eyes turned to the assistant medical examiner.

"Who is Rachel Cho?" Mason asked. "Or I guess, since she hung herself, I should be asking who *was* she?"

"She was my first suicide," Finola said in a matter-of-fact tone. "She came in right after I started working here with Dr. Armbruster. But of course, that was back before your time."

Her eyes flicked from Mason to Madeline.

"Although, I don't think Rachel Cho was the water-skiing

type. From what I remember, her parents said she had been a straight-A college student but had recently taken to staying in her room all the time and rarely got out. The only social interaction she had was on her computer."

Mason frowned.

"Did you ever find out where she'd gotten the rope?"

Finola shrugged.

"Like I said, I was brand new and I was just assisting Dr. Armbruster. He didn't like me asking too many questions."

Sensing her tacit disapproval, and that there was more she wanted to say, Mason raised an eyebrow.

"Was there something you wanted to ask Dr. Armbruster about Rachel's autopsy? Was there something he missed?"

She hesitated and then shook her head.

"Not really. I probably only remember the bit about Rachel staying in her room because she was my age at the time and a fellow straight-A student."

Her tone grew wistful.

"I can remember thinking how sad it was that she'd suddenly just given up like that. It seemed as if she had everything to live for."

Considering Finola's words as she turned away, Mason made a mental note to look into Rachel Cho's case just as Madeline cleared her throat.

"Sorry, but I've got to go," she said, looking at her watch. "I promised to meet someone for lunch."

Eloise cocked her head.

"Is it a date?" she teased, her eyes sparkling with mischief. "Is there a handsome new man in your life?"

"Oh, he's handsome alright," Madeline replied with a grin as she pulled the cap from her dark hair. "Unfortunately, it's not a date, just an interview, but I still don't want to be late so I'd better get going."

Leaving Eloise to continue sorting and connecting the bones on the table, Mason followed Madeline into the lobby.

"Hopefully, the DNA results from the bones won't take too long," he said as she reached the door. "I'll be sure to keep you updated."

"That would be great," Madeline replied. "Let's just hope they lead us to the bastard who shot our John Doe."

Pulling open the door, she gave him a grim smile and slipped out into the warm, windy day.

His eyes followed the CSI team leader as she hurried down the sidewalk and climbed into a small red sportscar that had been idling along the curb.

Despite Mason's best efforts, the car's darkly tinted windows prevented him from seeing who was driving as the little car sped away.

He was just turning away from the window when a shiny white Lexus pulled into the lot and parked in an empty space up front.

Mason watched as Cate Flynn climbed out and headed toward the front entrance, her auburn hair blowing and twisting in the strong wind as large reddish leaves from a nearby maple tree cart-wheeled past her legs.

Holding the door open for her, Mason waited until Cate was safely inside before planting a soft kiss on her lips.

"Was that Madeline Mercer I saw in the red sportscar out

there?" she asked. "What was she doing here?"

"Come into the back and I'll show you," Mason said, taking her hand. "We've actually had a very interesting development since you were here yesterday."

He led her down the hall and into the autopsy suite, where Eloise was still bent over the metal dissecting table.

"Put these on," Mason said, handing Cate a one-size-fits-all coverall and a face mask. "We're putting together remains that just might belong with the skull you saw yesterday."

Once she'd pulled the protective gear over her street clothes, Mason guided Cate forward, stopping beside the metal table to watch as Eloise positioned the radius bone and the ulna bone next to each other.

"I heard you came by yesterday and viewed the skull," the forensic anthropologist said as Cate stared down at the pile of bones with startled green eyes. "Did you get a chance to see the bullet hole?"

Cate shook her head.

"The poor guy sustained a gunshot wound to the left mastoid region," Eloise said.

Lifting a hand to her head, she tapped on the bony bump behind and below her left ear.

"The bullet was embedded in the petrous bone."

"The petrous bone?" Cate repeated, looking confused.

Eloise nodded.

"That's right. The name comes from the Latin word petrosus, meaning stone-like, which makes sense because it's the densest bone in the body. Too dense to allow the bullet to pass through."

Mason tried to catch his fiancé's eye, suspecting she might want to be rescued from the overload of information Eloise was sharing with her, but Cate appeared to be listening to the forensic anthropologist with keen interest.

"And what can you tell me about the bullet itself?" Cate asked. "Are you able to find out who manufactured it or where it was sold? Was there anything unique about it other than the markings from the gun?"

The barrage of questions seemed to stump Eloise.

"Those sound like wonderful questions to ask Madeline Mercer," she said. "She's more into the physical and trace evidence side of things. I mainly study human remains."

Bending over to pick up a femur bone, Eloise looked back at Mason as if seeking his help.

"I think Eloise is right," he said, stepping up behind Cate. "Other than Detective Fraser, I think only Madeline would have information about the bullets."

"But Madeline left a while ago," Eloise added helpfully. "She had a lunch meeting with a handsome writer."

Putting a hand on Cate's arm, Mason spoke in her ear.

"So that's who she was with in the sportscar," he said. "I guess your questions about the bullets will have to wait."

"They weren't really my questions," Cate admitted as she backed away from the table. "They were Bailey's questions. She told me to tell you that she'll be coming here to ask you about the bullet and the skull found at the Summerset Depot. She's determined to find the man who shot her."

Mason nodded.

"I don't blame her," he said. "Bailey will want to know

about the rope as well. In fact, I have a few unanswered questions about that myself."

"The rope?" Cate asked, raising an eyebrow. "What rope are you talking about?"

Deciding it was best not to voice his concerns in front of Eloise and Finola, Mason led Cate down the hall to his office and motioned to the chair across from his desk.

"I don't want to sit down," she said, crossing her arms over her chest. "I want to know about the rope."

Staring down into her stubborn green eyes, he sighed.

"A rope was tied around the bones they found last night," he said. "Apparently, a young woman used the exact same type of rope to hang herself a few years ago. Finola attended the autopsy and it seems she had doubts afterward."

"What young woman?" Cate asked. "Doubts about what?"

Mason ran a hand through his dark hair, not sure how much he should say before he had done some more digging.

He could be reading too much into Finola's reaction. But if there was any question as to Rachel Cho's manner of death, he was obligated to investigate.

And if there's a connection to Bailey's shooting, I owe it to her and her sister to find out what really happened.

"The woman's name was Rachel Cho," he said.

Circling the desk, he sank into the chair in front of his computer and began to type as he spoke.

"Finola didn't think Rachel Cho showed suicidal tendencies prior to her death. And she said Dr. Armbruster, the previous medical examiner, didn't like to be questioned, which makes me think he was insecure about his findings.

"Of course, at this point, I don't know enough about Rachel's death to overturn the suicide ruling or to conclusively link the rope she used to the rope wrapped around the bones. But Finola seemed certain that the rope they found at the depot was the exact same rope she saw during the autopsy."

Mason stared at Rachel Cho's autopsy report, which was now open on his computer screen. The date on the report showed that Rachel had died over three years earlier. Her cause and manner of death was listed as suicide by hanging.

He quickly read through the findings and scrolled through the photos Dr. Armbruster had taken at the death scene and during the autopsy, stopping at a photo that showed a close-up of the rope knotted around the young woman's neck.

His stomach dropped as he recognized the red and blue braided polypropylene rope he'd placed in the brown paper evidence bag that was now sitting in the cooler room down the hall.

Slowly, he turned the monitor around so that Cate could see the screen. Her face blanched as she studied the autopsy photo, which was clearly labeled with Rachel Cho's name and date of death.

Cate stared at the image for a long beat and then slowly walked to the chair across from Mason and sat down.

"Old Dr. Armbruster was a nice man but he wasn't the sharpest tool in the shed by the time he retired," she said in a weak voice, propping her elbows on the desk. "He could definitely have missed something."

Her words brought back the rumors Mason had heard

about the retired medical examiner when he arrived in Summerset County two years earlier.

"There were rumblings about Dr. Armbruster when I first came here," Mason said. "Several people told me that he'd been forced into retirement due to a series of mistakes, several of which were widely reported."

His words prompted a grimace from Cate.

"I suspected as much," she admitted. "Dr. Armbruster testified in a case I handled just before he retired and the poor man had trouble recalling simple facts about the victim and the cause of death. It was painful for everyone involved."

Leaning back in the chair, she sighed.

"To be honest, he couldn't even remember my name, much less detailed facts about the autopsy he'd conducted."

She glanced over at him.

"You think Dr. Armbruster might have made a mistake in ruling Rachel Cho's death a suicide, don't you?"

Mason looked decidedly uneasy.

"I don't know," he admitted in a grim voice. "But I'd say we have an obligation to Rachel and her family to find out."

CHAPTER TEN

Cate stepped out of the Audi and followed Mason along a winding path that led to the Belle Harbor Retreat by the Shore, the retirement community where Dr. Armbruster had been living for the last three years. The property was located several blocks from the shoreline but a strong breeze off the ocean managed to reach them as they followed the path around the main building to the back lawn.

A small man with a bald pate, white fringe, and wrinkled, sun-speckled skin sat beside a placid reflection pond.

As they approached, Cate recognized the retired medical examiner, who stood to greet them.

"Dr. Armbruster," Mason called out. "Thank you for agreeing to meet with us on such short notice."

Gesturing toward several lounge chairs, the old man gave Mason a fatherly pat on the back as if he knew him well.

"No problem, my boy," he said affably. "It's a pleasure to see you. A real pleasure. How have you been?"

Before Mason could answer, he turned to Cate.

"Why hello, young lady. Have we met before?"

"Yes, I'm Cate Flynn, assistant state attorney for Summerset County. You testified on a case I was prosecuting a few years ago," she replied. "It's good to see you again, Dr. Armbruster."

The older man studied her with a slightly bewildered expression before turning back to Mason.

"What was it you wanted to discuss, my boy?" he asked. "It's not often I get visitors seeking out my expertise anymore. Although, at one time, I was in constant demand."

The retired medical examiner shook his head as if he was still trying to make sense of his change in circumstances.

"I wanted to ask you about an autopsy you performed shortly before your retirement," Mason said, keeping his tone casual. "A young woman named Rachel Cho was found hanging by a rope in her family home. You ruled her death a suicide and I just had a few questions."

"What sort of questions?" Armbruster replied, instantly indignant. "Has someone said something to you? Have they been accusing me again?"

He stared at Mason suspiciously.

"No one's said anything," Mason assured the older man. "I just wanted to ask if you ever found out where Rachel Cho got the rope she used to hang herself. And was the rope tested for prints or trace evidence? Because there's nothing in the file about–"

"The girl was depressed," Armbruster blurted out. "Her parents didn't want to accept it, but in my mind, it was clearly a case of suicide."

"So, Rachel hadn't mentioned any suicidal thoughts to her parents?" Cate pushed. "There were no warning signs?"

Armbruster huffed in frustration at the question.

"Who was it who said, 'the dead might as well try to speak to the living as the old to the young'? Was it Thoreau?"

Cate stared at the man in confusion, not sure what he was talking about, but Mason quickly spoke up beside her.

"It was Willa Cather, I believe. But perhaps Ms. Cather never met a medical examiner. Because the dead *do* speak to the living. They just do it through the remains left behind."

But Mason's impassioned words were lost on Dr. Armbruster, who didn't appear to be listening as he sucked in an indignant breath.

"That girl's parents kept pushing me to give them answers," the old man grumbled, his face creasing into a frustrated scowl. "As if they expected *me* to somehow know what the girl had been thinking."

At this, Mason gave a sympathetic nod.

"Willa Cather also said, 'the heart of another is a dark forest, always, no matter how close it has been to one's own', and I have to agree.

"There's no way we can know for sure what was in Rachel's mind before her death. But we still need to speak to her parents to try to find out."

"Do you know where they went?" Cate asked

"Back to Seoul, I believe," Armbruster said. "I remember that because I was stationed in Korea in the late sixties. I was at Camp Casey, which is just north of-"

Mason cut him off.

"Did you get contact details for Rachel's parents?" he asked. "I'll need to reach out to them to discuss a possible exhumation. I didn't see anything in the files."

"Then I guess I didn't get contact details," the old man snorted. "If I had, they'd be in there."

His eyes narrowed.

"And why on earth would you need to exhume the girl's body? She was laid to rest years ago. Just leave it at that."

Ignoring Armbruster's comments, Mason frowned.

"What did you do with the rope?" he asked, beginning to lose patience with the old man's belligerence. "I need to confirm the manner of death was suicide and not homicide."

"The rope should still be in the evidence locker at the Belle Harbor PD," Armbruster said in a sullen voice. "That's where I sent all evidence for testing and secure storage."

Mason nodded.

"Fine, then we'll look there," he said. "Based on new evidence that has recently come to my attention, I believe an examination of the rope may force us to reopen the investigation into Rachel's cause and manner of death."

Drawing back his thin, rounded shoulders and jutting out his baggy chin, Armbruster glared at Mason with small, angry eyes.

"Are you questioning my findings, young man?"

A red flush filled his face as he struggled to suck in a breath and for a moment Cate feared he might be having some sort of attack. Then he sputtered, coughed several times into his balled fist, and exhaled.

When he spoke again, he had regained his composure.

"I stand by my work," he said. "Just as I did when they forced me to retire. Now, if that's all you wanted to ask?"

Mason opened his mouth as if to ask another question but

Cate put a hand on his arm and discreetly shook her head.

"I think that's all for now, Dr. Armbruster," she said, tugging Mason back toward the building. "We won't take up any more of your time."

As they walked back to Mason's Audi, he remained silent, his brow furrowed as if deep in thought.

"Do you think Dr. Armbruster was right about the rope they recovered during Rachel Cho's autopsy?" Cate asked as they pulled onto the highway. "Do you think it was stored in the BHPD evidence locker?"

"I hope so," Mason said, although Cate thought she could hear more doubt in his voice than hope. "But I'll have to ask Madeline to be sure."

Glancing in the rearview mirror, he changed lanes and prepared to take the exit toward Belle Harbor.

"There's one thing I *am* sure of," he said in a hard voice. "Dr. Armbruster failed to properly investigate Rachel Cho's manner of death. He ruled it a suicide before he'd done his due diligence and now I'll have to do it for him."

"You could start by going by the police station and asking Madeline about the rope," Cate suggested. "She should be back from her lunch meeting by now. And if you don't mind me tagging along, I can go with you."

Mason remained silent and kept his eyes on the road but he made a sharp turn on the next street, heading toward downtown.

Ten minutes later they were standing in the lobby of the Belle Harbor Police Department asking the desk sergeant if Madeline was available.

"I tried her extension and she's not answering," the uniformed officer behind the counter said in a bored voice. "I can give her a message if you want to leave one."

"No thanks," Mason said as he backed away. "I've got her number. I'll try her cell."

Following him back to the parking lot, Cate tried to keep up with his long, impatient stride, trying to remember how her earlier plan to talk to Mason about the wedding had ended with her standing outside the police station.

"Wait up," she called out as they reached the parking lot.

As Mason stopped and looked back, Cate saw a red sportscar pulling up to the curb. Seconds later, Madeline Mercer opened the door and climbed out.

A young, leanly muscled man with a light brown ponytail emerged from the driver's side door.

He glanced over at Cate and did a double take, his mouth curling into a surprised smile.

"You're Cate Flynn, aren't you?"

Not waiting for an answer, he held out a big hand, which she automatically took, feeling as if she should know him. As if she'd seen him before.

"I'm Garth Hamilton."

His hand was warm and firm as he gripped hers.

"I'm writing a book about the recent murders in Summerset County and have been meaning to contact you. I was hoping we could schedule some time to talk."

Digging out a business card, he handed it to her.

Cate stared down at his name on the card, realizing where she'd seen his face before.

"Your latest book *History of the Hangman* is on my bedside table," she said, feeling vaguely embarrassed by the admission. "I'm halfway through. It's very...compelling."

She didn't add that she'd recognized him from his photo on the back cover, or that she'd been considering giving up on finishing the book, which was filled with gory details about a serial killer who had targeted young couples in Virginia several years earlier.

She suspected the book was partly responsible for the increase in nightmares she'd been having lately.

Of course, her own harrowing history with serial killers could also have something to do with it. She couldn't let Garth Hamilton take all the blame.

"I'd love to meet up with you when you have some time," the writer said, summoning a hopeful smile.

Mason cleared his throat, prompting Garth to look over at the medical examiner for the first time.

"To talk about the book, of course," he quickly added as he saw the annoyed frown that had settled over Mason's face.

"As a prosecutor, I'm cautious about who I give interviews to," Cate said. "And I'm very busy with-"

"Please, just think about it," Garth cut in. "And if you change your mind, give me a call."

Turning back to Madeline, he whispered something in her ear that made them both laugh before saying goodbye.

As the writer jumped back into the red sportscar and sped out of the parking lot, three sets of eyes stared after him.

Once he'd disappeared around the corner, Madeline turned to Mason and Cate.

"The desk sergeant said you were looking for me," she said. "What do you need?"

"I need to see any evidence you have in storage related to the death of a young woman named Rachel Cho," he said. "The BHPD and the medical examiner's office responded to a death scene three years ago after the woman had been found hanging in her home."

Madeline frowned.

"That's the suicide Finola was talking about, right?"

She cocked her head.

"I guess you'll be looking for the rope, and I can check and see if we have it. But sometimes we send evidence over to our storage facility after a few years to free up space."

"Please, do what you can to find it," Mason said. "We need to make sure we don't have another homicide on our hands."

* * *

The courthouse was quiet when Cate stepped into the lobby and headed toward the elevator. It felt strange to be back at work after taking almost two weeks of personal leave.

Still thinking about the events of the morning, she paid little attention to her surroundings as she pushed the metal button and waited for the elevator.

When the sleek metal doors slid open, Cate was startled to see Tony Brunner standing inside.

It was the first time she'd seen the defense attorney in person since she had ended her campaign, and she noted that he was clean-shaven and wearing an expensive charcoal gray suit that appeared to have been tailored to fit his solid, muscular frame.

The judicial candidate was already dressing as if he'd won the race. Or perhaps he was just keeping up appearances in the run-up to the election.

"Well, if it isn't Cate Flynn," Brunner said as he stepped into the lobby. "What are you doing here? I thought you'd be at the hospital looking after your brain-damaged sister."

Using his thick body to block her way into the elevator, he raised his dark eyebrows in mock concern.

"Is it true that she's in a coma?" he asked, shaking his head. "What a shame. And she was such a smart girl."

Cate ignored his cruel remarks. Remaining silent, she tried to step around him but he held out a hand to stop her.

"Hold on, now. I've been hoping to run into you ever since I heard you'd dropped out of the race," he said as the elevator doors slid closed behind him. "I just wanted to say you made the right decision and I applaud you."

He produced a wide smile, revealing sharp white teeth.

"It makes no sense to stay in a race you have no chance of winning. Better not to humiliate yourself. But I am sorry to hear about your sister."

The mocking pity on his face said otherwise.

"I hope she learned her lesson and will be more careful in the future. I'd hate for anything else to happen to her."

"And I'd hate for you to be a judge in my county," Cate snapped, unable to hold back the anger Brunner always managed to rouse in her. "If there's any justice in this world, the voters of Summerset County will send you packing."

Obviously pleased to have gotten a reaction out of her, Brunner adopted a confused expression.

"That's strange. That's not what Mayor Sutherland said when he officially endorsed me this morning. But I'll be sure to pass your greetings on to the mayor when I see him at the country club. I'm heading there now for a round of golf."

Finally stepping out of her way, the lawyer headed toward the exit, leaving Cate to once again push the button to summon the elevator.

As she rode up to her office, Brunner's spiteful words replayed in her head, remaining there all afternoon as she tried unsuccessfully to focus on the work that had piled up on her desk while she'd been away.

Unable to concentrate, Cate left the courthouse at exactly five o'clock and headed toward her parent's house.

She had promised her mother she would stop by to pick up a box of *Mimi Harper for Summerset County Judge!* yard signs to distribute around the neighborhood.

Turning onto Claremont Street, Cate saw a white Mercedes sedan parked in the driveway. Inside the house, she found her mother sitting at the kitchen table with Mimi Harper.

Jackie's long-time friend appeared relaxed and cheerful in a tailored skirt and silky blouse that complimented her tall, willowy figure. Mimi's loose, silvery gray curls framed a tan, make-up-free face that showed no sign of stress, despite the fact that the election was little more than a month away.

Several cardboard boxes were strewn around the kitchen floor. Jackie's white Siamese cat Duchess loafed on one of the sealed boxes, staring around at the clutter in disdain.

Another box was open to reveal the campaign signs destined for front yards around the neighborhood.

"Are you okay?" Jackie asked once Cate had joined them at the table. "You look upset. You haven't received bad news from the hospital, have you?"

"No, nothing like that," Cate quickly assured her. "But I've had a stressful day. And running into Tony Brunner at the courthouse certainly didn't help."

Mimi raised an eyebrow.

"What did my opponent do to get you so worked up?"

"He stopped me from getting in the elevator and said he hoped Bailey had learned her lesson," Cate fumed. "He even implied she may have permanent brain damage. I tried not to let him bait me but he makes me so mad."

She banged her fist on the table, sending Duchess darting toward the door.

All at once, Cate felt her anger draining away.

Shaking her head in frustration, she sat back in her chair.

"I can't believe that a man like Tony Brunner has the mayor's endorsement," she said. "He said he's even playing a round of golf with Mayor Sutherland this afternoon at the club. It just doesn't make sense."

"I agree," Mimi said. "And I think Mayor Sutherland should stop worrying about Brunner's campaign and start worrying about his own. He's up for re-election in two years. And most people's memories are longer than that."

Suddenly her lips curled into a mischievous smile.

"I'm thinking maybe I should head over to the club myself and see if I can catch up with the mayor," she said, glancing at the slim gold watch on her wrist. "Although, he only plays the front nine before heading to the bar, so I may be too late."

She shrugged her slim shoulders.

"Oh well, I've got a round scheduled for Friday afternoon and Sutherland is usually there. I'll catch up with him then."

"You play golf?" Cate asked in surprise.

"Of course, I do," Mimi replied. "If you want to beat these sort of men at their own game, you have to know how to play it. And how to win."

Before Cate could respond, her phone buzzed in her pocket. Bailey had sent a text.

Come to the hospital first thing in the morning. And bring me a change of clothes. I'm getting out of here.

CHAPTER ELEVEN

Bailey took a hesitant step forward, her legs trembling as she drew closer to the small, pink tennis shoe peeking out of the underbrush around the little pond in Summerset Park. Crouching down, she reached toward the tangle of weeds and branches, her mouth dry with fear. Had she arrived too late to save twelve-year-old Dolores Santos?

Moving quickly, Bailey pushed back the branches to reveal a small motionless form and a pale, doll-like face.

She knew right away that she had found the girl who had been reported missing only hours before.

"Dolores?"

Bailey leaned forward to take the girl's arm, resting her index and middle fingers on one delicate wrist, feeling for a pulse in the radial artery. There was no movement beneath the cold skin. No reassuring warmth or rhythmic beat.

As she sat back on her heels with a soft, despairing sigh, the little girl's eyes flew open and a small hand reached out to grab Bailey by the arm.

Gazing up at her with bright, accusing eyes, Dolores Santos spoke in a high-pitched, childish voice.

"He's coming for you next, Agent Flynn."

The warning sent a shiver down Bailey's spine.

"Soon, you'll be dead, too. Just like the others."

As soft footsteps crunched through the grass behind her, Bailey spun around, expecting to see Ronin Godfrey, the predator she'd just killed.

Had the girl's abductor come back from the dead, too?

Confusion rose as she saw Godfrey still sprawled on the bank of the pond where he'd fallen moments before.

The bullet hole between his eyes was oozing blood just as it had been when she'd run past him to get to Dolores.

Rustling noises sounded within the shadows cast by a large pine tree. As Bailey began to move cautiously forward, a dark figure suddenly loomed over Godfrey's dead body, lifting an arm to point in Bailey's direction.

A familiar, bitter voice echoed through the air.

"You killed him. Now it's your turn to die!"

It was the same voice she'd heard in the audio recording from the coffee shop. The voice of her shooter.

As the figure lunged toward her, Bailey woke and sat up with a cry, startled to find herself lying in bed, safe in her hospital room.

She sucked in a deep breath and sank back onto the pillow, shaken by the nightmare that had seemed so real.

The rapid *beep, beep, beep* of the machine beside her bed began to slow as her breathing returned to normal.

Closing her eyes, she pictured the dark figure in her dream emerging from the shadows and again heard his voice.

Was her subconscious mind playing tricks on her by merging the memories of the shooting at the coffee shop with the events at Summerset Park the day Dolores Santos had been abducted and killed?

Or had someone else really been there that day with Godfrey? Had the shooter been at the park, hiding in the shadows? Had he seen everything that had happened?

She concentrated hard, trying to recall everything she could remember about the awful day.

Special Agent Sid Morley had been first on the scene, following his search and rescue dogs to the little pond, where he'd spotted Ronin Godfrey by the lake.

He had confronted the predator, who by that time had already panicked and killed the little girl he had snatched earlier in the day from the sidewalk outside her home.

Bailey had arrived at the pond just in time to see Godfrey take aim at Morley. She'd shot Godfrey between the eyes in an effort to save her fellow agent's life, but the killer's wayward bullet had severed a major artery in Morley's leg.

Guilt at not arriving in time to save either Dolores Santos or Morley's leg had lived with Bailey ever since.

Regret had consumed her. But had it also blinded her to what had really happened that day?

Is it possible Godfrey didn't act alone? Could he have had a partner in crime? Maybe even the shooter at the coffee shop?

"That's crazy," she murmured. "It couldn't be. Could it?"

No, it was just a dream. A terrible nightmare.

Or perhaps she was still suffering from the aftereffects of her head injury. Perhaps her brain was mixing up the memories from the two traumatic scenes.

Perhaps Dr. Pendergrast is right. Maybe I do need more rest.

Forcing the unsettling thoughts of Godfrey from her mind, she sat up and looked toward the window, where clouds were again gathering in the east.

Hurricane season was in full swing and another tropical storm was now churning in the Atlantic, heading toward South Florida.

With a soft groan, Bailey swung her legs over the side of the hospital bed. She frowned down at the IV tube in her arm and exhaled as she looked over at the call button.

Before she could reach for it, she heard a soft knock, and then a smiling face appeared in the doorway.

She thought she recognized the man who stepped into her room but she couldn't remember his name.

She automatically returned the smile anyway, having quickly become accustomed to a rotation of doctors, nurses, and orderlies coming and going from her room at all hours.

"Dr. Pendergrast promised I would be getting out of here first thing this morning," Bailey told him, deciding a little white lie was in order. "My sister will be here shortly and I need my IV removed."

As he crossed the room and stopped beside her bed, she saw that the man wasn't wearing scrubs or a lab coat and that his longish, light brown hair skimmed the broad shoulders of his chambray shirt, unfettered by a medical cap.

"You don't work here, do you?" Bailey asked as she reached for the call button. "Who are you?"

"I'm a writer," the stranger said, gesturing to the book in his hand. "My name is Garth Hamilton and I'm working on a book about Summerset County. I was hoping to ask you a few questions and...well, I also brought you a signed copy of my latest book. I thought you might enjoy it."

He held out the book but Bailey made no move to take it.

Glancing down, she saw that the name on the spine was *History of the Hangman* and suddenly realized why the man had looked familiar. The author's photo had been printed on the back cover. There was no doubt the man in the photo was the same man standing beside her bed.

"I've already read it," she finally said, recalling the true crime account of a serial killer who had targeted young couples in Virginia several years earlier.

She had passed her copy of the book on to her sister after she'd finished reading it. The last time Bailey had seen it, the book had been lying on Cate's bedside table.

"Well, I hope you enjoyed it," Garth said, tucking the book under his arm. "I'll be sure to send you an advance reader copy of my next book once it's completed."

When she didn't respond, he cleared his throat.

"In fact, that's actually why I'm here. Before I can complete *Slaughter in Summerset County*, I need a little more information. I was hoping you could–"

"What in the world are you doing in my sister's room?"

Both Garth and Bailey jumped at the furious voice.

Cate had silently entered the room and was now standing in the doorway with her hands on her hips and her face flushed with anger.

"Do you have no boundaries?" she demanded. "Can't you see she's hospitalized and–"

"It's okay, Cate, I'm fine," Bailey cut in. "I'm getting out of here this morning. In fact, Mr. Hamilton is welcome to have my room if he likes. Only, he'll need to leave so I can get dressed first."

She stood up to take the bag of clothes from Cate's hand and turned to the writer, who was staring at her in wide-eyed surprise.

"Do you mind?" she asked, raising an eyebrow.

Looking surprisingly unflustered, Garth inclined his head.

"I've obviously come at a bad time, so I'll let you have your privacy. But perhaps we could meet up later. This afternoon would work for me if-"

"Go!" Cate snapped, losing patience.

Garth shrugged and took out a card from his pocket. He gently laid it on the foot of the bed.

"Call me when you're ready to talk," he said as he backed toward the door. "You have important information that my readers need to know. Think about it."

With those final words, he pushed open the door and disappeared out into the corridor.

"I'll make sure he's gone," Cate said, following the writer out into the corridor as Bailey quickly pulled on her clothes.

She was eager to leave before the doctor arrived for her morning rounds. She hadn't exactly been cleared for discharge as she'd led her sister to believe.

"I got rid of him," Cate assured her as soon as she returned. "But aren't they supposed to wheel you downstairs in a wheelchair?"

"Oh, that's not necessary," Bailey said as she began stuffing her few possessions into the bag. "I can walk just fine and we don't want to bother anyone."

Opening the door, she glanced down the corridor in both directions to make sure Dr. Pendergrast was nowhere in view before leaving the room.

As she and Cate headed toward the elevator, Bailey walked closely beside her sister, surreptitiously using her as a shield as they neared the elevator.

When the doors slid open to reveal Dr. Pendergrast talking to another woman in a white lab coat, Bailey looked away and lowered her head, bracing herself for a confrontation.

But the doctor was too caught up in her conversation to notice Bailey standing behind Cate as she passed by.

As she stepped onto the elevator and watched the doors close behind her, Bailey exhaled in relief.

"Okay, let's get out of here," she said, jabbing a thumb at the ground floor button. "I need to get to the Miami field office. Time to find out if I've still got a job."

* * *

Bailey stared through the windshield of Cate's white Lexus as they neared the ultramodern glass building that housed the FBI's Miami field office.

"Are you going to be able to get a ride home?" Cate asked.

"I'm sure I'll manage," she said, sounding more confident than she felt. "Hopefully, they'll let me take the same Expedition I was using before if it hasn't been reassigned."

She had returned the black SUV to the Bureau's pool of vehicles when she'd gone deep undercover and she knew there was no guarantee it would still be available.

In fact, she'd been thinking there was also no guarantee that she would even still have a job.

She'd heard nothing from Special-Agent-in-Charge Ford Ramsey since she'd regained consciousness in the hospital, and Will Griffin had never returned to finish debriefing her as he'd promised.

As she climbed out of the Lexus, she noticed that she was still wearing her hospital bracelet and turned back to Cate.

"You have any scissors?" she asked, holding up her wrist.

With a sigh, Cate dug into her purse and pulled out a portable manicure kit, which contained a small pair of cuticle scissors.

"Thanks," Bailey said as she cut off the bracelet and handed back the scissors. "You're always ready for any emergency. Always there when I need you."

Their eyes met and Bailey blinked away sudden tears.

"I mean it, Cate. You've always been there for me."

Cate smiled as she slipped the case back into her bag.

"And I always will be," she said matter-of-factly. "Cause you'd be lost without me."

Rolling up the window, Cate sped away, leaving Bailey standing outside the intimidating building.

She hesitated, suddenly realizing that no one knew she was coming into the office. She wasn't sure how her sudden appearance would be received.

I guess there's only one way to find out.

Pushing through the front door, she reached into her pocket, pulled out the security badge that Cate had brought along with her clothes, and was relieved to find it still allowed her to access the building.

Feeling slightly more confident, she took the elevator up to her usual floor. She was relieved to find the door open to SAC Ford Ramsey's office and glad to see Special Agent Aisha Sharma sitting across from Ramsey at his desk.

Sharma's light brown eyes lit up with pleasure as she stood and hurried to the door. Her long, dark hair fell over one shoulder as she leaned forward to give Bailey a warm hug, which was accompanied by the faint vanilla scent of her signature perfume.

"I didn't know you would be here today," Sharma said as she backed away to make room for Ramsey, who offered Bailey a firm handshake instead of a hug.

The SAC was unusually fit for a man on the wrong side of fifty. The long, lean muscles of his body contrasted sharply with his thinning hair and the network of deep wrinkles around his eyes.

"So, what's the prognosis?" Sharma asked. "Are you going to be okay? How are you feeling?"

"I'm feeling lucky to be standing here," Bailey admitted. "And lucky not to have sustained permanent brain damage."

"So, there are no residual effects from the injury?" Sharma asked, looking hopeful. "All's good now?"

Bailey quickly nodded.

There was no need to mention the memory loss. No need to tell them about the strange dreams she'd been having or the phantom voices she'd been hearing.

That would only worry Sharma and Ramsey.

And if they were concerned about her readiness to return to duty, it could interfere with her plans.

"I'm ready to get back to work," she said firmly. "And I'm ready to find the man who tried to kill me."

There was an awkward moment of silence before Sharma cleared her throat and got to her feet.

"I think I better leave you two alone so that you can talk."

She walked to the door, hesitated, and looked back to meet Bailey's eyes.

"I'm really glad you're okay," she said. "I was worried. When you're done here, come see me."

Opening the door before Bailey could respond, she slipped out into the hall, leaving her alone with Ramsey.

"So, what is it you need to tell me?" Bailey asked. "It must be pretty bad to run Sharma off like that."

Ramsey circled back around his desk and sank into his chair with an ominous sigh, motioning for her to take a seat across from him.

"Based on orders from above, Griff's unit has been disbanded," he said, making no attempt to soften his words. "And we've been ordered to open an internal investigation. We need to find out how Operation Tombstone was compromised. We need to determine who was responsible."

His pronouncement left Bailey momentarily speechless.

She'd expected Ramsey to question her ability to objectively lead the search for Jordan Stone. After all, Stone was the man who'd ordered the hit on her.

But she hadn't expected Ramsey to tell her that the Bureau was now investigating her team rather than her assailant.

"Griff didn't say anything to me about the team being disbanded when he came by the hospital on Monday," Bailey said, feeling betrayed. "And he didn't say anything about an internal investigation either."

Thinking back to the conversation she'd had with Will Griffin, she wondered what else he'd kept from her.

"It isn't his fault," Ramsey said. "Griff was only informed this morning. He wasn't too happy, as you can imagine. Not about his unit being disbanded, not about the investigation. I'd been hoping we could figure something out but..."

He gave a disgruntled shrug as the words trailed off.

Bailey felt a surge of sympathy for Will Griffin and the rest of the team. Then her thoughts turned to her own future.

"What does that mean for me?" she asked. "Will I be sent back to the D.C. field office?"

A sudden idea took root.

Maybe I can talk SAC Roger Calloway into letting me head up a search for Jordan Stone out of the D.C. office.

But Ramsey was already shaking his head.

"Turns out that after you accepted the undercover assignment down here in Miami, Roger Calloway recruited another agent to backfill your position within his special crimes unit. They aren't budgeted to take on another agent. At least, not right now."

"Oh," Bailey said as all the breath left her lungs. "So, what happens to me now? Am I being suspended?"

The slight headache she'd had all morning turned into a dull throb as she waited for Ramsey's response.

"No, not suspended," he said. "But you will have to be

reassigned to a new field office with an open position."

"A new office? Which one?" she asked. "Do you know where I'll be going?"

Bailey braced herself for his reply, knowing she could be given an assignment somewhere far removed from family and friends, picturing somewhere cold and desolate.

"Well, for now, you'll stay in Miami. You've been temporarily reassigned to our field office," he said. "Once we've concluded the investigation as to what went wrong in the undercover operation and have reviewed the findings, a decision will be made as to a permanent reassignment."

Bailey sensed there was something he wasn't saying.

Her heart suddenly dropped.

Did they suspect she'd made a mistake, or worse?

"Do you think *I'm* responsible for the operation's failure?" she asked. "Has someone implicated me?"

Resisting the impulse to jump to her feet and defend herself, to shout out she hadn't been the one who'd made a mistake or leaked information, she stayed seated in her chair.

After all, she had no memory of that day. No memory of what had actually happened.

All she had to go on was an audio recording of the shooter in which he claimed he'd recognized Morgan Tate and known her as Special Agent Bailey Flynn.

Her cover as a bespectacled barista had failed her.

Of course, that wasn't necessarily her fault. Someone on the Operation Tombstone team could have outed her, either intentionally or inadvertently.

But who was the shooter and how did he know her?

And why is he holding a grudge against me for killing Godfrey?

She'd need the answers to those questions if she hoped to prove she wasn't the one who'd blown the operation.

"Don't take this personally. It's standard protocol to conduct an investigation after a fatal shooting," Ramsey said but his somber tone wasn't reassuring. "While the investigation is in process, I suggest you stay safe and keep out of trouble."

"But what about Jordan Stone?" she asked. "Who's going to find him? Who's going to take down his operation now?"

Ramsey ran a hand through what was left of his hair.

"We believe Stone may have left the country," he admitted. "The Bureau's in the process of forming a transnational task force to track him down. Of course, now that we have reason to believe Stone put a hit out on you, it's clear you can't be involved in the search."

Bailey started to protest but he held up a hand to stop her.

"If you've got medical clearance to return to work, Agent Sharma has been looking into a money laundering ring just south of Miami Beach. You can assist her with the investigation."

Sensing she'd been dismissed, Bailey nodded numbly.

As she left Ramsey's office, she made a decision.

If I can't track down Stone myself, I'll find someone who can.

CHAPTER TWELVE

D alton West paced back and forth in front of his desk, moving with the tense, brooding grace of a panther trapped in a cage. He'd asked Sid Morley to meet him at his office after lunch and the retired FBI agent was seated in a chair by the window, the outline of the West Security Services logo visible on the glass pane behind his head.

Morley's eyes followed Dalton as he paced, as did the eyes of the German shepherd he'd brought with him.

Ludwig shifted restlessly at Morley's feet as if he wasn't sure what they were doing inside the cramped little office on Davenport Drive when the day outside was sunny, windy, and gloriously warm.

Stopping next to a whiteboard on the wall, Dalton lifted a dry-erase marker to add another name to his growing list.

He'd asked Morley to come by and help him put together a dossier on Jordan Stone to help with his search.

He wanted to document everything he knew or could learn about the billionaire that might help him track down Stone's current whereabouts.

They had started off by listing all the associates and partners in crime who might be helping Stone.

These were the people who had helped him perpetrate his crimes and enabled his corruption in the past.

The effort had naturally progressed into a discussion of all the known victims Stone was suspected to have played a part in killing over the last few years.

Since they suspected the crypto billionaire had worked with Chuck Ashworth before the Tumba Cartel boss met his fate in the Summerset Detention Center, the list was long.

It included dozens of people from all walks of life, ranging from street-level drug dealers to high-profile lawyers.

Morley read the last name Dalton had written on the whiteboard out loud.

"Mario Rocco," he said slowly. "Yes, that's right. Mario was representing Chuck Ashworth before his death. Bailey believes Stone ordered a hit on Ashworth and Mario was collateral damage."

Circling his desk, Dalton sank into the chair in front of his computer, performing an online search on Mario Rocco.

An avalanche of results was returned.

The first few pages included coverage of his sudden death.

Photos from his funeral showed a packed church of mourners, most of whom were either famous for their celebrity status or infamous for their criminal connections.

Later pages of results included hundreds of photos of the wealthy defense attorney attending various high-profile events. Mentions of his romantic conquests on celebrity gossip websites were interspersed with news items covering the latest sensationalized trial of the notorious clients he'd represented over his career.

Scrolling back to the top of the search page, Dalton clicked on a photo of a portly older man in a finely tailored black suit exiting the church after Mario's funeral.

"That's his dad, Giovanni Rocco," Morley said.

He was leaning forward to look at the computer screen.

"His father defended a few of the scumbags I arrested back in the day," he added as he stared down at the photos.

"Yeah, I've heard that Giovanni Rocco's a real character," Dalton said. "I guess anyone with the nickname *Loco Rocco* is bound to be a bit eccentric."

"He actually seemed like an okay guy," Morley said. "That is if you disregard his habit of successfully defending mob bosses and career criminals."

Leaning back in his chair, Morley shook his head.

"It's strange how I'm sitting here feeling sorry for Giovanni Rocco when he's still got both his legs and a bazillion dollars in the bank."

"Yeah, I guess none of that matters when you lose a son."

Dalton cocked his head.

"You think Mr. Rocco would be interested in helping us find Stone? Maybe even fund the search?"

The question brought an interested shine to Morley's eyes.

"Now that you mention it, I *do* know where he lives."

The retired agent scratched thoughtfully at the stubble on his sagging chin.

"I actually went there once to take one of his clients into custody. The perp agreed to surrender as long as he had his lawyer with him. Turned out Loco Rocco was his lawyer."

He raised a shaggy gray eyebrow.

"Rocco owns a house in West Palm Beach. It's ridiculously big. More like a palace than a house. I remember thinking it was a real waste of space for a single man. And it seemed so...*empty*."

His voice took on a musing tone.

"It's like he's spent his life chasing fame and fortune at the expense of his family and friends, and now he's ended up alone, trapped inside a palace that feels more like a prison."

Getting to his feet, Dalton headed toward the door.

"How about we take a road trip?" he suggested, smiling as Ludwig jumped to his feet in excitement. "Let's go to Palm Beach and see if we can get an audience with *King Rocco*."

As Morley adjusted his prosthetic leg and pushed himself to his feet, the door swung open.

To Dalton's surprise, Bailey stood in the doorway.

Before either of them could say anything, Ludwig gave an excited bark and sprang toward Bailey, running in joyous circles around her and wagging his tail furiously in an exuberant greeting.

Kneeling beside the German shepherd, Bailey hugged him to her and patted the tan and black fur on his back.

"I guess I'm not the only one here who's been missing you," Dalton said as he watched the happy reunion between the search and rescue dog and his handler.

"Come on now, Ludwig. Let Bailey inside," Morley said.

He crossed the room and tugged on the dog's collar, pulling him back so that Bailey could enter.

"You sure you should be out and about already?" he asked, studying Bailey's pale face with concern. "I mean, I'm as thrilled to see you as Ludwig here, but shouldn't you be at home resting?"

"I'm fine," Bailey said, waving away his concern. "In fact, I went into the office this morning. I even managed to get my old Expedition back from the vehicle pool."

Morley frowned.

"From what I was told, you had a pretty serious head injury. Did the doctor really clear you to go back to work so soon? That seems like an awful big risk to me."

Dropping her eyes, she didn't respond, choosing instead to bend over and enthusiastically ruffle Ludwig's fur.

Dalton knew Bailey well enough by now to know that she had a tendency to ignore questions she didn't want to answer, and he immediately suspected she might not have gotten her doctor's blessing after all.

But before he could question her further, she quickly moved on, adeptly changing the subject with a blunt announcement.

"My undercover unit has been permanently disbanded," she said. "So, it looks like I'll be staying in Miami for the foreseeable future."

She spoke in the stilted, cheerful voice she always used when she was upset but didn't want to admit it.

"And my old position in D.C. has been filled so I've been temporarily reassigned to the Miami field office."

There was a moment of surprised silence in the room, and then Bailey sank into a chair with a heavy sigh as if the pretense that everything was fine had suddenly become too tiresome to continue.

"For now, I've been assigned to work on a local money laundering case," she continued in a weary voice. "Although to be honest, I'm not sure I'll have a job after the internal investigation into the shooting is concluded."

"They won't let a sharp agent like you go," Morley assured her. "The suits calling the shots aren't that clueless."

Slumping back in the chair, Bailey didn't seem convinced.

"They're investigating my actions in relation to the shooting instead of focusing on finding the actual shooter," she said. "And they've told me I'm not allowed to look for Jordan Stone. That all sounds pretty clueless to me."

Dalton didn't argue with her. He was too busy struggling to hide his relief that she was back in Belle Harbor and would be staying in the area, perhaps permanently.

He knew he should feel ashamed of himself for being happy at her news when it was clearly making her miserable.

But having Bailey back in Belle Harbor felt good. Too good for him to let anything happen to her again. And there may be something he could do to make her feel better.

Standing beside her, he gestured to the whiteboard.

"I don't want you to worry about finding Jordan Stone," he said. "Because Morley and I are going to do that for you."

Bailey scanned the list of names he and Morley had written with interest and nodded her approval.

"That's a good starting point," she said. "But I want to help with your search for Stone as much as I can. Or as much as I can without getting into trouble with Ramsey."

Her forehead creased into a frown as she lifted a hand to the back of her head and rubbed absently.

"I just wish I could remember everything that happened," she said. "I wish I could remember the face of the man who shot me. I wish I could remember his name. I'm sure he could lead you straight to Stone."

A pang of worry filled Dalton at her words. The shooter might be thinking the very same thing. And if the shooter thought she may be able to identify him, he could decide to come after her again.

And next time, she might not be wearing a bullet-proof vest.

But there was no point just worrying about it. He needed to do something about it. And the best thing to do was to find Stone and bring him in. If they had Stone, they had a good chance of bringing in the shooter as well.

"You guys looked like you were getting ready to leave when I came in," Bailey said. "Where were you going?"

"We were heading over to West Palm Beach to visit Giovanni Rocco," Dalton said. "We're thinking of asking him if he wants to fund our search for Stone."

Bailey nodded slowly.

"I can see why he'd want to help. He must be eager to find the man who played a key role in the death of his only son," she said. "Just be careful. From what I've heard about Loco Rocco, he can be a dangerous man."

* * *

Dalton stepped on the brake, bringing the Dodge pickup to a sudden stop outside the wrought iron gate that blocked the long drive up to Giovanni Rocco's house in West Palm Beach.

A stone plaque outside named the mansion *Villa Rocco*.

Rolling down the window, Dalton leaned out and pressed the call button on the security panel.

He expected to be greeted by a voice over the intercom but instead saw a uniformed guard the size of a defensive lineman stepping out of a small door set into the stone wall surrounding the property.

"Do you have an appointment with Mr. Rocco? Because I don't see anything on his calendar."

The security guard surveyed the truck and the men inside with hostile, suspicious eyes.

"Actually, we didn't call ahead," Dalton admitted. "We were hoping to talk to Mr. Rocco about an important matter involving his son and-"

"Mr. Rocco isn't at home," the guard said. "And he doesn't receive uninvited visitors in any case. Now get lost."

Before Dalton could react, the guard turned and made his way back to the door, slamming it behind him.

"That certainly went well," Morley said as they stared through the wrought iron gate at the opulent house beyond. "I guess maybe I'll have to put in a call to some of my old connections and see if we can get an introduction."

But as Dalton started to roll up the window, a friendly voice called out to him.

"Don't let Yuri bother you. He's just moody sometimes."

Looking around, Dalton saw a small man standing behind the gate holding a pair of pruning shears.

"Who's Yuri?" he asked.

The man smiled.

"Yuri is the security guard here and I'm the gardener," he said. "And Mr. Rocco really isn't home right now. He's at the golf club down the street. If you stop by, he'll probably let you buy him a drink. He's been drinking a lot lately."

The man put a small finger to his lips.

"But don't tell him I said that."

With a jaunty wave, the gardener was gone, leaving Dalton staring after him.

"You think he was telling the truth?" Morley asked. "Or just trying to send us on a wild goose chase?"

Looking up at the clear blue sky, Dalton shrugged.

"It's a nice day for golf," he said. "Might as well find out."

Thirty minutes later they were speeding along a narrow cart path in a golf cart they'd rented from the overpriced shop. As they neared the thirteenth hole, Dalton caught sight of a portly man with a thick mane of gray hair lining up his tee shot and stopped the cart.

"That's him," Morley said. "That's Giovanni Rocco."

They both winced as the old man shanked the ball into a thick line of trees down the side of the green. Letting out a string of curses, Rocco threw his golf club to the ground.

"Yikes," Morley muttered under his breath. "Maybe we should wait for him up at the club house."

Dalton quickly agreed and restarted the golf cart.

When Rocco finally finished the course and arrived at the club house an hour later, they were waiting for him at the outside bar.

"Gin and tonic," he called to the bartender as he sat down at a nearby table. "Make it a double."

Picking up the beer he'd ordered, Dalton stood and walked over to Rocco's table.

"Hello, Mr. Rocco, I was wondering if you might have a minute to talk with me and my friend," he said, motioning for Morley to join him. "I think we have a mutual interest."

The older man raised an eyebrow.

"Let me guess. You have a company I'd be a fool not to invest in, right? Believe me, I've heard it all and I'm not interested. Now, if you'll leave me to enjoy my drink."

Ignoring the request, Dalton sat down at the table, laying one of his cards in front of Rocco.

"I'm a private investigator with West Security Services and my friend here is a retired FBI agent. We're searching for Jordan Stone. One way or the other, we plan to find him and bring him to justice. We thought you might want to help."

The bartender brought over the gin and tonic and set it on the table as Rocco stared at Dalton, momentarily speechless.

He picked up the glass, drained it, and then called out to the bartender, asking for another.

"Thanks to that filthy bastard Jordan Stone, my bloodline and my legacy will die with me," Rocco said, studying Dalton with bloodshot eyes. "It's his fault my Mario is gone."

"Stone's running his own cartel now," Dalton said. "But he's gotten himself in a bit of trouble and he's hiding out."

Rocco nodded.

"Yes, I know. And I've been trying to find him."

"Any luck?" Dalton asked.

The question was left unanswered as the bartender came back and set the second drink on the table.

"As I said, we plan to find Stone with or without your help," Dalton said. "But he could be anywhere in the world right now and your connections could speed things up, as could your funding. It takes money and resources to run a search like that."

Leaning forward, Dalton propped his elbows on the table.

"I'm sure you're wondering why you should trust me when you could hire any firm. But you won't find anyone as motivated as I am."

Rocco raised an eyebrow.

"And why is that?"

"Because Stone tried to have the woman I love killed," Dalton said. "And if I don't find Stone, he may try again."

He watched Rocco pick up his drink. But the man hesitated before putting the glass to his lips.

"Here's to my boy Mario," he said, lifting his glass toward Dalton, who clinked his beer bottle against it. "And here's to our new partnership. May you find Stone quickly and may he rot in jail."

By the time Dalton and Morley left the golf club, Rocco had agreed to hire West Security Services. He wanted them to find the man responsible for the death of his only son.

Pleased with the day's outcome, Dalton pulled into the parking lot of the Armory apartments to find Sabrina's van parked outside.

Realizing he hadn't seen his sister all day, he stopped and knocked on her door, wanting to check on her and make sure everything was okay.

Instead of opening the door, she called out in a loud,

almost hostile voice he barely recognized.

"Who is it?"

"It's me, your brother," Dalton said. "What's going on?"

Sabrina wrenched open the door and pulled him inside, quickly closing the door behind him.

"He's threatening to kill me."

She slid the deadbolt into place.

"He might be out there now."

Staring at his sister in surprise, Dalton thought at first she must be kidding. That she was playing some sort of joke.

But then he saw the anger and the fear on her face and was instantly concerned.

"Who's threatening to kill you?" he asked with a frown. "Who might be outside?"

Sabrina tapped on her phone and held it up so that he could see the message on the screen.

Are you ready to die?

Anger coursed through Dalton as he took the phone from her hand and read the words.

"I was contacted by a woman named Krystal Devine last week," Sabrina said. "She was being harassed and threatened by someone online and wanted me to produce a report about online trolls. She thought that might make the troll stop.

"But when I sent a message to the troll asking for a statement to put in the report, I started getting these death threats, too."

Shaking his head in disgust, Dalton looked more closely at the message. His heart dropped when he saw the sender's username.

SirGrendel88.

His mind flashed to the bones in the old boxcar and the graffiti tag spraypainted on the wall.

He read the message again with a growing sense of dread.

Are you ready to die?

CHAPTER THIRTEEN

Sabrina stalked over to the front window and peeked out between the closed blinds, not really expecting to see a stranger standing on her doorstep ready to carry out the threats she'd been receiving. She didn't know who SirGrendel88 was yet, but she already knew the troll was a coward. Someone who didn't have the guts to confront his targets directly or to show his face in broad daylight.

As she had suspected, there was no one lurking outside.

Turning back toward Dalton, she realized her brother hadn't said anything since he'd seen the message from SirGrendel88 on her phone.

Surprised by his silence, she spun around to face him.

"What's wrong with you?" she asked.

All the color had drained from his face.

"Are you okay?"

"When did you get this?" he demanded, his eyes still riveted on the little screen.

"Like I told you, Krystal Devine contacted me last week," she said, trying to stay calm. "I reached out to the troll who's been harassing her and he turned on me. He's sent a dozen messages since then. Why, what's wrong?"

"What I'm about to tell you has to be off the record," Dalton said. "I don't want to hear this on the evening news."

His eyes held hers and his voice was deadly serious.

"Fine," Sabrina snapped. "Just stop freaking me out and tell me what you saw."

"Remember I told you I was at the Summerset Railroad Depot two days ago when the BHPD went to investigate a skull they'd found?" Dalton said. "The skull had a bullet in it. It belongs to an unidentified homicide victim."

Sabrina's heart dropped.

"Okay, so what about the skull with a bullet in it?"

"Well, someone had spraypainted graffiti all over the place," he said. "The tag SirGrendel88 had been painted on the wall. Right above the bones."

Dread settled in Sabrina's chest.

"Bones? As in...*human bones?*" she stammered.

Dalton gave a grim nod.

"We've got to tell Detective Fraser about the threats you've been getting from this troll," he said decisively. "Fraser was at the railroad depot with me. I believe he's asked Madeline Mercer and Eloise Spellman to analyze the bones and try to find out who they belong to. Your information could help his investigation."

Following Dalton out to his pickup truck, Sabrina numbly climbed into the passenger's seat and allowed him to drive her to the Belle Harbor police station to file a report.

As they turned onto Grand Harbor Boulevard, Dalton reminded her that what he'd told her about the skull and bones discovered at the railroad depot was off the record.

"That information can't be shared or broadcasted," he insisted. "If they think I'm leaking information to the press, they won't ask me to help out with future searches."

Sabrina nodded absently as they parked in the station's lot and went into the lobby.

She wondered where the skull and bones were being kept as Dalton went up to the desk sergeant and asked to speak to Detective Fraser.

Are they here somewhere or at the medical examiner's office?

The thought that the human remains might be down the hall in an evidence locker sent a shiver down Sabrina's spine.

"They said Detective Fraser will be out to speak to us shortly," Dalton said as he turned away from the desk.

Just then the door to the back opened and a dark-haired woman walked out, heading toward the exit.

Recognizing Madeline Mercer, Sabrina remembered that she had been meaning to talk to the CSI team leader about the interviews she'd been giving to Garth Hamilton.

But before she could react, Dalton had already walked over to Madeline, who greeted him with a cautious smile.

"If you're here to ask about the items we recovered at the depot, you've come to the wrong place," she said. "Those items have been taken to the M.E.'s office. And as far as I know, they haven't gotten any results back yet."

As Madeline continued on, pushing through the front door, Sabrina impulsively followed after her, telling Dalton she'd be right back.

Once outside, she called to Madeline, who was heading to her van. The CSI team leader stopped and turned around.

"Sorry to bother you, but I wanted to ask you about Garth Hamilton," Sabrina said. "I heard he's writing a true crime book on Summerset County and that you're one of his prime sources of information."

Madeline beamed.

"I hope I've been of help," she said. "It's so important that the people around here know what happened. As Garth always says, those who study the criminal mind and how it works are better able to protect themselves in the future."

Trying not to roll her eyes, Sabrina nodded politely.

"In fact, I'm giving him another interview tonight," Madeline said. "He's paying me back for my time by taking me out to dinner. Isn't that sweet of him?"

"I'm sure it seems that way to you," Sabrina said, biting her lip. "But I'm worried Mr. Hamilton might be taking advantage of your kindness. Are you sure he hasn't been manipulating you into giving him information?"

The comment caused Madeline's back to stiffen.

"No one is taking advantage of me," she said in a cold voice. "And I'm not one to be easily manipulated, despite what you might think. Now, I've got to go."

Spinning on her heel, Madeline continued on to her van, her angry strides telling Sabrina she was unlikely to convince the woman to give her an interview when she actually started writing her own book.

As she stared after the CSI van, Sabrina heard someone calling her name. Dalton was standing at the station door, motioning to her.

"Fraser's ready for us now," he called out.

With a sigh, Sabrina hurried back inside, where Fraser was waiting to lead her and Dalton into an interview room.

Once they were all seated around a small table, the detective crossed his thick arms over his solid chest and raised his eyebrows.

"Okay, Ms. West, I understand you want to file a report?"

Sabrina nodded.

"Someone has been sending me death threats online," she said. "It's the same troll who has been harassing a woman named Krystal Devine. She contacted me in hopes I would cover her story on the news.

"She thought it might shame the troll into silence. What she didn't realize is that trolls like this one have no shame."

Leaning back in his chair, Fraser frowned.

"Online threats, harassment, and other cybercrimes need to be reported to the FBI's Internet Crime division, IC3," he said. "They handle all that stuff and-"

"This is a bit more complicated than that," Dalton cut in.

He looked at Sabrina and motioned to her phone.

"Show him the message," he said.

With a sigh, Sabrina tapped several times on her phone screen, scrolled to the message from SirGrendel88, and placed the phone on the table in front of Fraser.

The detective's eyes widened as he read the message and registered the username.

"Of course, this could just be a hell of a coincidence," he said. "But we can't dismiss the possibility that this troll was involved in the death of our John Doe at the railroad depot. Either way, we need to loop in the Bureau...now."

CHAPTER FOURTEEN

Bailey rubbed the back of her head as she sat across from Special Agent Aisha Sharma, reviewing the evidence collected so far in the money laundering case she'd been assigned. Perpetrating such a crime consisted largely of falsifying written reports and digital records. Proving the crime required close attention to detail, something Bailey was finding difficult given the headache she'd been battling for the last twenty-four hours.

Glancing down at Ludwig, she saw that the German shepherd had taken up a post by the table, keeping an eye on her as if he was afraid she might suddenly disappear again.

She had just bent down to scratch at the fur behind his ears when Ford Ramsey appeared in the doorway.

"Agent Flynn? I need to see you in my office."

Without waiting for a response, he turned and disappeared down the hall, leaving her little choice but to stand and follow him. She shot Sharma a *what-did-I-do-this-time* grimace as she shrugged and walked out of the room.

When she reached Ramsey's office, she saw that a lanky man with thick blonde hair, a full beard, and a mustache was standing by the window.

"Agent Flynn, I'd like to introduce you to Dr. Mitch Ellis," Ramsey said in a gruff voice. "He's a psychiatrist and he comes highly recommended. He's worked with several agents who were injured or involved in shootings and–"

"I know Dr. Ellis," Bailey cut in. "I met with him before. After the Ronin Godfrey shooting."

She glanced at the psychiatrist.

"It's good to see you again, Dr. Ellis."

"What has it been?" he asked. "Three years?"

Bailey nodded and turned back to Ramsey.

"Is this mandatory?" she asked. "Are you saying that I need to see Dr. Ellis in order to return to work?"

Ramsey looked surprised.

"Well, no," he admitted. "Seeing Dr. Ellis is up to you. But I highly recommend that you do so."

Clearing his throat, the psychiatrist took a business card out of his pocket and held it out to her.

"Here's my contact information."

After an awkward pause, she reluctantly plucked the card from his hand and tucked it into her pocket.

"Give it some thought and call me if you decide you'd like to talk," he said. "You'd be surprised how cathartic it can be to have a chance to talk things over with an objective party."

"Okay, I'll think about it," Bailey agreed. "Thank you."

Her pocket buzzed as she turned to leave Ramsey's office.

Pulling out her phone as she headed back down the hall, she saw that Jimmy Fraser was calling.

"Fraser? What's up?" she asked as she stepped back into the conference room. "I'm here with Agent Sharma."

"And you're on speaker on my end," Fraser replied. "I've got Sabrina West here with me. She came into the station with her brother Dalton to file a report. She's been receiving online death threats."

His words prompted an instant reaction. Adrenaline surged through Bailey as he continued.

"It seems an internet troll has been harassing and threatening a woman named Krystal Devine. She reached out to Sabrina hoping she'd do a story on trolls and online bullies in the area."

Bailey figured she already knew what had happened next.

"Let me guess. The troll then turned on her?"

"That's right," Fraser said. "But more importantly, Dalton saw that the troll's username was SirGrendel88, which matches a graffiti tag spraypainted on the wall out at the old railroad depot."

He drew in a deep breath.

"The tag was painted on the wall of the caboose where we found the bones and the rope. And since those bones very likely belong to the skull that had the bullet in it...well, I thought you'd want to know right away."

Bailey stared down at her phone, realizing he was referring to the bullet that ballistics had matched to the bullet found at the coffee shop.

The one that would have ended her life if not for the vest.

"Why did Ms. Devine contact the press about the threats instead of going to law enforcement?" Sharma asked, speaking up for the first time.

Suddenly, Sabrina West's voice filled the room.

"Krystal said she'd reported the threats to the FBI's Internet Crime Tip Line but didn't hear back," the reporter said. "She got frustrated and thought maybe the troll would be shamed into silence if we ran a story on the news."

Bailey opened her laptop.

"What's the influencer's name?"

"Krystal with a K," Sabrina said, spelling the last name. "D-E-V-I-N-E."

After typing in the information, Bailey nodded.

"Yes, I see her complaint in the system."

She read through the woman's complaint with Sharma looking over her shoulder.

"Most people never officially report this type of thing. They'll try to ignore it or handle it themselves," Sharma said. "The word *trolling* makes it sound as if it's a game or a prank so most people write it off as harmless."

"Well, Krystal Devine is an online influencer and activist who speaks out about a bunch of different causes," Sabrina said. "She's not the type of person who ignores things or chooses to stay silent for long."

Bailey opened an attachment on the file, which contained screen captures of the messages Krystal Devine had received.

She studied the messages, which had grown increasingly threatening over time, noting that they had all been sent by *SirGrendel88*.

"Could Grendel be the troll's last name?" Bailey asked.

Sharma spoke up behind her.

"I doubt it," she said. "More likely it's a reference to the evil troll in the poem *Beowulf*, who was described as a descendant of Cain, the original murderer in the Bible."

The idea wasn't comforting.

"That must be where I've heard the name before," Bailey said. "I thought it was familiar. We had to read *Beowulf* in high school but I don't really remember what it was about."

"It was written by an anonymous poet in Old English over a thousand years ago," Sharma said. "There are hundreds of translations out there and each one is a little different."

"Depending on which version you read, Grendel is described as an ogre, a monster, a troll, a fiend, and a beast. I think a few translations even refer to him as a hater and a stalker. However, they all agree he was evil.

"He was merciless, driving his victims to such depths of despair they began praying to the *slayer of souls* to help them. Which is sort of like asking the devil to fight on your side."

She pronounced the words with relish as Sabrina shivered.

"The Grendel in the poem sounds horrible," she said. "Maybe SirGrendel88 used him for inspiration."

"Whoever sent the threats to Krystal Devine and Sabrina likely uses the name Grendel as a way to intimidate and mock people," Sharma theorized. "But the Grendel in the poem actually killed a lot of people. Hopefully, the online version won't take it that far."

As she stared at the hateful messages, Bailey had an idea.

"Let's check Krystal's social media around the time she started getting the messages," she said. "She must have encountered the troll online. Maybe we can find something that will tell us why she was targeted."

Opening a browser, Bailey began scrolling through Krystal

Devine's most recent social media posts and timeline.

She stopped on a photo of Krystal at Summerset Park.

The young woman was dressed in a metallic jumpsuit and had a short cap of platinum blonde hair.

Bailey's pulse quickened as she realized that, in the photo, Krystal was standing in front of the recent memorial held for Dolores Santos, holding up a sign.

STOP GUN VIOLENCE!

She frowned, wondering if the woman could have angered the troll with her sign. Was it just a coincidence that she'd been at the park where Godfrey had died around the same time she'd started receiving death threats?

Deciding she didn't believe in coincidences, Bailey glanced over at Sharma.

"We need to check the database for other references to the username SirGrendel88. I have a feeling we'll find that other complaints have been filed."

Her fingers moved quickly over the keyboard as she performed the search. As the screen filled with results, she inhaled sharply.

"There's been over a dozen complaints in the last two years," she said, her heart quickening as she recognized the last name on the list. "A woman named Luisa Santos filed a complaint two months ago. She's Dolores Santos' mother."

An image of the grief-stricken woman flashed through Bailey's mind as she opened the screen captures attached to Luisa's complaint.

Each one contained a different message from SirGrendel88. Most threatened death but the last message contained only a reference to a bible verse.

Psalm 27:10

Navigating back to her browser, Bailey looked up the verse. She stared at it in confusion before reading it aloud.

"For my father and my mother have forsaken me, but the Lord will take me up."

"What do you think it means?" Sharma asked.

Bailey's stomach felt sick as she studied the words.

"I think it's meant to imply that Dolores' parents failed their daughter," she said. "The troll's taunting them, implying God took Dolores because they had forsaken her."

Closing Luisa's file, she scanned the rest of the complaints, all of which were made by people living in Summerset County. None had resulted in an arrest.

She sent the screenshot of the names to the printer and jumped to her feet to grab the printout.

Suddenly, the room began to spin, forcing Bailey to reach out and hold on to the table.

"Oh dear, you look really pale," Sharma said. "Sit back down and have a rest. You just got out of the hospital."

Her voice was filled with concern.

"I'm sorry Detective Fraser, but I think we'll need to reconvene and continue our discussions tomorrow," she said as she stood and leaned closer to the phone. "Bailey needs to go home and get some rest. She's not looking so good."

"That's fine," Fraser said. "Just make sure she gets home safely. We don't want anything else happening to her."

Feeling foolish, Bailcy tried to protest that she was fine,

but Sharma wouldn't listen. She insisted on escorting Bailey and Ludwig to the Expedition, even offering to drive them home but Bailey refused.

Reluctantly, Sharma waved them off. She watched as they pulled onto the highway and headed back toward the coast.

As she drove toward Belle Harbor, Bailey groaned, remembering she had promised her mother she would sleep at her parents' house that night just to make sure she really was okay.

Speeding east along the highway, she mulled over everything that had happened that day, wondering who SirGrendel88 was and if the troll was somehow involved with the skull and bones found at the railroad depot.

And the bullet. What about the bullet?

When she finally pulled onto Claremont Street, she reminded herself that the troll wasn't the only monster she had to worry about.

Where is Jordan Stone, and where is the man he hired to kill me?

The shooter's voice, the one she'd heard on the recording, echoed through her head, making it throb.

I've been dying to get this chance ever since the day you killed my old partner Ronin Godfrey at Summerset Park.

Bailey's mind whirled with questions.

Who is the shooter? Could he really have been Godfrey's partner? Is he out there right now plotting his next move?

CHAPTER FIFTEEN

G rendel watched Krystal Devine's house with growing rage, his hands clenching and unclenching as he imagined wrapping the rope around her neck and pulling it tighter and tighter. How satisfying it would be to squeeze every self-serving word from the influencer's mouth and every last breath from her lungs.

Earlier that evening, he'd received a message from the silly woman saying that she had been contacted by the FBI.

She'd boasted that she would be meeting with agents the following day to provide them with information, ensuring he would be found and exposed as the vile troll he was.

Grendel suspected he knew which agent she would be meeting with and his teeth clenched in anger at the thought.

No doubt Special Agent Bailey Flynn would be doing the questioning. But what exactly could Krystal tell her?

The influencer knew nothing about him.

But then, perhaps she would tell Bailey that she'd gone to the memorial at Summerset Park several months earlier.

That was where he had first seen Krystal in person, waving her ridiculous sign, pretending she cared about the death and suffering of others when she cared only for herself.

That's when he'd first felt the urge to kill her.

After waiting for her to leave the park, he had followed her home, biding his time as he started the delicious process of learning everything he could about her.

Where she worked. What she ate. When she slept.

His plan was to use it all to troll her over the coming days, weeks, and months, haunting her with his constant presence until she had been driven mad with worry and fear.

Only then, when the exquisite torture had reached its crescendo, would he give her the release she'd be begging for.

At least, that had been his original plan. It was a plan that had worked beautifully before, not so long ago.

The trouble was, that Krystal Devine wasn't easily scared.

If he'd learned anything about the woman over the last few months, it was that she wouldn't go down easily.

And if she does go down, she'll go kicking and screaming. And she'll do everything in her power to take me down with her.

But it was too late to back down now. His sense of pride would never allow it. His pride had caused him to do much worse in the past. In fact, if he thought about it, his pride had been responsible for the first murder he'd committed a decade earlier at the old railroad depot.

Of course, he knew the old saying about pride going before a fall. He'd actually learned the proverb behind the saying back when he was a child. Before the trouble had started.

"Pride goes before destruction, a haughty spirit before a fall," he muttered to himself as he watched the window for signs of life from within. "And *Ms. High and Mighty* in there is certainly set to take a fall."

Then again, the FBI agents might make the connection between the memorial she'd attended and the first message he'd sent to her the following day.

If they were smart, they would start looking at her photos from the memorial online and maybe even photos from others who'd been there that day. Someone could have captured a shot of him looking at her with hate in his eyes.

And with his recent screw-up at the coffee shop, he couldn't afford to have the FBI showing up on his doorstep.

Jordan Stone might hear about it and think he was talking to the feds, trying to make a deal. The billionaire didn't need another reason to end Grendel's life.

Catching sight of headlights coming up the street behind him, Grendel quickly ducked down as a car pulled onto Krystal's driveway.

He watched furtively as the car stopped and a delivery man stepped out. The man unloaded several bags of groceries, carried them up to the front porch, and knocked. Turning on his heel, he got back into his car.

As the car pulled out of the driveway, Grendel decided there was only one way to make sure Krystal never told the feds about the memorial.

His father's Berretta was in the glove compartment. He took it out and stuck it into the waistband of his pants before reaching into the backseat to grab the bag of supplies he always had at the ready.

Climbing out of the vehicle, he crossed the street, slipped through the shadows along the side of the house, and mounted the porch steps.

He picked up one of the plastic grocery bags and held it out in front of him, hoping to pass for an incompetent delivery man as Krystal Devine opened the door wearing baggy ripped jeans and a pink t-shirt with the words *BE KIND* written across the front.

She froze when she saw him, her eyes wide with surprise under her platinum pixie cut.

"Sorry, I think something broke inside this one," he said, managing an apologetic smile as he glanced past her into the house, confirming she was alone. "If you report it to the store, they'll give you a refund."

Krystal stared out at him, instantly suspicious as she picked up the remaining bags, set them inside, and then reached for the bag he was holding.

She looked out at the dark driveway and frowned.

"I thought you drove away...did you come back to-"

Her words abruptly ended when she saw the Beretta, with its stainless steel finish, shining under the porch light.

The gun was pointing directly at her chest.

"Get inside," Grendel said as she gaped at him in horror.

Pushing her into the house, he kicked the door shut behind him, knocking the bag of groceries from her hand, and spilling two cans of soup and a bag of frozen peas onto the floor.

"You'll never get away with this," Krystal said as he grabbed her arm and shoved her down the hall.

He followed behind her, holding the gun to her back.

Stumbling over the discarded bag, he went down hard on one knee. Instantly, she was running for the kitchen, screaming at the top of her lungs as he jumped up and aimed the gun at her back, his finger tight on the trigger.

But no, he didn't want it to end that way.

That wasn't the way he had planned it.

Shoving the Berretta back into the waistband of his pants, he charged after Krystal, tackling her to the ground just before she reached the back door.

"Where do you think you're going?" he panted as he straddled her back, using all his body weight to pin her to the floor. "That's not how to treat a guest in your home, is it?"

"Get off me," she gasped. "I can't...breathe."

With a nasty laugh, he bent over and hissed in her ear.

"I'm going to make sure you never breathe again."

Wrapping both hands around Krystal's neck, he squeezed until she stopped struggling and then got up to retrieve his duffle bag from the hallway where he'd dropped it.

Still panting, Grendel unzipped the bag, took out a coil of the same red and blue braided rope he kept on his little fishing boat, and walked back to the kitchen.

As he knelt down beside the influencer's limp body, he saw the gentle rise and fall of her breath and smiled. She was unconscious but still alive.

That was good. He wasn't done with her yet.

Looping the rope around her neck, he tied the ends into a clove hitch knot and pulled it tight, but not tight enough to block off all air flow.

Once that was done, he dragged Krystal into the garage, hefted her into the trunk of her old Chevy Malibu, and slammed the lid closed.

He went back into the house and sat in front of her computer, which was already turned on and logged in.

It took him only a few minutes to delete the handful of photos she'd taken at the memorial as well as the comments about the event that she'd posted online.

Hopefully, that would be enough to stop Bailey Flynn and her fellow agents from making a connection between the memorial and the messages Krystal had been receiving.

Searching through the desk drawer, Grendel found a notepad and a pen. He carefully studied the grocery list that had been written on the top sheet of paper before tearing it off and laying it beside the notepad.

With great care, he wrote out a short note, using the grocery list as a guide to mimic Krystal's handwriting.

Everyone I love has forsaken me.
May God save my soul.

After wiping his fingerprints from the keyboard, he stuck the pen in his pocket and carried the note out to the garage.

Climbing into the Malibu, he heard a faint banging from the trunk. Krystal was awake.

He grinned as he used the remote to open the garage door and backed down the driveway with the car lights off, hoping not to attract the attention of any nosy neighbors.

Minutes later he was speeding down the highway headed toward Summerset Pier, reviewing his plan in his head, reassuring himself he'd thought of everything.

After all, the ruse had worked before.

It would work again.

CHAPTER SIXTEEN

Detective Jimmy Fraser sat at the little kitchen table between Tiana and Sasha, watching his daughters play with the lumpy cinnamon and raisin oatmeal Linette had made them. Checking his watch, he polished off his own breakfast of marmalade on wholewheat toast and drained the last drops of black coffee from his #1 *Dad* mug.

"C'mon, girls. You're going to be late for school again if we don't get on the road soon," he said.

Before he could get to his feet, his phone buzzed on the table. He groaned as the dreaded words *BHPD Dispatch* appeared on the display.

"This is Detective Fraser," he said, holding the phone to his ear as he stood. "What's happened?"

"Officers have responded to reports of a fatality on Summerset Pier," the dispatcher said. "They've requested a detective on the scene."

Fraser frowned.

"What kind of fatality?"

Glancing down, he saw both his daughters staring up at him with wide, interested eyes.

"A woman was found hanging by the pier," the dispatcher

said. "Officer Boswell called it a possible suicide."

"Okay, I'll be there shortly. And I'll call Detective Gallagher myself and get him to meet me there."

Ending the call, he sighed.

"Looks like Mommy's going to have to take you two to school today," he said. "You'd better finish up that oatmeal before she gets in here and sees what you've done to it."

He left them groaning in protest behind him as he tapped on Gallagher's number.

His partner's phone rang a half dozen times before Eloise Spellman answered the phone.

"Sorry, Gallagher's in the shower right now," she said. "Can I give him a message?"

Fraser hesitated, momentarily flustered.

He'd first suspected that the forensic anthropologist had moved in with Gallagher and his daughter Annabelle some time ago but hadn't been sure until now.

"Um, can you tell him we have an unnatural death down at Summerset Pier?" Fraser said. "Tell him to meet me over there as soon as he can. I'll be waiting."

After ending the call, he moved down the hall while calling up the stairs to Linette.

"Honey? I'm going to need you to drop off the girls."

His wife's unhappy face peered down from the landing.

"I'll probably need you to pick them up, too," he said before she could protest. "We've recovered a woman's body hanging from Summerset Pier, so it's most likely going to be a long day and a late night."

Linette sighed and nodded, silently conceding that the

viewing she'd scheduled couldn't compete with a dead body.

Twenty minutes later, Fraser pulled into the Summerset Pier lot, which was just south of the Belle Harbor Inlet.

Parking his Interceptor next to the medical examiner's van, he stepped out and surveyed the view before him, taking in the waves crashing endlessly on the sandy white beach and the gulls screeching in the blue sky overhead.

"Lovely day, isn't it?"

Fraser turned to see a man climbing out of a little red sportscar. He wore dark sunglasses and had his light brown hair pulled back in a ponytail.

"You know what's going on down there?" the man asked.

He gestured to the yellow tape, which was blocking the path down to the beach and the steep wooden steps leading up to the pier.

Recognizing the man as Garth Hamilton, the writer Madeline Mercer had been obsessing over, Fraser frowned.

"It's a crime scene," he said bluntly. "Like it says on the tape. I figured a hotshot writer would know how to read."

Fraser didn't give the man a chance to respond as he strode toward the pier and ducked under the tape.

Before he could start up the stairs, Officer Boswell's short, stocky frame emerged from the shadows under the pier.

"We're over here," he said, looking vaguely queasy. "We're just getting ready to cut her down."

The officer led Fraser to the other side of the pier, where a small group of people stood below the deck, looking up.

The body of a woman hung from a wooden support post, swaying in the wind off the churning ocean.

Fraser could see that the end of a rope had been tied around her neck. The rope's other end had been fastened to one of the wooden posts supporting the rail along the deck.

Moving closer, he saw the woman had short, platinum-blonde hair framing a swollen, discolored face.

She wore ripped jeans and a pink t-shirt with the words BE KIND printed across the front. Her feet were bare.

"We've taken the necessary photos of the body in situ," Mason Knox said, coming over to stand beside Fraser. "Now we need to transport her to my office. But first, we have to figure out how to get her down from there."

"How about we stand on the pier and use the rope to pull her up?" Finola Lawson suggested. "That might be quicker than trying to find a way to cut her down."

Fraser considered the idea and then looked over at Mason.

"I'm willing to give it a try if you are," he said.

The M.E. nodded.

"Let's do it."

He turned and headed up the stairs with Fraser following close behind him. Once they were on the pier, they scanned the edge of the deck, quickly spotting the rope tied around a wooden post along the handrail.

Kneeling on the hard boards of the deck, Fraser grasped the rope and began to pull. Mason knelt beside him and gripped the rope, positioning his hands several inches below Fraser's, adding his strength to the effort.

Slowly, and with much grunting and straining, they lifted the woman's body up and over the side of the pier, gently lying her down on the rough wooden boards at their feet.

Mason asked Finola to take several more photos of the rope as he retrieved a sharp knife from his bag.

He first sliced through the knot that had been tied to the post, and then he moved back to the dead woman on the ground, slicing through the rope just below the knot still fastened around her neck.

"We need a collection bag for the rope," he called back to Finola as he lowered the rope to the deck.

Bending over the body, he studied the dead woman's hand.

"Several of her fingernails have been torn off," he said with a frown. "And there's discoloration on her upper arms."

He looked back at Fraser.

"Looks like perimortem bruising," he said. "I'd say she was involved in some sort of struggle before she went over the side."

Mason motioned to the red and blue rope on the deck.

"And we've all seen this type of rope recently," he said.

Both Finola and Fraser nodded in agreement.

"That was the same rope we found at the railroad depot the other day," Fraser said. "The one with the bones."

"It may also be the same type of rope used in a suspected suicide a few years ago. Back when Dr. Armbruster was still running the M.E.'s office," Mason said. "I suspect the woman's death may have been staged to look like a suicide."

Before Fraser could ask any questions, Gallagher appeared beside him. The big man avoided looking down at the dead woman on the pier as he spoke.

"Boswell caught me as I was coming up here. He said there's something you need to see in the parking lot."

"What is it?" Fraser asked.

But Gallagher was already heading back to the stairs.

With a sigh, Fraser followed him to the parking lot where Boswell was standing beside a Chevy Malibu.

"The responding officers say this car was the only one parked here when they arrived on the scene early this morning," Boswell said. "I came over to run the plates and saw that inside."

Opening the car door, he pointed to a handwritten note lying on the sunbaked dashboard.

Fraser leaned in and read the note without touching it.

Everyone I love has forsaken me.
May God save my soul.

He frowned at the old-fashioned formality of the note. Did people really write that way anymore?

"The car's registered to a twenty-six-year-old woman named Krystal Devine," Boswell said. "Based on her driver's license photo, I'd say she's the one we found hanging up there, and the one who wrote that note."

"Krystal Devine?"

Fraser glanced at Gallagher in surprise.

"I heard that name yesterday," he said. "Sabrina West came into the station to file a report about receiving death threats online. She said a woman named Krystal Devine had received several threats, as well.

"When we looped in the FBI, it turned out there was a whole list of people who'd reported getting threats from some troll calling himself SirGrendel88."

"You think an internet troll had something to do with that woman killing herself?" Gallagher asked.

"Who said she killed herself?" Fraser shot back. "Mason Knox sure doesn't think this was a suicide."

Gallagher raised his eyebrows.

"You think this is a homicide? You think someone tied a rope around that woman's neck and threw her off the pier?"

He looked doubtful.

"That's exactly what I think," Fraser said, pulling out his phone. "And I bet Bailey Flynn is going to think the same thing once she hears that Krystal Devine is dead."

CHAPTER SEVENTEEN

Bailey woke to a dull pounding in her head and a sharp buzzing in her ears, confused as to where she was. Opening her eyes, she squinted against the harsh sunlight streaming in through a crack in the window blinds. It took a second to remember that she was in her parents' house, sleeping in the guest room that had once been her childhood bedroom.

Reaching toward the nightstand, she felt around until she found her phone. When she saw that Jimmy Fraser was calling, she sighed and held it to her ear.

"Krystal Devine is dead," he said as soon as he heard her voice. "Beachcombers found her this morning hanging from Summerset Pier. Looks like she was there all night."

Bailey frowned as she registered the name.

"Krystal Devine? You mean the woman who-"

"Yeah, the one who was being trolled by SirGrendel88," Fraser cut in. "The one who was getting death threats."

He sounded angry.

"The one the FBI ignored until she went to the press."

Bailey didn't bother to argue or make excuses for the Bureau's failure to protect the woman. Not when every word she spoke made her head pound a little more.

"Mason Knox is already here at the pier and he's saying it's likely a homicide. Although, it was clearly setup to look like a suicide."

Squeezing her eyes shut, Bailey exhaled.

"Okay, I'm on my way."

She ended the call and lay perfectly still, willing the pain in her head to subside.

When it didn't, she inhaled deeply and sat up.

Ignoring the queasy pounding that radiated from the back of her head all the way down to her stomach, she stood and made her way into her parents' bathroom, where she rifled through the medicine cabinet.

She was tempted by a bottle of hydrocodone her father had been prescribed for a slipped disc over the summer but settled instead on the extra-strength Tylenol at the back of the cabinet. Bending over the sink, she scooped up a handful of water and swallowed two of the pills.

After returning to the bedroom, she pulled on the clothes Cate had brought to the hospital, glad her sister had opted for an appropriate work outfit consisting of black pants, a white blouse, and a lightweight jacket with deep pockets. Comfortable loafers completed the outfit.

If only she had her Glock in its holster and her little Ruger strapped to her ankle. She felt somehow naked and vulnerable going to work without them.

Following the scent of fresh coffee, Bailey went downstairs to the kitchen, where Ludwig was busy eating his breakfast and ignoring Duchess, who sat sullenly beside him.

Her mother's Siamese cat gave Bailey a disgruntled glare as she bent over to scratch the cat's silvery white fur with one hand and Ludwig's black and tan fur with the other.

"I'm surprised to see you up so early."

Bailey turned to see her mother standing in the doorway.

"After the way you looked when you came in last night, I expected you to sleep most of the day," Jackie said.

"Actually, I'm heading out to a scene," Bailey admitted. "There's been a fatality at Summerset Pier."

Her mother's voice filled with disapproval.

"You're heading to a *crime scene*?" she asked. "In your condition, you should be heading back to the hospital, not to the scene of an accident or a-"

"It's probably a homicide," Bailey cut in as she headed toward the coffee machine, hoping some caffeine would help clear the fuzzy ache in her head. "And it may be related to...well, to another case I'm involved with."

It was best not to tell her mother that the other case in question was the shooting at the Holbrook Coffee Company, or that she suspected the shooter who had tried to kill her may have already struck again.

"Well, at least have some breakfast," Jackie insisted. "You look weak as a kitten and as pale as a ghost."

"I feel fine," Bailey said, despite the pounding in her head. "And I don't have time to stop and eat anything. I'll take a banana and a granola bar with my coffee."

She called to Ludwig, who eagerly ran to the door, wagging his tail in excitement. The poor dog likely thought they were heading out on the five-mile run that had been part of their morning routine.

But that had been before Bailey had accepted her undercover assignment and before she'd ended up in the hospital with a traumatic brain injury.

"No running today," Bailey said as she led Ludwig out the front door. "You'll just have to settle for a quick walk around the block until I'm back in fighting shape."

Struggling to keep up with the energetic German shepherd as he led her down Claremont Street toward Rampart Road, she noticed a young girl running down the sidewalk.

Bailey stared at the girl's retreating back and long dark hair, reminded of her recent dream about Dolores Santos. She shivered as she pictured the dead girl's accusing eyes.

She'd dreamed of that terrible day so many times, reliving the agony of arriving too late, of not getting to Dolores in time to save her. Always thinking *if only...*

If only I'd done something different. If only I'd run faster...

The possibility of what might have been had haunted Bailey for years, and the self-recrimination had only grown stronger, driving her to run farther and faster on her morning runs with Ludwig.

If she was strong enough and fast enough, the next time a little girl or an innocent victim needed her, she would be ready. With this thought always in the back of her mind, she had pushed herself to the limit.

And now, here I am, barely able to walk.

If the shadowy figure from her recent dream jumped out at her now, she'd be unable to fight or to get away.

The thought sent a chill down her spine and she

instinctively reached for the Glock in her holster before she remembered it wasn't there.

She made a mental note to retrieve her weapons from the gun safe in Cate's apartment as soon as possible while she waited for Ludwig to finish his business, and then she settled the German Shepherd into the backseat of the Expedition and climbed behind the wheel, heading east toward the coast.

Opening all the windows, she selected *Stranger on the Shore* from a smooth jazz playlist, clearing all thoughts from her mind as the soothing saxophone washed over her and the warm wind blew all around her.

By the time she arrived at Summerset Pier and parked the SUV behind Fraser's Interceptor, her headache had faded into the background.

A crowd had started to gather, and as she opened the door for Ludwig and headed toward the pier, she was forced to push her way through a cluster of reporters, tourists, and concerned local citizens.

Quickly ducking under the crime scene tape, she climbed the stairs to the old wooden pier and immediately saw Mason Knox and Finola Lawson preparing to load the body of a woman into a black body bag.

Fraser stood beside them ready to lend a hand if needed. He turned as Bailey approached.

"Sorry to call you out here so early," he said. "But I thought you'd want to see this."

He gestured to the dead woman lying on the pier.

Although the woman's face was bloated and discolored, Bailey recognized her short platinum blonde hair from the photos she'd seen of Krystal Devine at the memorial for Dolores Santos.

"A few beachcombers called 911 just after .dawn saying someone was hanging from the pier," Fraser said. "The first responders saw right away she'd been dead for a while so they called the M.E., thinking she was a suicide.

"Her car was in the lot. The tag and registration identified her as Krystal Devine. There was also a note in the car. Madeline and the CSI team have already bagged it. I'll ask them to bring it up so you can see it."

Pulling out his phone, he tapped in a message.

"And you don't think it was a suicide?" Bailey asked. "Even though there was a note?"

"Judge for yourself," Fraser said as Madeline appeared at the head of the stairs.

As the CSI team leader approached, Bailey could see that she was carrying a clear evidence collection bag.

"We found this on the car's dashboard," Madeline said.

She handed the bag with the handwritten note to Bailey, who read it aloud.

"Everyone I love has forsaken me. May God save my soul."

There was a moment of silence and then Mason Knox spoke up behind her.

"I've never found a note like that at any suicide scene before. If she had been in unbearable emotional pain, it seems unlikely she would have taken the time to neatly write out a note that is so...impersonal."

He frowned and cleared his throat.

"From my initial examination, I'd say that Krystal Devine

was involved in a violent struggle before she died."

Bending over the dead woman, he pointed out several reddish abrasions on her body, as well as a collection of small round bruises on her upper arm. They appeared to have been left by the grip of strong fingers.

"And there's the matter of the rope," Mason added, gesturing to the rope tightly tied around Krystal's neck.

"This rope appears to match a rope we recently found with human remains at the Summerset Railroad Depot," he said. "A clove hitch knot was used to tie the rope at both scenes."

He stood and stared at Bailey with a grim expression.

"I also believe Krystal's death may be linked to another suspected suicide," he said. "I have doubts about the initial ruling in that case."

Bailey cocked her head.

"What do you mean?"

"A college student named Rachel Cho was found hanging in her family's attic three years ago," Mason explained. "Dr. Armbruster was the M.E. for Summerset County at the time and he ruled the death a suicide."

He sighed.

"I'm not so sure that was the case. Rachel had only recently started showing signs of depression and-"

Mason turned to Madeline.

"Were you ever able to locate that evidence I requested?" he asked. "The rope collected during Rachel Cho's autopsy?"

Madeline grimaced and shook her head.

"I haven't had a chance to look yet," she admitted. "But this sure does look like the rope found at the railroad depot."

Bailey reached into her pocket and pulled out a crumpled piece of printer paper.

It was the printout of the names of the people who had reported being trolled by SirGrendel88.

Rachel Cho's name was the third name on the list.

"I think you may be right," she told Mason. "I don't think either Rachel or Krystal killed themselves. I think whoever trolled them wanted it to look that way."

Her stomach dropped as she read the last name on the list.

"I've got to go," she said, already backing away. "I've got to warn Luisa Santos."

* * *

Bailey headed west in the Expedition, cutting through downtown Belle Harbor, and passing Summerset Park.

As far as she knew, Dolores Santos' parents still lived less than a mile from the site of their daughter's death.

Turning onto Cascadia Drive, she pulled onto an oil-stained driveway in front of a small, concrete block house.

Although she'd only been to the house once before, she recognized the green shutters and matching flower boxes. At one time they had been full of bright yellow marigolds, but the flowers were now gone and the boxes were empty.

As Bailey opened the car door and stepped onto the cracked sidewalk where Dolores Santos had ridden her skateboard that fateful day, she looked up at the windows, noting that the blinds were drawn.

She could still remember walking up to the front door

three years earlier and seeing Luisa Santos standing in the doorway waiting for news about her little girl.

The look on her face had haunted Bailey ever since.

Leaving Ludwig in the car with the windows rolled down, Bailey slowly walked up the path to the front porch.

When she lifted her hand to knock, she noted Dolores' parents had mounted a small security camera over the door.

She imagined the new security measures had been prompted by the abduction and murder of their daughter, and that to Luisa and Rodrigo Santos, the world must now seem like a very dark and dangerous place.

Bailey tensed as soft footsteps sounded inside the house and the door swung open. Luisa Santos peered out.

"Detective Flynn?"

Her eyes narrowed.

"What are you doing here? What's happened?"

Struggling for words, Bailey stared at Luisa.

In the last three years, the bereaved mother's face had aged. Deep creases marred her forehead and the network of lines around her eyes revealed the grief she'd suffered, making her seem older than her thirty-four years.

"I need to speak to you," Bailey said. "Can I come in?"

Luisa hesitated and then stepped back, waving a thin arm to usher her visitor into a small living room.

As she stepped inside, Bailey noted a heavy dead bolt had been installed on the door below the chain lock.

The living room was sparsely furnished and tidy. As Luisa motioned for her to take a seat on the sofa, she turned off the television, which had been tuned to a talk show.

"I'm sorry to just show up like this unannounced," Bailey said. "But I wanted to talk to you about the complaint you filed last month. The one about the harassing messages and threats you received. Are you still being trolled online?"

"Yes, I am," Luisa said. "But I never thought the FBI would send *you* to look into my complaint. I thought you were assigned to serious crimes, like homicides and abductions."

Her voice faltered on the last word and she blinked hard to clear the shine that had come into her eyes.

"I've actually been getting trolled for years by the same guy," she continued before Bailey could respond. "He uses the name SirGrendel88."

She plucked a tissue from a box on the table.

"Rodrigo installed a security system and those locks, and he told me to stay off social media. But I shouldn't have to," she said, raising her chin defiantly. "Why should I let some online troll bully me and keep me from doing what I want to do? Besides, now that I've lost my Dolores, what more do I have to lose?"

Bailey hesitated. She couldn't blame Luisa's husband for being cautious. After all, his daughter had been murdered. It was natural he'd be scared of losing his wife, too.

"I think Rodrigo has a point," she said, trying not to sound judgmental. "I pretty much stay off social media myself."

She had first made the decision to quit social media after her name had been published in news coverage about a case she'd been working on, resulting in a barrage of online comments and opinions, many of which were disturbing or even threatening.

No doubt Luisa would be wise to do the same.

"At first, I thought the messages were just the work of some nut...just some harmless trolling by a sick, bitter man," Luisa said. "But once the death threats started...well, I finally decided I'd better report him."

She suddenly frowned at Bailey.

"But that was over a month ago. Why are you just coming to ask me about it now? Has something happened?"

Bailey nodded.

"There have been other reports of this SirGrendel88 sending death threats," she finally said. "And now several of the people filing complaints have turned up dead."

Sucking in a deep breath, she continued, knowing that Luisa could be in danger and needed to know the truth.

"In fact, you'll be seeing on the news that a woman's body was found this morning on Summerset Pier," she said. "The woman reported death threats similar to the ones you've been receiving."

"So, you came here because you think I could actually be in real danger?' Luisa asked. "You think this guy could do something to me in real life?"

The beginnings of panic filled her eyes.

"I'm here to advise you to be careful," Bailey said. "Our agents will be looking into your complaint and trying to track the messages back to whoever is sending them. But in the meantime, you need to take precautions."

She pointed toward the front door.

"Keep your doors locked. And don't hesitate to call 911 if you feel threatened in any way."

Luisa's face hardened.

"I called 911 when Dolores was taken," she said, getting to her feet. "But that didn't save my little girl."

The bitter words stung as Bailey stood and followed the woman to the door.

"Please, take the threats seriously," she stressed as she stepped onto the porch. "This guy's not just an online troll. He's stalking people in real life."

As Bailey turned and made her way back to her Expedition, her phone buzzed in her pocket.

She'd missed several text messages while she'd been speaking with Luisa Santos.

One message was from Aisha Sharma.

Where are you? Are you coming into the office today?

Another was from Mason Knox.

Krystal Devine is being prepped for autopsy now. If you want to observe, you need to hurry.

Climbing back into the Interceptor, Bailey thought for a moment and then tapped on Sharma's number.

"Krystal Devine died last night," she said when Sharma answered the call. "You want to come to the autopsy?"

CHAPTER EIGHTEEN

Mason Knox had already donned his protective gear and was heading down the hall toward the autopsy suite when the door leading out to the lobby swung open. He turned to see Finola Lawson usher Bailey Flynn and Special Agent Aisha Sharma through the doorway.

"Coveralls, masks, and shoe covers are in the prep room," Finola said, pointing the two agents in the right direction. "When you're ready, we'll be next door."

The assistant medical examiner turned to Mason.

"Krystal Devine is ready on the table," she said, hurrying past him into the autopsy suite.

Following her across the room to the stainless-steel dissecting table, Mason pulled on a second set of gloves and positioned his face shield as Finola double-checked the tray of instruments needed for the task ahead.

Soon Bailey and Sharma emerged from the prep room, silently taking their places around the table.

The FBI agents stared down at the stiff white sheet covering Krystal Devine's body.

As Mason prepared to pull down the sheet, he caught sight of Bailey's green eyes, which were the only part of her face not covered by her mask and hesitated.

"You sure you're up for this?" he asked. "You've only just gotten out of the hospital and-"

"I'm sure," Bailey quickly cut in, sounding impatient. "I'm ready when you are."

With a slight nod of surrender, Mason motioned for Finola to start the recorder and then pulled back the sheet.

Clearing his throat, he stared down at the dead woman.

"The decedent is a well-nourished white female measuring sixty-six inches and weighing one hundred forty-eight pounds," he said. "External appearance is consistent with the victim's age, which is known to be thirty years. Lividity is fixed in the distal portions of the limbs."

He began the external examination by inspecting Krystal Devine's head and face for injuries or abnormalities.

Moving on to the eyes, he used a gentle finger to first open the left eye and then the right.

"Petechia is present in both eyes," he said, referring to the tiny red tell-tale spots that often resulted from blood vessels rupturing during strangulation.

Once he had examined Krystal's mouth, ears, and nostrils, Mason pulled the sheet down to reveal her neck and torso.

The rope was still knotted tightly around her neck.

Using a sharp scalpel, Mason carefully cut and removed the length of red and blue braided rope, dropping it into the evidence collection bag Finola had prepared.

He studied the skin that had been hidden under the rope as Finola took several photos for the autopsy file.

"A series of deep contusions and abrasions are visible

around the neck," Mason said. "The pattern is complex, indicative of both manual strangulation as well as asphyxiation due to hanging. There also appears to be a cluster of bruises across the upper left arm."

After Mason inspected the remainder of Krystal's body, noting several perimortem contusions consistent with a struggle, he moved on to the internal examination.

Cutting open her chest and rib cage, he removed and examined her internal organs, including her lungs and heart, and studied her neck and spine, verifying that none of her cervical vertebrae had been fractured.

"Finola will collect blood and tissue samples needed for a complete toxicology screening as usual, but I see nothing to indicate that we'll find anything unexpected.

"I'd estimate Krystal Devine's time of death to be somewhere between midnight and two a.m., although it's impossible to know an exact time. It looks as if she was hanging under the pier all night exposed to the elements.

"The cause and manner of death is homicide by asphyxiation due to hanging. Although it appears there was a struggle before she was killed and she may have suffered damage to her throat prior to being suspended by the neck from the pier."

He looked over at the rope in the evidence collection bag before turning his eyes to Bailey.

"The rope is definitely the murder weapon," he said. "And from what I can tell, it closely matches the rope we found earlier in the week at the Summerset Railroad Depot."

* * *

Mason had removed his protective gear and now sat behind the desk in his office, facing Bailey Flynn and her fellow FBI agent, Aisha Sharma, as they reviewed the autopsy findings.

"So, according to your theory, the perp assaulted Krystal, manually strangled her, knotted the rope around her neck, and then threw her over the side of the pier?" Bailey asked.

"Well, I wouldn't go so far as to say she was *thrown* over," Mason corrected her. "The second vertebrae in Krystal's spine, what we call the C2 or axis bone, wasn't fractured.

"A fracture of the C2 is called a hangman's fracture because it often occurs when a hanging victim is dropped from a distance, causing the neck to hyperextend and snap."

Leaning back in his chair, he tried to imagine the scene at the pier that would have led to the injuries he'd seen during the autopsy.

"If I had to guess, I'd say the assailant attacked Krystal somewhere else, strangled her into unconsciousness, and transported her to the pier. He could have knotted the rope around her neck and lowered her over the side.

"After that, he may have even gone down to the beach to stand below the pier, watching her struggling to breathe, taunting her as she slowly died."

Sharma shuddered in revulsion.

"That's horrible," she said. "But it would fit with the theory that Krystal's killer is the same sadistic troll who's been sending her death threats."

"And it makes me even more determined to find out if her murder is somehow connected to Rachel Cho's death," Mason said. "Although, at this point, I can't even be sure Rachel Cho's death wasn't a suicide. Not until I have a chance to examine the rope and the body in detail, which would require an exhumation."

He shook his head in frustration.

"So, just talk to the family," Bailey said as she absently rubbed the back of her head. "Explain what you need."

Mason wished it were that easy.

"Based on Dr. Armbruster's very unreliable memory and the brief search I was able to conduct online, it seems as if Rachel's parents relocated to Seoul, South Korea a year or so after her death," he explained. "I haven't been able to find contact details for them yet, so we'll likely have to work through the courts if we want to exhume her body."

"We may have no other choice," Bailey agreed. "Not if we want to find out what really happened to her."

Mason nodded grimly and punched a button on his desk phone, activating the speaker.

"Well, we'd better call your sister then," he said, punching in one of the only phone numbers he knew by memory. "She went with me to speak to Dr. Armbruster so she already knows I have doubts about Rachel Cho's autopsy."

Cate answered his call on the first ring, sounding cheerful.

Her voice quickly dimmed when Mason said Bailey and Sharma were with him and explained why they were calling.

"We need your help with a court-ordered exhumation," he said. "I need to examine Rachel Cho's body. And it can't wait until we track down her parents. There's no telling how long that could take."

"Why the rush?" Cate asked. "Has something happened?"

Propping her elbows on the desk, Bailey leaned toward the phone.

"A woman named Krystal Devine was found hanging from Summerset Pier this morning," she said. "We believe her death may be connected to the death of Rachel Cho."

"Connected how?" Cate asked.

Bailey winced and rubbed her head again as she explained.

"Both Krystal and Rachel were found hanging by the same type of rope," she said. "And both women reported being threatened online by the same troll."

"You guys think an online troll convinced Rachel and Krystal to kill themselves?" Cate asked.

She couldn't hide her surprise.

"No, we think he did the job for them," Mason cut in.

Anger surged through him at the thought of the two young women whose lives had been ended much too soon.

"As you know, I already suspected Rachel's death had been incorrectly ruled a suicide. Now, I'm even more convinced that something isn't right.

He sucked in a calming breath.

"In order to be sure, I need to perform a postmortem. And as far as I can tell, Rachel's parents are no longer in the country. Can you find a judge willing to issue a court order?"

There was a moment of silence on the other end of the call. Mason looked up at Bailey and Sharma. Both agents looked as tense and worried as he felt.

"I'll do what I can," Cate finally said. "But no promises. Send me over the details and I'll work up a petition to the court asking for a court order to exhume the remains. If I'm lucky, Judge Walsh might still be in his chambers."

As Mason ended the call, he looked up to see Eloise Spellman standing in the doorway. Jimmy Fraser hovered in the hall behind her.

"You both can come in," Mason said.

As the newcomers stepped into his office, he waved toward two chairs by the window but they both shook their heads.

"We won't be staying," Eloise said. "But I tried to call you and you didn't answer so...well, I thought you'd want to hear this as soon as possible."

Mason raised his eyebrows.

"I'm all ears, what is it?"

"The DNA tests came back on the bones we found at the Summerset Railroad Depot," she said. "They were a match to the skull. The bones and skull belong to the same victim."

All thoughts of Krystal Devine and Rachel Cho retreated to the back of Mason's mind as he processed Eloise's words.

"We also managed to find a familial match in a publicly available DNA database," she added. "The mitochondrial DNA extracted from the skull and the bones match a woman named Hannah Rosenbaum."

Opening the file she was carrying, Eloise continued.

"Hannah's only son was an ex-con named Ezra Rosenbaum. He had a long criminal record before he suddenly just dropped off the radar about ten years ago.

"At the time, he was in his early twenties. Mrs.

Rosenbaum filed a missing person report but there was no real search from what I could find. He's never been found."

"So, we can assume the skull belonged to Ezra Rosenbaum, then?" Bailey asked.

Eloise nodded.

"The timeline for Ezra's disappearance roughly matches the length of time we estimate the skull had been at the railroad depot before we found it."

"I'd say the next step is finding out what Ezra Rosenbaum was doing ten years ago and who he was with," Fraser said. "If we track his movements, we could find the shooter who killed him. Which means we could also find the gun used in the Holbrook Coffee Company shootings."

All eyes turned to Bailey.

Mason was startled to see her wincing in pain.

"Are you okay?" he asked, getting to his feet and circling the desk. "I think we're done here for now. Why don't we get you home so you can rest?"

He expected her to resist, but she nodded and allowed Mason and Sharma to walk with her out to the lobby, where Ludwig was waiting with the receptionist.

"I'll drive her home," Sharma assured him.

"And I'll wait there for Cate," Bailey said. "She should be there soon. I'll let you know if she was able to talk Judge Walsh into issuing a court order."

CHAPTER NINETEEN

Cate scanned the petition one last time, making sure she had included the correct information about Rachel Cho's original autopsy and burial before sending the document to the printer. Getting to her feet, she collected the document and headed to the elevator, hoping to find Judge Walsh still in his chambers.

Stepping off the elevator, she hurried down the hall and slipped into the outer office where Inez Flores sat at her desk.

"How can I help you, dear?" the law clerk asked.

She continued typing as she looked up and smiled.

"I'm looking for Judge Walsh," Cate said. "I have an emergency petition to exhume a body in-"

"Judge Walsh went home early," Inez said, quickly cutting her off. "He scheduled a long weekend away and won't be back in the office until Monday. But I think Judge Nelson is still in his chambers if you want to stick your head in."

Suppressing a grimace, Cate thanked Inez and turned away, not sure what to do. She could either wait until next week to speak to Judge Walsh, who would be more likely to grant her petition, or she could walk straight into Judge Nelson's chambers and plead her case.

Slowly and without much enthusiasm, she began to move toward Judge Nelson's Chambers.

The new judge had been appointed by the governor to replace Judge Brett Inglebert on the bench after the man had resigned due to public outrage over pending bribery charges.

Glenn Nelson would now serve out the remaining two years of Inglebert's original six-year term, and Cate was already giving serious thought to challenging the pompous man for his seat. But two years was a while away. She would need to play nice with Nelson in the meantime.

Following Inez's advice, Cate stuck her head into Nelson's chamber and found the judge pulling on his suit jacket, preparing to leave for the day.

He was a barrel-chested man with salt and pepper hair and a thick mustache that hid his upper lip. His normal facial expression was one of casual disdain, which closely matched his predominate attitude toward the world.

When he saw Cate standing in his doorway, he didn't bother to hide his annoyance.

"Inez said I might be able to catch you before you leave."

Holding up her printout, she spoke quickly.

"I've got an emergency petition for an exhumation. A young woman named Rachel Cho was buried three years ago. Her death was ruled a suicide. The new M.E. and the BHPD now have reason to believe she's a victim of foul play.

"They want to conduct another autopsy, but they need a court order to exhume the body first. They've asked the State to petition the court so...here I am."

"Can't they just ask the family for permission?" the judge

asked. "That would be the proper procedure in this type of situation, wouldn't it?"

Cate nodded.

"Yes, in most cases that would be the preferred option," she agreed. "But it seems in this case, the family is no longer in the country. And time is of the essence."

"Yes, of course, it is," Nelson said sarcastically, shaking his head in contempt. "*Everyone's* in a rush. *Everything's* an emergency. *Every decision* is a matter of life or death."

Clearing her throat, Cate forced herself to remain calm.

"Actually, Judge Nelson, this just might be a matter of life or death," she said. "The medical examiner and the police believe Rachel Cho's death is connected to a homicide that took place just last night. This is an active investigation and they need that court order as soon as possible."

"And I really need you to follow proper protocol," the judge snapped. "Try to track down the family and get their approval first. If they won't agree, you can come back and present your petition for a court order. But I'll need more than just a medical examiner's hunch to let you dig up a body that's been in the ground for over three years."

He buttoned his jacket and gestured toward the door, giving Cate no choice but to step into the hall.

As she walked back toward the elevator, she decided that maybe it was time for her to go home, too.

But first, she owed Mason a call. She needed to tell him that she'd failed to get the court order. She needed to let him know there would be no exhumation.

* * *

Cate turned into the Sanctuary Apartments and parked her white Lexus in its usual spot.

Leaning her forehead on the steering wheel, she closed her eyes, trying to block out the voices that were echoing in her head. She didn't want to think about Judge Nelson's sarcastic denial of her petition or Mason's disappointment when she'd told him there would be no exhumation.

Lifting her head, she wearily opened the car door, climbed out, and then stopped in surprise to see that her sister's black Expedition was parked in its usual spot.

What is Bailey doing here?

Wasn't her sister supposed to be staying at her parents' house? Was something wrong? Was she okay?

All thoughts of Judge Nelson and the denied petition vanished as Cate ran toward the apartment.

Unlocking the front door, she swung it open to find Bailey sitting at the kitchen counter.

"What are you doing here?" Cate asked as she hurried into the living room and dropped her computer bag on the sofa. "Are you okay? I thought you were staying with Mom and Dad until you were in the clear."

"I *am* in the clear," Bailey insisted. "I'm fine. And I don't need anyone babysitting me. Besides, I ordered pizza."

She opened the box on the counter and picked up a slice.

"It's your favorite, cheese and mushroom."

As Bailey took a big bite, Cate exhaled with relief and suddenly realized she was famished.

"Judge Nelson wouldn't even consider my petition for an exhumation, much less issue a court order," she said as she helped herself to a slice. "He wants us to find Rachel Cho's family and ask for their permission. I already called Mason and let him know. He sounded pretty disappointed."

Taking a big bite of the cheesy pizza, she joined Bailey in companionable silence while they chewed.

She found herself smiling as she looked at her sister, suddenly grateful to have her there, not caring about the denied petition or anything else for the time being.

"I'm glad you're okay," Cate said. "And I'm glad you're back. I missed having you here."

Bailey smiled, revealing a half-chewed mouthful of cheese.

"I'm glad I'm back, too," she said. "Although, I do feel bad about you ending your campaign because of me. And it's a shame you aren't running against Brunner anymore. You would have kicked his ass."

"It wasn't the right time," Cate said.

She produced a mischievous grin.

"But just wait until Judge Nelson is up for reelection. I think that will be the perfect time to relaunch my campaign."

"And by then you'll be an old married woman," Bailey teased. "And hopefully, I'll still have a job. Although, if Ramsey finds out what I'm working on..."

Cate frowned.

"What do you mean? What doesn't he know?"

The question earned her another moment of silence as Bailey stuffed the last bite of her pizza in her mouth and spent an inordinate amount of time chewing and swallowing.

When she was done, she crossed the room and sank down on the sofa with a sigh.

"I guess the good thing about my temporary assignment to the Miami field office is that I'll still be in Belle Harbor for your wedding," she said, skillfully managing to change the subject. "Tell me, have you found a wedding dress yet?"

"Actually, I did see a few dresses I liked at the Belle Harbor Bridal Boutique," Cate admitted.

Unable to resist telling Bailey all about the dresses she'd tried on, Cate was still talking when she realized that Bailey had fallen asleep.

CHAPTER TWENTY

Bailey sat at the kitchen counter sipping milky coffee from a chipped mug, her head thudding dully as the rising sun shone in through the apartment window. She had dozed off on the sofa while talking to Cate the night before and had woken at dawn. Unable to go back to sleep, she had decided she might as well get an early start.

As she drained the last drops from her coffee mug, she was surprised to see Ludwig come into the kitchen.

"Why are you up so early?" she asked the German shepherd as she bent to scratch him behind his ears. "Did I wake you up? Or were you having a bad dream, too?"

Crossing to his food bowl, Ludwig sniffed at the empty container and looked back at her with dark, expectant eyes.

"Oh, you're hungry, is that it?" she asked, filling his bowls with food and water before heading into Cate's study-turned-bedroom to get dressed.

She pulled on a pale pink blouse, navy blue pants, and matching jacket, and then studied herself in the mirror, noting that her face was still pallid and that her dark blonde hair fell limply to her shoulders.

Sucking in a deep breath, she pulled her hair back into a

low ponytail, swiped on a rosy blush to give her cheeks color, and coated her lashes in black mascara in an attempt to mask the shadows that lingered under her eyes.

"That will have to do," she murmured to her reflection. "Now, there's just one more thing you need."

Bailey turned to the closet and opened the door, bending down to unlock the gun safe where Cate had secured her Bureau-issued service Glock and her personal Ruger while she'd been in the hospital.

It felt good to strap on her holster and secure her Glock. And as she slipped the little Ruger into her ankle holster, she immediately felt less vulnerable.

Walking out to the kitchen, she found her sister, still in her nightgown, rooting through the refrigerator.

"I thought we had some milk left."

"I actually drank the last of it in my coffee," Bailey admitted. "Sorry, I can get some more on the way home."

Her sister turned to glare at her. The annoyed expression on Cate's face quickly morphed into concern.

"You look pale. Are you sure you're feeling okay?" Cate asked. "And why are you up so early? You need more sleep. I bet Ramsey will give you more time off if you ask."

Bailey rolled her eyes at the suggestion.

"He already wants me to see a shrink," she said. "I can't let him think I'm not up to the job."

Ignoring her sister's protest, Bailey picked up her computer bag and headed toward the door.

"Come on, Ludwig," she called to the German shepherd, who was still lapping water from his bowl. "Let's go."

She followed the dog outside, allowing him to lead the way as they walked down Sanctuary Street and circled the block, enjoying the warm wind that blew in from the east.

It seemed that hurricane season wasn't over yet.

Once Ludwig had taken care of business, Bailey opened the back door to the Expedition and waited for the dog to climb inside and settle in by the window.

An hour later she was walking into the FBI's Miami field office, proud of herself for arriving on time for the meeting she'd scheduled with Aisha Sharma and Ford Ramsey.

Standing in front of the SAC's door, Bailey inhaled deeply, mentally preparing herself to argue her case.

Before she could knock, a teasing voice sounded behind her, making her jump.

"Wow, you're here early. I think this is a first."

She turned around to see Sharma dressed in warm fall colors that set off her long dark hair and big brown eyes.

"I guess I'm just eager to talk to Ramsey," Bailey said.

Sharma laughed.

"Now, *that* is definitely a first."

"I want his approval to focus solely on finding the online troll," Bailey said. "I don't want to be distracted with the money laundering case. The troll is escalating and-"

Suddenly, the door swung open. Ford Ramsey stood in the doorway, his weathered face creased into a scowl.

"What are you two whispering about out here?" he demanded. "Do you want me in this meeting or not?"

Hurrying inside, Bailey and Sharma sat at the desk across from Ramsey, who continued to glower at them.

"Now, what is it you want to discuss?" he asked.

"I want to discuss the online troll who I believe has already killed at least two of his targeted victims," Bailey said.

She'd decided it would be best to get straight to the point.

"I want to help the Belle Harbor PD investigate this creep and bring him in before anyone else has to die. And I want your approval to give the investigation top priority over the money laundering case."

"Online troll?"

The wrinkles around Ramsey's eyes deepened.

"Shouldn't complaints about online harassment be passed on to the Internet Crime division?"

Having anticipated Ramsey's objection, she had already prepared a response.

"This guy has progressed way beyond harassment. He's escalated to homicide...at least twice," Bailey said. "And Sharma and I will keep IC3 in the loop. They can participate as much or as little as they like. But this is a homicide investigation now, and the local PD needs our help."

She kept her eyes on the SAC, not daring to look over at Sharma, who remained silent beside her.

"Okay, I'll give you a week to investigate and report back. If this really is what you think it is, I'll see about reassigning the money laundering investigation."

Relief flooded through Bailey.

"Thank you," she said. "And while I'm here, can I ask how the investigation is going into the shooting at the Holbrook Coffee Company? Are there any leads so far?"

Holding her breath, she wondered if he would mention the

ballistics report or the audio recording Will Griffin had shared with her.

"There's nothing you need to be concerned about at this point," Ramsey said. "But I can assure you the investigation is still ongoing and you will be updated in due course."

"And the search for Jordan Stone?" Bailey asked.

The SAC's face tightened.

"A task force has been formed. That's all I can say."

Fighting the urge to rub the back of her head, which had started to ache again, she nodded.

"Very well," she said, getting to her feet. "I'll update you on the troll investigation within the week as agreed."

Before she could follow Sharma out of the door, Ramsey held up a hand, gesturing for her to wait.

"How are you feeling?" he asked in a low voice. "Frankly, you don't look well. Now, I know you've been through a lot."

He shifted uncomfortably in his chair.

"Are you sure you haven't come back to work too soon?"

Bailey gave a stiff shake of her head.

"No," she said firmly. "I'm perfectly fit to work."

"Have you thought any more about seeing Dr. Ellis?" he asked. "Maybe, if you're having trouble sleeping or-"

"I appreciate your concern," Bailey interjected. "But I've thought about it and have decided it isn't necessary."

After an uncomfortable pause, Ramsey sighed and nodded.

He didn't stop her as she stood and left his office.

Returning to her desk, she spent the morning searching online for Rachel Cho's parents without luck and trying not to stew over Ramsey's refusal to give her any sort of update on the search for her shooter or Jordan Stone.

It was already noon by the time Sharma appeared in her office doorway.

"You want to grab some lunch?" she asked.

Bailey checked her watch.

"Thanks, but I've got an errand to run."

Rising from her chair, she stretched her stiff legs and called to Ludwig. Leaving the building, they climbed back into the Expedition and headed toward Davenport Drive.

* * *

Bailey parked the Expedition in the lot beside West Security Services and followed Ludwig to the main entrance.

As she pushed through the front door, she saw Dalton sitting in front of his computer, studying a map.

Holding up a bag from Summerset Subs, Bailey smiled.

"I brought sandwiches," she said. "You hungry?"

"I'm always hungry," Dalton said, getting up from his desk and hurrying over to plant a kiss on her forehead. "And I never pass up a free lunch."

He took the bag from her and began unpacking the sandwiches, chips, and napkins inside.

His eyes lingered on her face.

"Are you feeling okay?" he asked

With a groan, Bailey sank into a chair and exhaled.

"That must be the million-dollar question," she said. "Because *everyone* keeps asking. And I keep saying *I'm fine.*"

Dalton stared down at her, unconvinced.

"We're all just worried about you," he said. "No one would blame you for taking more time to recuperate or even seeing a psychiatrist to deal with-"

"I'm not seeing a shrink," she cut in, knowing she sounded childish but unable to stop herself. "Ramsey already tried to pressure me into seeing Dr. Ellis and I told him no."

Raising his hands in surrender, Dalton sighed.

"Okay, it's your decision," he said. "But if you want my advice, I'd say you should give this Dr. Ellis a chance."

As he turned back to his desk and unwrapped a sandwich, Bailey decided it was time to change the subject.

"I didn't come here to talk about my health," she said. "I came to tell you that I've been assigned to a new case. I'm officially investigating SirGrendel88."

Dalton raised an eyebrow.

"You're investigating the graffiti artist who spraypainted the tag in the caboose at the Summerset Railroad Depot?"

He laid down his sandwich as if he had lost his appetite.

"Well, no," Bailey admitted. "I'm investigating the online troll who uses SirGrendel88 as his username to threaten and harass people. And he's doing more than just trolling people online. He's suspected in at least two homicides."

She glanced over at him.

"Of course, it might turn out to be the same person who painted the graffiti on the wall..."

"And Ramsey is okay with that?" Dalton asked. "He doesn't mind that you're investigating a perp who may have a connection to your own shooting?"

Picking up a piece of cheese from her sandwich, she fed it

to Ludwig.

"He doesn't know about the scene at the railroad depot," she admitted. "I haven't told him about the graffiti, or the bones, or the ballistics on the bullet."

"So, he doesn't know the bullet in the skull at the depot was fired from the same gun used in the shooting at the Holbrook Coffee Company?" Dalton asked.

Bailey shook her head.

"And he doesn't know anything about SirGrendel88," she admitted. "Not yet. Although, I'll have to turn in a full report within the week."

She stood and began to pace the room.

"If I tell him the online troll I'm looking for killed a victim with the same gun used in the coffee shop shooting, Ramsey may figure out the troll and my shooter are the same guy."

Stopping in front of Dalton, she stared up at him.

"He may figure out the troll is working for Jordan Stone."

A look of stunned understanding filled Dalton's face.

"The online troll who's killing people is the same guy who shot you...and he works for Stone?"

"I'm sure of it," she said. "Only, I can't prove it yet."

She bit her lip and sighed.

"And I can't tell Ramsey that I'm looking for the man who shot me," she said. "He'd pull me from the investigation."

"But you've got to tell him," Dalton protested. "You need protection. This guy could come after you again."

Bailey shook her head.

"I can't just sit around hoping that Ramsey and the team he's supposedly got searching for this guy come through."

Resting her hand on her gun, she produced a grim smile. "Besides, this time, I'll be ready for him."

The smile faded as she saw the worry in Dalton's eyes.

"Investigating this troll is the only chance I have of finding the man who shot me," she said with a weary shrug. "And if I happen to find out where Stone is hiding along the way, well, Ramsey can't very well blame me for that."

"I'm not worried about who Ramsey will blame," Dalton said, taking her hands and pulling her close. "I'm worried about you getting hurt again. Last time I almost lost you."

His voice thickened with emotion.

"I always knew that someday you'd get reassigned and that I'd have to let you go, at least for a while. But I didn't think I'd lose you permanently. I never imagined when you left that you might be gone forever."

Brushing a strand of hair back from her face, he sighed.

"I know I can't stop you from doing what you need to do. But please, promise me you'll be careful."

"I promise," Bailey said, offering him a faint smile. "I won't do anything you wouldn't do in my place."

Dalton rolled his eyes and laughed, giving her a tight hug before he released her and turned back to his desk.

He didn't notice her dizzy spell, and he didn't see her grabbing for the desk to steady herself as he told her his initial meeting with Giovanni Rocco had gone well.

"Rocco agreed to fund the search for Stone," Dalton said. "In fact, I'm going to meet with him again this afternoon. And I need to leave soon if I'm going to make it on time."

"Now it's my turn to tell you to be careful," she said. "We

now know that Emil Lazar killed Mario Rocco and Chuck Ashworth with a cocktail of fentanyl and xylazine. And I'm convinced Lazar was acting on Jordan Stone's behalf.

"I'm also convinced that Stone has other associates willing to do the same to anyone who gets in his way.

"So, if I were you, I'd try to find out where those key associates are now. One of them is sure to turn on Stone or be careless and lead you straight to him."

CHAPTER TWENTY-ONE

Dalton West pulled up to the wrought iron gate outside Villa Rocco and rolled down the window of his Dodge, prepared to face the same stone-faced security guard who had summarily dismissed him the last time he'd visited Giovanni Rocco's mansion in West Palm Beach.

But as he leaned out to press the call button on the security panel, the gate swung silently and smoothly open, allowing him access to the long drive up to the luxurious house.

He steered the dusty black truck onto the property, half-expecting to be stopped by the muscle-laden Yuri, but saw only the portly, gray-haired figure of Giovanni Rocco standing at the head of the long driveway waiting for him.

"Let's take a walk on the beach," Rocco said as Dalton stepped out of the truck. "I've always found it to be the safest place to talk in private. There's no chance of a bug or a hidden microphone."

Making his way around to the side of his majestic home, Rocco led his guest down a scenic stone pathway toward the churning Atlantic Ocean.

When they reached the shoreline, he stopped and looked out at the water with a brooding expression.

"Mario always loved the ocean," he said softly. "All he wanted to do was enjoy life. He never hurt anyone. Not like the bastard responsible for his death."

He turned anguished eyes on Dalton.

"You need to find Stone and stop him. He's been allowed to hurt too many people. It has to end."

Nodding in agreement, Dalton lifted a hand to shield his blue eyes from the sun. The wind lifted his fair hair and ruffled it as he turned to Rocco.

"You told me before that you had been looking for Stone," he said. "But you didn't say if you'd had any luck."

A gull flew overhead, emitting a high-pitch call.

"Do you have any information you want to pass on?" Dalton asked. "Do you know of anyone Stone might turn to for help? Someone who would hide him?"

Dalton cleared his throat.

"Or better yet, is there someone who might turn on him?"

Rocco frowned.

"There was a woman named Tamara Vincent," he said slowly. "She contacted me several months ago, claiming to have been working for Lazar and Stone."

The older man's voice grew hard.

"She said they'd killed my boy, although she swore she hadn't known what they'd done until it was too late. She said she had nothing to do with Mario's death."

He shook his head in disgust.

"The woman had the nerve to ask for my help. She wanted me to represent her. She asked me to work out a deal with the feds. Immunity in exchange for helping to bring in Stone.

"She said she was on her way to meet him. That she would be finding out where he was hiding. She said she knew I would want to see Stone brought to justice since he was responsible for the death of my son."

Dalton stared at Rocco in astonishment.

"And what did you do? What did you say?"

"I stalled, trying to keep her on the phone, playing for time," Rocco said. "But, of course, I never even considered her offer. Despite what she claimed, I couldn't help but believe she was involved in the plot to kill Mario."

His voice softened as he said his son's name.

"I've had to associate with some depraved, dangerous people in my time. It's a necessary evil in my line of work. But I have yet to sell my soul to the devil.

"That's what it would feel like for me to represent a woman who played even a small role in ending Mario's life."

Hearing the raw pain in the grieving father's voice, Dalton felt a surge of sympathy for Rocco, pitying the man despite his elegant house and breath-taking view.

"I can understand why you wouldn't want to represent Tamara Vincent," Dalton said. "She was involved in the abduction and assault of someone I hold very dear. She cares for no one but herself. And it's my understanding that she was complicit in the events leading up to Mario's death."

His hands clenched into fists at his side as he thought of the licensed funeral director who had worked for TBC Corp, the company Stone and his silent partner had formed with the goal of buying up struggling funeral homes around Summerset County.

The company had acted as a front, allowing Lazar and his partner to launder money and traffic in drugs, weapons, and humans. Tamara had helped Lazar in the quest to build his new business, enabling him to commit a series of grisly homicides, including that of Mario Rocco.

"Of course, if Tamara Vincent knows where Stone is hiding, she could be useful."

Rocco nodded stoically.

"Yes, I realize that. And I had decided that the next time she called me, I would try to lure her back to South Florida. I hoped that maybe she would be picked up by the police. That maybe she'd provide whatever information she knew about Stone so that he could be captured and brought to justice."

He shrugged.

"But she never called back."

Hiding his disappointment, Dalton looked out at the surf.

"Did Tamara give you a number or email address? Did she tell you how to contact her?"

"No, she called me using an unlisted number," Rocco said.

He hesitated.

"I actually had a contact in law enforcement try to trace the call," he admitted. "But the phone was one of those burner phones all the crooks use."

His eyes narrowed as he looked over at Dalton.

"I have another contact who believes Stone may be holed up in D.C. or somewhere nearby. I guess Tamara Vincent could have gone there to meet him. Maybe he stopped her from calling me back."

Dalton nodded slowly.

"You think your contact would tell me what he knows?" Dalton asked. "If it sounds promising, I could go up to D.C. and take a look around. See if I can find Stone or Tamara."

"I'll tell him to call you," Rocco said. "And if Tamara calls back, you'll be the first one to know."

After Dalton finished up the meeting at Villa Rocco and headed back to Belle Harbor, he thought of another of Stone's associates who might prove useful.

He remembered Bailey telling him that Tamara and Tony Brunner had been seen together in a bar around the time Chuck Ashworth and Mario Rocco had been killed.

Tony Brunner may still be in touch with the woman. Perhaps the slimy defense attorney was the key.

Maybe he would know how to get in touch with Tamara.

And based on what Giovanni Rocco had just told him, it seemed almost certain that Tamara knew where Jordan Stone was hiding.

CHAPTER TWENTY-TWO

Tamara Vincent sat on the plush sofa with both her feet tucked beneath her and the glass of wine Jordan Stone had poured still untouched on the mahogany coffee table. Her dark, glossy hair hung in thick waves over one shoulder as she gazed around the luxurious room with bitter eyes, thinking back to the night two months earlier that had led to her current predicament as a prisoner in a gilded cage.

Tamara ran out of the crematorium at the Ashworth Funeral Home without looking back, ignoring the shouts from behind her as she slipped into the woods and darted through the trees.

Soon she was stepping out of the forest onto an old rural road.

Sticking to the shadows, she took out the burner phone she kept tucked in her knee-high boots and scrolled through the list of recently dialed numbers, not sure who she could trust.

Finally, knowing she didn't have much time, she tapped on Tony Brunner's number and held the phone to her ear.

The lawyer answered in a wary voice.

"I can't talk now but if you don't want the feds knocking at your door tonight I suggest you get over here fast," she said. "I'll explain everything when I see you."

She gave him the name of the street up ahead and fifteen minutes later, she was sitting in his sleek BMW.

After making a two-minute stop at her rental home to throw some clothes into an overnight bag and collect her passport, they were back on the highway heading down the South Florida coast.

"I need to get out of town," she said. "Sonny's gone crazy. He's not using cadavers like we planned. He's actually killing people so that we can use their dead bodies and caskets to ship drugs. He even threatened to kill me and the Muldoon Brothers."

Hearing sirens in the distance, she looked over her shoulder, but the police cars were heading in the opposite direction.

"The feds and the cops must be at the funeral home by now. God knows what they found," she said. "I need to get out of Florida. I need to hole up somewhere for a while."

She stared down at the single bag she'd taken with her.

"But I'm going to need some money first. And quite a lot of it."

"I can give you the cash I have on me but that's about it," Brunner said. "All my finances are under scrutiny right now. I'm running for a seat on the Summerset County bench, remember?"

Tamara shot him a resentful glare, tempted to threaten to expose his connection to Jordan Stone's trafficking operation.

That would certainly tank his campaign.

But she knew better than to wave a red cape in front of a bull like Brunner.

"If I can get to Chicago fast enough, I can get enough money to tide me over," she said. "But I can't fly. They'll be looking for me at the airport."

"What's in Chicago?" Brunner asked.

"A dead tourist in a casket filled with a whole bunch of little blue

pills that are worth a million dollars on the street."

Leaning back in her seat, Tamara pictured Theodore Young.

"He drowned while on vacation and we shipped his body out to a funeral home in Chicago a few days ago. If I can get there in time to retrieve those pills before they bury the casket six feet under, I can still offload them to the buyer and have enough money to start over somewhere new."

"And what about Stone?" Brunner asked. "What'll he say about you stealing his shipment?"

"I'll handle Stone," she said, sounding more confident than she felt. "Just get me to the Amtrack station."

Brunner took her to the station and used cash to purchase a ticket for a two-day train ride to Chicago.

He grudgingly handed over a small stack of hundred-dollar bills, no doubt desperate to get her out of the area before she could blab to the cops about his role in the trafficking ring.

When Tamara reached Chicago, she went straight to Primrose Park Mortuary, where a sour-faced mortician confirmed that Theodore Young had been flown in from South Florida and that he was in the cooler and ready for the viewing, which would be held the next day.

He confirmed that after the family said their goodbyes, Mr. Young would be buried at Primrose Park Cemetery outside the city.

Trying to figure out how she could persuade the mortician to allow her and her overnight bag into the funeral home's cooler for a few minutes alone with the corpse, Tamara concocted a sob story about having to leave town before the viewing the next day.

Tears flowed easily as she told him she'd traveled thousands of miles to say goodbye to the dead man.

But the mortician wasn't swayed by her tears.

He only acquiesced after she pulled out one of the hundred-dollar bills Brunner had parted with at the station.

Tamara barely looked at Mr. Young as she pushed his embalmed body to one side and removed the hidden drugs from the padding under his corpse.

Once she'd dumped all the pills into her overnight bag, she checked into the Primrose Park Hotel.

It took her less than twenty-four hours to offload the drugs to the waiting buyer and deposit what she felt was a fair cut of the cash proceeds into a safe deposit box.

Then came the tricky part.

Using the phone number Sonny had instructed her to call in the event he was ever arrested or injured, she contacted Jordan Stone.

Once she'd reminded him who she was and what she knew, she told him about the shootout at the funeral home.

"Sonny's gone crazy," she said.

"Actually, Sonny is dead," he countered. "And the two idiots he had working for him have been arrested. Luckily, the Muldoon brothers don't know much."

She wondered what he thought she knew but decided not to ask.

"I'm in Chicago," she said instead. "I delivered the package to the buyer as planned and I have your cut. I can bring it to you if you like. Or you could pick it up."

There was a brief silence on the other end of the connection.

"Why don't you take a taxi out to the Safe Harbor Executive Airport this afternoon," he said smoothly. "I'll have someone meet you there. They'll bring you to me and we can have a little talk."

"Okay," she said, thinking fast. "I'll be there."

As soon as she hung up, Tamara called Giovanni Rocco.

If she could talk the famous lawyer into representing her, he might be able to work out a deal for her to get immunity in exchange for her testimony against Stone.

She might still have a chance to get out of the mess Sonny had created with her life and her freedom intact.

After presenting her proposal to Mario Rocco's father, she'd told him she would be in touch once she'd learned Stone's whereabouts.

She'd have the upper hand with the feds if she could hand them the billionaire on a silver platter.

Shutting off the phone, she slipped it back into her boot next to what remained of the cash Brunner had given her and took a taxi to the Safe Harbor Executive Airport outside the city.

Just as Stone had promised, a little Cessna with a cheerful yellow stripe down the side was waiting to take her to him.

She boarded the plane carrying only her overnight bag, which was filled with Stone's share of the cash.

They'd been in the air for just over two hours when the plane started to descend, landing on a long runway in what appeared to be the middle of nowhere.

When Tamara asked the unsmiling pilot where they were, he only gestured impatiently for her to exit the plane.

And as she walked down the steps, she was met by two men in security uniforms. When she saw that they were openly carrying guns, she braced herself, expecting to be shot but they only frisked her and searched her overnight bag without comment.

She was then led to a car and driven into the woods, relieved that the men hadn't detected the slim phone in her leather boots.

The security goons ignored her questions as to where they were going. The only indication of her current location was a sign they passed that said Welcome to Providence Gap.

Minutes later they jerked to a stop at a deserted crossroads, where they left her waiting with her overnight bag.

Moments later, a dusty Land Rover pulled up.

Jordan Stone was sitting in the driver's seat.

"Let's go," he said. "We can talk once we're safely inside."

As Tamara strapped on her seatbelt, he drove down a narrow dirt road that wound through the gently sloping hills of a forest, stopping only once to punch in a code to open the gate of a chain-link fence topped with barbed wire, before continuing on.

Suddenly, he brought the SUV to a stop under the cover of a large Maple tree, its leaves red with the prospect of the winter to come.

"Welcome to my new home," he said.

Tamara looked around.

"What home?"

"Come with me and you'll find out."

Leading her down a path to a hidden opening in the hillside, he stopped in front of a large metal door blocking their way.

Stone looked down at his phone and tapped in a code.

As the door swung open to expose a stairway leading down into the ground, he ushered Tamara forward, explaining that he had been hiding in an underground bunker that had been designed to be used in the event of a catastrophe.

"Oh, I've heard of this kind of thing before," Tamara said. "This is one of those billionaire bunkers, isn't it?"

As he gave her a tour, Stone proudly told her that the underground bunker occupied over five thousand square feet and included a luxuriously furnished living space, a state-of-the-art control room to run the automated security system, a filtered air supply system, and a decontamination chamber.

It was secured by blast-proof doors, shatterproof windows, and a biometric entry and security system, while the storeroom contained a full wardrobe of personal protective equipment, first-aid supplies, and enough medications to fill a pharmacy.

Tamara tried to act impressed as she followed Stone through the bunker, but she was growing increasingly alarmed.

And despite her many questions, Stone refused to tell her where the bunker was located. All she knew for sure was that it was located within a two-hour flight from Chicago.

"This is really cool," she said when they ended up back where they'd started. "But I've got to get going. I just wanted to drop off the money I owed you and I'm actually a little claustrophobic."

"Oh, you're not going anywhere," Stone said calmly. "You see, I can't afford to have you going around telling everyone what you know. Especially now that you've seen my little bunker."

He crossed to a bar against the wall and poured red wine into two large wineglasses. With a smile, he handed one to her.

"You'll come to love it here," he assured her. "And I could use the company. It can get lonely here all by myself."

As he clinked his glass against hers, Tamara realized she was trapped and she didn't know if she would ever get to leave.

Tamara shifted on the sofa and picked up an iPad that was preloaded with a whole catalog of books ranging from classics to just released best-sellers.

Unable to concentrate on the latest thriller from her favorite author, she gritted her teeth and tried to think.

She couldn't be trapped there forever, could she?

Not when she was rarely allowed outside, enjoying only a few blissful minutes to bask in the sunshine or to gaze up in frustration at the passage of time reflected in the changing phases of the moon.

She didn't know if she could stand it much longer, despite the luxurious surroundings. Not without going stir-crazy.

During one of her rare trips outside, Tamara had managed to use her burner phone to try to call Giovanni Rocco, hoping the rich lawyer would find some way to help her, but the cell signal had been too weak.

I'll have to think of another way to get out of here, even if it takes me killing Stone in the process.

Throwing down the iPad, she picked up a remote and turned to the large screen on the wall, flicking through the many channels available through the powerful satellite dish Stone had installed.

There were hundreds of channels from around the world but none of them could hold Tamara's attention for long.

When she found Channel 3 News in South Florida, Sabrina West was reporting live from the Summerset Pier.

"A woman's body was found hanging from Summerset Pier and police have yet to announce the cause of death although sources tell us that foul play is suspected and a full investigation is underway."

Ignoring the reporter's solemn voice, Tamara stared at the big screen, her eyes widening as she saw Special Agent Bailey Flynn standing on the wooden stairs leading up to the pier.

Resentment flooded through Tamara.

If the stupid woman had done her job and stopped Stone long ago, I wouldn't be in this mess. It's all Bailey Flynn's fault.

The FBI agent obviously didn't know or even care what had happened to Tamara Vincent.

Bailey Flynn's still out there living her life without a care in the world. Of course, there's still a chance that Stone will find her and take care of her once and for all.

CHAPTER TWENTY-THREE

Bailey stood on the deck of the Summerset Pier, looking out at the turbulent Atlantic Ocean. As she listened to the waves crashing endlessly against the shore, she realized Krystal Devine would have heard the same sound as she'd hung from the pier with her life slowly ebbing away.

Crossing to the edge of the pier, Bailey held onto the rail and looked down at the sand and water below, picturing the events leading up to Krystal's death just as Mason Knox had described it during her autopsy.

It wouldn't have been easy for the troll to carry Krystal's unconscious body up the stairs and drag it to the edge. But once he'd knotted one end of the rope around the post and the other end around her neck, it wouldn't have taken much to push her over the side.

Only he didn't push her over. He lowered her, making sure she was still alive so he could watch her struggle at the end of the rope.

The effort must have taken considerable strength and patience, and Bailey suddenly realized the troll had likely been planning out the murder in his mind for months, fantasizing about every detail, anticipating the moment he would stand on the shore and watch Krystal Devine die.

Feeling slightly sick to her stomach, Bailey led Ludwig back to the stairs. She wasn't sure why she had decided to stop by the pier before going back to the office, but she was glad that she had since she now had a better understanding of the man she was looking for.

The troll was a planner who bided his time as well as a sadist who enjoyed making others suffer, which meant he had likely already targeted someone else as his next victim.

He's out there right now somewhere making new plans.

As she descended the stairs, Bailey saw that Sabrina West was set up in the parking lot reporting live at the scene.

And leaning on a little red sportscar a few spaces away, Garth Hamilton was jotting down something in a notebook.

Making a concerted effort to avoid eye contact, Bailey quickly crossed to her Expedition and opened the door for Ludwig to jump in.

"Agent Flynn, has the FBI opened an investigation into Krystal Devine's death?" Sabrina asked as she hurried over to stick the microphone in front of Bailey.

"No comment," Bailey said, slipping behind the wheel.

"Has her death been ruled a suicide?" Sabrina yelled. "Or is it possibly a homicide?"

Bailey started the engine and backed out of the parking space. She couldn't give a public statement about the troll or her suspicions that he'd killed Rachel Cho as well as Krystal Devine. At least, not yet.

For now, the only thing she could do was get back to work.

She needed to concentrate on finding the man who had hung Krystal Devine from the pier.

As she pulled onto the highway and headed toward Miami, she wondered how Dalton's meeting had gone with Giovanni Rocco. Had he managed to find out anything new to help him track down Jordan Stone?

Would the billionaire ever be brought to justice for killing Lorraine Holbrook and Claude Kessler? Would he ever pay for all the people he'd hurt and the lives he'd ruined?

And will he ever pay for what he did to me?

Questions about Stone and his current whereabouts continued to plague her all the way back to her office, exacerbating the aching in her head.

Once she sat down at her desk, she opened up her laptop and logged into the central server, hoping that she still had access to the department's evidence records, case notes, and investigation files.

Navigating to the main folder for the Holbrook Coffee Company shooting task force, she clicked on a subfolder and was relieved when it opened as usual to display a list of files.

With a twinge of guilt, Bailey clicked on the latest update file and began to read, even though she suspected Ramsey would be angry if he found out she still had access.

She spent the next hour perusing the recent case files and had just started to scan the list of calls and messages that had been downloaded from Lorraine Holbrook's phone when Bailey saw something that made her heart stop.

SirGrendel88 had sent Lorraine Holbrook a direct message the morning she had been killed.

Suspecting she already knew what kind of message the troll had sent, Bailey opened it and read the single sentence with a growing sense of dread.

Are you ready to die?

Staring at her computer screen, she realized that she needed no further proof that the troll who'd terrorized Rachel Cho and Krystal Devine, among so many others, was the shooter she'd encountered in the coffee shop.

And there could be no doubt now that his online threats had escalated into murder.

Hearing footsteps in the hall, she quickly closed the file.

She was convinced that if Ramsey found out the troll worked for Stone, he would take her off the case, disrupting the investigation that had just started.

Can it hurt to have two teams searching for the same killer? Maybe it will help to look at the case from two different angles.

As Bailey attempted to rationalize her decision to keep the information she'd learned about the shooter from Ramsey, Sharma appeared in the doorway.

"I'm going home," she said. "You sure you're okay? You look a little flushed. You don't have a fever do you?"

"No, I'm good," Bailey assured her. "And Ludwig and I were just heading out as well. I told Fraser I would stop by the station on the way home. I want to let him know the Bureau is now officially investigating SirGrendel88."

* * *

Bailey spotted Jimmy Fraser as soon as she and Ludwig walked into the Belle Harbor police station.

"Ezra Rosenbaum's mother is waiting for me in an

interview room," the detective said after hurrying over to greet her. "She was notified this morning that her son's remains were found at the Summerset Railroad Depot. She's pretty upset as you can imagine."

"I can sit in on the interview Mrs. Rosenbaum if you'd like," Bailey offered. "I was actually coming here to let you know SAC Ramsey has given me and Agent Sharma his blessing to investigate SirGrendel88. If Ezra is one of his victims, it'll be helpful to hear what his mother can tell us."

With a grim nod, Fraser led Bailey and Ludwig to his office, allowing the German shepherd to settle in by the window, before moving on to an interview room down the hall.

After knocking softly, he opened the door.

A petite woman sat at the wooden table.

She had steel gray hair pulled back into a neat bun and wore a navy blue track suit and scuff-free white tennis shoes, which appeared to be brand new.

"Mrs. Rosenbaum, this is Special Agent Bailey Flynn with the FBI," Fraser said. "She'll be joining us today."

As Bailey took a seat across the table, she could see that the woman was in obvious emotional pain.

Hannah Rosenbaum sat with her arms wrapped around her body as if for comfort and she rocked slowly back and forth as she told them about her son in a dazed voice.

"Ezra was a sweet child but he had difficulties at school from the start. He never quite fit in with the other children but he wanted so badly to have friends. I think that's why he ended up falling into the wrong sort of crowd.

"He ended up getting into trouble as a teenager. I was

heartbroken when he was sent away to the Summerset Juvenile Detention Center for a year.

"He hated it there. He would call me and beg for me to get him out, saying he was being bullied and mistreated. But there was nothing I could do. Once he did get released, he was...different. His whole life seemed to go off track.

"He was in and out of jail. There was always something going on, although he wouldn't talk to me about it. And then one day, he said he was going to meet up with someone he hadn't seen in a long time and he just...vanished."

She looked at Bailey with forlorn, red-rimmed eyes.

"I reported him missing but I don't think the police did much to look for him. I tried to tell myself he must have decided to start fresh...somewhere new. I held out hope he might show up on my doorstep one day out of the blue."

Taking a crumpled tissue from the pocket of her track suit jacket, she dabbed at her eyes.

"I think that's why I sent in my DNA to that company. I was hoping something might turn up. But I never thought..."

Her voice trailed away and she lifted the tissue again.

"Did Ezra ever mention anyone who might have threatened him?" Bailey asked. "Anyone he was afraid of?"

"Just those boys in the detention center with him," Mrs. Rosenbaum said. "But that was nearly twenty years ago."

Fraser frowned.

"So, Ezra had been out of the detention center for about seven or eight years before he went missing in 2014?"

The older woman nodded.

"And did he tell you anything about the person he was

going to meet that last time you saw him?" Bailey asked. "His name? Where they planned to meet? Anything at all?"

"Ezra said he hadn't seen the guy in a long time, and he seemed surprised that he'd called," Mrs. Rosenbaum said. "I got the impression he didn't particularly like him, although I don't know what made me think that."

She shifted in her chair.

"Now, can I pick up my boy's remains?"

"The medical examiner's office is still investigating the cause and manner of death," Fraser said. "But once they've concluded their investigation, someone will call you. They'll send the remains to a funeral home or mortuary for either burial or cremation."

Hannah Rosenbaum nodded numbly before standing and silently following Fraser out of the interview room.

When he returned, he told Bailey he was planning to drive out to the Summerset Juvenile Detention Center where Ezra had been incarcerated as a teen.

"It seems that's where it all went wrong," he said. "I think whoever contacted him that last day must have been one of his fellow inmates when he was there."

Bailey looked at her watch.

"It's almost quitting time," she said. "But I'll ride along with you if you want an update on what I've found out about the troll so far."

"Sounds like a plan," Fraser said, already heading toward the door. "I'll let Linette know I'll be a little late."

As Bailey followed him into the lobby, a voice called out.

She turned to see Madeline Mercer coming toward them.

"I found the rope in the evidence locker," the CSI team leader said. "The one collected at Rachel Cho's house the day her body was found."

She lowered her voice.

"From what I can tell, Finola was right. It's the same red and blue polypropylene braided rope that was used to hang Krystal Devine."

Bailey glanced at Fraser, who didn't look surprised.

"I'll be running the usual tests on the rope later today, but I don't expect to find fingerprints. And I didn't see any hair," she said. "There could be traces of blood, I guess. I'll keep you guys posted."

She didn't sound hopeful.

In fact, Bailey thought the CSI team leader sounded depressed. As Fraser continued on toward the door, Bailey laid a hand on Madeline's arm.

"I'm sure we'll find the troll who killed Rachel Cho with or without trace evidence from the rope," she said. "Don't let it stress you out."

"Oh, I'm not stressed about the rope," Madeline said.

She looked around the lobby and lowered her voice.

"It's just that Garth Hamilton canceled the interview we had scheduled. We were supposed to meet for happy hour. Now I'll have to find another way to spend my Friday night."

Bailey opened her mouth to respond and then closed it again, not sure what to say.

She watched Madeline disappear into the back before turning and following Fraser out to the Interceptor.

As they pulled out of the parking lot, heading toward the

Summerset Juvenile Detention Center, Bailey decided to tell Fraser everything she knew about the troll.

"I haven't told Ramsey this, but I think the man who shot me at the coffee shop is the troll we're looking for," Bailey admitted. "Which means he's working for Stone."

Fraser stared at her as if she were crazy.

"You've just had a head injury and..."

"I'm not imagining all this," Bailey insisted. "I saw a message on Lorraine Holbrook's phone. SirGrendel88 sent her a death threat the day of the shooting."

Sucking in a deep breath, Fraser was silent for a long beat.

"And Ford Ramsey is okay with you working on the case?" he finally said. "If the troll really is the shooter–"

"He is," Bailey said firmly. "But Ramsey doesn't know that. Not yet. If he finds out, I'll be off the case and kept in the dark. And I don't think I could handle just sitting around waiting for the troll to make his next move."

CHAPTER TWENTY-FOUR

As Fraser steered the Interceptor through downtown Belle Harbor's perpetual knot of traffic, he frowned over at Bailey, who looked drawn and pale, wondering if she was ready to lead an investigation into another serial predator so soon after suffering a traumatic brain injury.

But the stubborn tilt of Bailey's chin as she stared out the window told him she was done discussing the issue, at least for the time being, so he kept the question to himself.

Driving east toward the coast, he turned onto Haverfield Road and followed the two-lane highway until he saw the sign for the Summerset County Juvenile Detention Center.

The two-story redbrick building was faded and weathered, having withstood decades of coastal winds, tropical storms, and blazing sun. It stood behind a chain link fence, which was topped with coils of rusty barbed wire.

Wedging the Interceptor into an empty space in the parking lot, Fraser jumped out and opened the back door for Ludwig before hurrying around to check on Bailey.

She looked at his offered hand and sighed.

"I told you I'm fine," she said with a hint of exasperation. "I can get out of a car on my own. No help required."

But he walked closely behind her just the same, not liking the grayish pallor of her cheeks or the habit she'd suddenly developed of rubbing the back of her head.

Hurrying into the administration entrance with Bailey and Ludwig on his heels, he stopped at the reception desk.

"I have a meeting scheduled with Warden Pacheco," he said. "He should be expecting me."

"You're late."

A deep voice spoke from behind him and Fraser turned to see a short, burly man with a thick tuft of graying hair.

"I'm Warden Pacheco," the man said, offering a hand. "And you're Detective Fraser from Belle Harbor, I assume. I was expecting you a full ten minutes ago."

Fraser took the warden's hand and smiled uncertainly.

"Sorry for calling out your tardiness, but I was in the military long enough to expect punctuality," Pacheco said, returning Fraser's smile. "It seems I'm often disappointed."

He turned his attention to Bailey.

"And who have you brought with you?"

"This is Special Agent Bailey Flynn with the FBI," Fraser said. "And her search and rescue dog, Ludwig."

The warden inclined his head toward Bailey and then issued a curt command to Ludwig.

"Shake hands!"

The German shepherd obediently lifted a paw, earning a hearty laugh of approval from the warden.

"He's a fine dog," Pacheco said as he led them down the hall to his office.

Once they were seated at his desk, he looked at Bailey and

cocked his head.

"We've met before, haven't we?"

Raising both eyebrows, he pointed a finger at her.

"I know...you're the FBI agent who shot Ronin Godfrey at Summerset Park, aren't you?"

Before Bailey could reply, he continued.

"I might be aging myself, but I was a guard back when Godfrey was one of our inmates. I guess it's been almost twenty years now. I'd been discharged from the service and was looking for a new career.

"I'd pretty much just started here when Ronin Godfrey arrived at the detention center. He went by the name Ronnie back then. And he was a real bully. Evil through and through.

"I hadn't thought of him for decades and then there was that incident at the park. The shooting and the little girl. I've followed the case closely and, well..."

He lowered his voice to a confidential tone and looked at Bailey with an approving nod.

"You did the world a favor the day you took him out, I have to say. He was a bad apple from the start."

Sensing Bailey's discomfort, Fraser jumped in.

"That *is* an interesting coincidence," he said. "I didn't know Godfrey had been incarcerated here but-"

"You're not here to talk about Ronin Godfrey?" Pacheco asked, looking confused. "I guess I just assumed...since that writer came by earlier in the week and was asking all sorts of questions."

"What writer?" Bailey asked.

"He said his name was Garth Hamilton."

Pacheco rifled through the mess on his desk, picked up a small card from under a pile of papers, and handed it to her.

She glanced down at the card, noting that it contained Garth Hamilton's name and contact details.

"I told the guy I couldn't tell him anything that wasn't already in the public records," Pacheco assured them. "But he mainly wanted to know what kind of prisoner Godfrey had been. What kind of food he ate. How he got along with the other inmates. Stuff like that."

His eyes lit up with interest.

"Apparently, he's writing a true-crime book about infamous killers in Summerset County."

Glancing over at Bailey, Fraser saw that she was as surprised as he was to hear that Garth Hamilton had visited the detention center.

He cleared his throat.

"I'm afraid this is a lot more serious than collecting information for a book," Fraser said. "We're here as part of an investigation into another of your former inmates."

Pacheco raised an eyebrow.

"Which one?"

"Ezra Rosenbaum."

Fraser took out a mugshot, which was the only photo he had of the dead man, and handed it to the warden.

"Ezra was sent here back in 2006 as a fifteen-year-old on a conviction of burglary of an occupied dwelling. His mother said he came out of here suffering emotional damage. She said he wouldn't talk about it, but she was pretty sure he'd been bullied. Maybe even abused."

As Pacheco stared down at the photo of a sullen teenager with a buzz cut and an unfortunate case of acne, Fraser quickly did the mental math, calculating that Ezra must have been an inmate at the detention center around the same time Godfrey had been there.

"Sorry, I don't remember him," the warden said, handing the mugshot back to Fraser. "Why are you guys looking for him anyway? What did he do?"

"He got himself killed," Fraser said.

Setting the mugshot on the desk, he sat back in his chair.

"One day about ten years ago, Ezra told his mother he was going to meet up with an old acquaintance. Someone he hadn't seen in a while. He never came back. He just sort of vanished. There was no sign of him for almost a decade.

"Then earlier this year, we found his skull at the old Summerset Railroad Depot. There was a 9mm bullet in it. A forensic anthropologist estimated the skull had been there for at least a decade or more.

"We were hoping you might be able to tell us what you know about him. We were wondering if he had any friends here that he might have been going to meet. Anyone who might know what happened to him prior to his death."

The warden shrugged.

"Like I said, I don't really remember the guy, but I can pull up his record," he offered. "We can see if there's anything in the system that might help with your investigation."

Pacheco turned to his computer.

After a few minutes of tapping on the keyboard, a printer beside the desk whirred to life and began spitting out a thin stack of paper.

Scooping up the pages, he handed them to Fraser.

"That's all there is," Pacheco said. "Not much there, I'm afraid. Ezra Rosenbaum ended up getting released early due to overcrowding, which is pretty normal around here."

Fraser picked up the pages and flipped through them as Bailey read over his shoulder.

A quick scan of the document revealed that Ezra had been sentenced to serve twelve months at the detention center but only served nine.

Bailey pointed to a note on one of the pages.

"Looks as if he was involved in a fight," she said. "According to this, he used one of the weights in the rec area to assault a fellow inmate."

She turned the page to the collected witness statements. Fraser's eyes widened as she read the first statement aloud.

"*Ezra picked up a twenty-pound dumbbell and threw it at Ronnie G's head. The weight struck his shoulder instead.*"

Bailey glanced up at Pacheco, who was nodding slowly.

"Actually, I think I remember that incident now. Ronnie liked to target younger boys and we all figured the other kid had been acting in self-defense.

"But none of the witnesses had the guts to speak up against Ronnie so there wasn't much we could do."

Fraser stared at the name written on the statement.

"Ronnie G..." he murmured.

Taking out his phone, he scrolled through the photos of the graffiti he'd taken inside the caboose at the Summerset Railroad Depot.

He held out the phone so that Bailey and Pacheco could see one of the images where the graffiti tag *RonnieG* had been spraypainted on the wall across from the big letters spelling out *SirGrendel88*.

"Did any inmates go by the name Grendel?" Fraser asked. Pacheco shrugged.

"That doesn't ring a bell," he said. "But I can see if there's anyone by that name in the system."

After a few minutes of typing on his keyboard, the warden shook his head.

"Nothing in here for anyone named Grendel," he said. "Sorry I couldn't be more helpful."

"Actually, I think you've given us some very useful information," Fraser said. "We appreciate your time."

After asking the warden to contact him if he thought of anything else, he followed Bailey and Ludwig outside.

Once they were back in the Interceptor, Fraser checked his messages. A call had come in from Eloise Spellman.

"We've finished our evaluation of the bones found at the railroad depot. I think there's something you should see."

* * *

Fraser winced as he tapped in a text to Linette, advising her and the kids to go ahead and eat dinner without him.

His wife wasn't going to be happy with him now whatever time he ended up getting home.

Stepping out of the Interceptor, which was now parked in front of the medical examiner's office, he followed Bailey inside to find Eloise Spellman looking somewhat unsettled.

"Sorry to call you over here so late on a Friday afternoon," she said. "But I thought you'd probably want to know what we've discovered as soon as possible."

Leaving Ludwig behind by the receptionist's desk, the group walked into the back and down the hall to the prep room to pull protective coveralls over their clothes.

Once they moved into the autopsy suite, Fraser saw a metal dissecting table set up at the far end of the room.

Eloise stood at the head of the table.

"We've reconstructed Ezra Rosenbaum's skeleton," she said. "And we found something unusual when we examined the C1 and C2 vertebrae."

"Where are the C1 and C2 vertebrae?" Fraser asked, staring down at the bones. "Anatomy wasn't my best subject."

He watched with interest as Eloise gestured to several bones positioned just below the jaw of the skeleton.

"The bones in the neck and spine are called cervical vertebrae," she explained. "They protect the spinal cord and are numbered C1 through C7. This is C1."

She pointed to a ring-shaped bone at the top of the neck.

"This bone helps us hold our heads upright, so it's often called the atlas bone."

Looking at Fraser, she smiled expectantly. When he didn't respond she raised an eyebrow.

"You do know Atlas, don't you? He was the Titan in Greek mythology who carried the heavens on his shoulders."

Without waiting for a response, she looked down at the skeleton on the table.

"This second bone here is the C2 vertebrae, which is also called the axis since it helps the head to rotate," she continued. "And a fracture of any of the cervical vertebrae is called a broken neck."

She looked up at Fraser.

"Cervical fractures are usually caused by high-impact accidents or falls. You can see in this skeleton that both the atlas and the axis bones have been fractured with some sort of sharp blade. They both show multiple cut marks."

Fraser frowned.

"What are you saying?"

"I'm saying this victim suffered multiple high-impact cuts to the neck area," Eloise said with a heavy sigh. "I'm saying there's a reason you found the skull on the track and the rest of the bones in the caboose."

Her eyes met Fraser's.

"I'm saying whoever shot Ezra also chopped off his head."

Wincing at her words, he stared at Eloise in surprise.

"I thought you should know right away since that means there has to be another weapon out there," she added. "An axe or sword or something capable of taking off a head."

"And that weapon could have forensic evidence on it," Bailey said, speaking up for the first time. "I'd say we need to organize another search."

Fraser looked over at Bailey and slowly nodded.

Within minutes, they were back in the Interceptor.

Pulling out his phone to send yet another update to Linette, he saw the photos he'd shown Warden Pacheco.

The photos of the graffiti he'd taken during the previous

search. Wondering if they'd missed the second weapon, he studied the photo of the graffiti tags, remembering what Arturo Pacheco had told them.

"I'd say we can assume that Ronin Godfrey is RonnieG," he said, holding the phone so that Bailey could view the image. "But who the hell is SirGrendel88?"

CHAPTER TWENTY-FIVE

Grendel turned the white van into All Souls Cemetery, ignoring the sign that said no visitors were allowed after sundown, well aware that the perpetually open gate that stood at the entrance was for show only and that the local church that owned and ran the cemetery didn't have the budget for twenty-four-hour security guards.

Heading toward the far side of the cemetery, he followed the narrow road that wound its way through row after row of gravestones, some of which had been in the ground long before Grendel had been born.

As he reached the rickety wooden fence that separated the tidy, manicured cemetery from the weed-strewn stretch of land beyond, he brought the van to a stop and shut off the engine and lights.

Voices sounded from somewhere past the fence, causing Grendel to stop and listen. He jumped as he heard the excited bark of a dog in the distance.

The police had returned to the depot.

He slipped through an opening in the fence, sticking to the cover of the scraggly trees that filled the abandoned land as he made his way to the old railroad depot.

Using binoculars, he saw a black SUV and a CSI van from the Belle Harbor PD parked outside the abandoned station.

Flood lights had been set up, illuminating the scene.

His pulse quickened as he saw a slim blonde woman in a pink blouse, navy blue pants, and a matching jacket.

It was Special Agent Bailey Flynn.

Instinctively, Grendel laid a hand on the gun in the hidden holster on his belt. The Beretta had been his father's gun.

It was the same gun he'd taken with him to the Holbrook Coffee Company. The one he'd used to kill Lorraine Holbrook and Claude Kessler. The one he'd used to shoot Bailey Flynn.

As he stood there looking at the railroad depot, he realized it was also the same gun he'd used to kill Ezra Rosenbaum all those years ago at the very same site.

Keeping his hand on the beretta, he frowned, wondering what the FBI and the local police could be searching for.

They'd already found Ezra's skull and bones, so what more could they be hoping to find?

The question gnawed at him as he snuck through the trees and around the back of the abandoned boxcars, wanting to get close enough to hear what the searchers were saying.

Familiar with the terrain, Grendel moved forward quickly, having used the railroad depot for his own purposes since he'd been a teenager.

He stopped and darted behind a tree as he heard a dog barking up ahead. Peering around the thick tree trunk, he recognized Bailey Flynn's search and rescue dog.

As the German shepherd ran toward the dark woods, Grendel prepared to turn and run. He heard Bailey Flynn call out before he could make his move.

"Ludwig! Come, boy!"

The German shepherd stopped and obediently raced back to his handler as Grendel exhaled in relief.

Remaining hidden behind the tree, he listened to the searchers as they went from one boxcar to the next.

It sounded as if they were looking for some sort of weapon. Something sharp enough to cut bone.

As he heard someone say Ezra Rosenbaum's name, he thought back to the day the stupid kid had attacked Ronin Godfrey at the detention center.

When Grendel had attempted to step in, Ezra had thrown a wild punch at him, managing to knock him to the ground.

A flush of embarrassment and rage had spread across his face as Ezra had walked away, calling back a threat.

"Mess with me again and I'll knock your head clean off!"

All the inmates around them had laughed as Grendel promised himself he would get Ezra back for the humiliation.

He hadn't known it would be many years before he had the opportunity to fulfill the promise.

Now, as he watched the search at the railroad depot continue, he allowed his mind to return to the day he'd finally taken his revenge.

Grendel waited in the sweltering caboose, his anticipation growing with every passing hour, sweat dripping from his face as the summer sun rose to its highest point in the blue Florida sky.

He'd arrived four hours before the arranged meeting time, knowing that Ezra Rosenbaum would also undoubtedly arrive early. He'd surely want to check out the place in advance.

After all, anyone with any sense of self-preservation would want to make sure a trap hadn't been laid.

Unfortunately for his intended victim, Grendel had already taken up his position in the last train car when Ezra arrived at the depot.

Carrying a switchblade in one hand and a phone in the other, Ezra stopped beside the train tracks and looked around.

"He's not here yet," he said into the phone. "I'll wait inside the depot for him. I've got my blade if he tries anything funny."

He shoved the phone back into his pocket as he continued walking along the track.

Hardly recognizing his old jail mate, who had become a grown man in the years since they'd been at the Summerset County Detention Center together, Grendel watched from his hiding place, assessing Ezra's now-broad shoulders and muscular legs, glad he'd thought to bring along the old Berretta.

There was little chance he'd be able to carry out his plan without the gun. Little chance he could kill Ezra in a fair fight.

But Grendel wasn't intending to fight fair.

As soon as he'd seen Ezra's post online the day before, he'd known this was his chance to get his own back.

His former fellow inmate had quickly fallen for the lie he'd fed him about working on his twelve-step program and making amends to those he'd wronged.

When Ezra had agreed to meet, Grendel had immediately thought of the deserted depot, where he and his old partner in crime, Ronin Godfrey, had spent many a happy day getting high and planning out their next burglary.

Finally, Ezra was going to pay the price for humiliating him.

Grendel waited for Ezra to walk past the caboose.

Stepping down off the platform, he stuck the muzzle of the gun to the back of Ezra's head, just below his left ear.

"Thanks for coming," he said as the big man in front of him froze in fear. "I've been waiting a long time to see you again."

"What's with the gun?" Ezra asked.

He remained rigid, standing totally still as he spoke.

"You said you wanted to make amends. That you were in AA. That you wanted to apologize for-"

"I lied," Grendel said. "I'm not in AA, you moron. It was a trick. I don't even like to drink. And I'm not the one who should be making amends...you are. You're the one who needs to apologize."

Ezra nodded slowly.

"You're right," he said, his voice shaking. "I'm really sorry."

"Yeah, you're going to be sorry when I'm done with-"

Before Grendel could finish the thought, Ezra was spinning around, moving fast as he thrust an elbow into Grendel's stomach.

Reflexively gasping for breath, Grendel clenched his trigger finger, sending a bullet into Ezra's head with a deafening bang.

Blood spurted into the hot summer air as the big man's body fell to the ground, jerking and spasming as his life drained away.

"You idiot!" Grendel yelled as he stared down at the dying man. "Now you've ruined everything!"

The perfect revenge he'd imagined wouldn't happen now. He wouldn't get the pleasure of watching the life slowly drain from Ezra's eyes as he dangled from the end of his rope.

It wasn't fair. Ezra Rosenbaum had barely even suffered.

But Grendel could still have his grand finale.

Crossing to the caboose, he retrieved the track chisel he'd scavenged from the roundhouse.

He knew at one time the tool, which consisted of a long wooden handle and a sharp metal cutting blade, had been used by workers to cut and remove old, rusted rails.

It would serve a different purpose now.

Walking back to where Ezra lay, Grendel rested the sharp edge of the blade on his neck.

Using all his strength, he lifted the chisel into the air and then brought the blade down with full force.

Blood spurted into the air and spilled onto the ground.

Exhilarated, Grendel brought the track chisel down again and again, until the blade buried itself into the sodden earth.

Reaching down, he grabbed a handful of blood-soaked hair.

With a grunt of satisfaction, he flung Ezra's head with all his might, following its trajectory with shining eyes as it landed on the tracks, disappearing between the old rails.

The buzzing of his phone interrupted Grendel's memories.

Digging his phone from his pocket, he saw that Jordan Stone was calling. The billionaire must be getting impatient.

Grendel quickly silenced the call, hoping no one in the search party had heard the sound, unsure how he'd explain his presence at the depot if the searchers found him there.

It would be best to leave before he got caught.

As he had done with Ezra, he would patiently bide his time. Eventually, he would get Bailey Flynn alone. And when he did, she would pay for what she'd taken from him.

CHAPTER TWENTY-SIX

Bailey looked around at the darkened depot, discouraged that neither the human nor canine searchers had found anything new to help with the investigation. After discovering a collection of old tools in the roundhouse, which at one time had been used to service the trains coming through the depot, she had been hopeful.

But after closer inspection, none of the tools had a blade sharp enough to sever a head from a body. They'd found no discarded axes or swords. No bloodstained weapons or tools of any kind. The search had proven to be a waste of time.

Deciding to call it a day, Bailey and Fraser ended the search and headed back to the Interceptor, passing Madeline Mercer standing beside the CSI van on the way.

"When I told you I needed to find something else to do tonight, I didn't exactly mean this," the CSI team leader called out to Bailey with a wry smile.

Fraser raised an eyebrow but didn't question what Madeline had been talking about as they drove back to the police station in silence.

They were both too weary from the long day and discouraged from the unsuccessful search to talk.

But when Fraser dropped Bailey off at her Expedition, he roused himself enough to remind her to be careful.

"The troll is out there, and if your theory is right, he's already come after you once," he said. "There's always the chance that he'll try again."

Resting her hand on her Glock, Bailey nodded.

"If and when he does, I'll be ready."

She stepped out before he could respond. She was exhausted and her head was aching. All she wanted to do was go home and get some rest.

But when she walked into the dark, empty apartment, Bailey suddenly realized that it was Friday night and she was all alone. Dalton had gone off somewhere searching for Jordan Stone and Cate was out with Mason, probably enjoying a romantic dinner.

Even Ludwig abandoned her after eating his evening meal, curling up on his cushion by the window to sleep rather than staying up to keep her company.

As she opened up a can of tomato soup, she was too tired to pour it into a pan and heat it up.

Taking a spoon from the drawer, she began to eat the soup straight from the can, thinking about the disappointing search for the second weapon at the depot and the investigation into the troll's true identity, which seemed to be going nowhere fast.

And now that she knew the troll was the same man who'd shot her, she found it even more frustrating that she had seen the shooter, had even stood face to face with him, but couldn't remember him at all.

If only she could make her tired, aching brain remember.

After she showered, changed into jeans and a t-shirt, and poured a glass of wine, Bailey sat in front of her computer, feeling the need to organize and sort through all the information she'd gathered during the investigation so far.

She decided she would start by typing out a detailed list of everything she knew about the troll.

It would be a start on the report she owed to Ford Ramsey by the end of the week. It would also do her good to get all the information out of her head and down on paper.

Starting with a section on the Summerset Railroad Depot, she included the original discovery of the skull on the tracks, the ballistics for the bullet in the skull matching the bullet found at the Holbrook Coffee Company, the graffiti found in the caboose where Ezra Rosenbaum's bones were hidden, and the red and blue braided rope knotted around the bones.

She noted that the graffiti tags *SirGrendel88* and *RonnieG* had been spraypainted on the walls, suggesting that both the troll and Ronin Godfrey had been inside the boxcar.

Next, she added a section about Krystal Devine's death, including her complaint about death threats from SirGrendel88, the discovery of Krystal's body hanging at the pier by the same red and blue braided rope found at the depot, and the strange suicide note found in her car.

This was followed by a section on Rachel Cho, including her complaint about death threats from SirGrendel88, her supposed suicide, the use of red and blue braided rope matching rope found at the two other death scenes, and the need for an exhumation of her body to prove homicide.

The final section referenced the Holbrook Coffee Company shooting, including the message in Lorraine Holbrook's inbox from SirGrendel88, the ballistics for the bullet on the shop floor matching the bullet in Ezra Rosenbaum's skull, and the shooting of two associates working for Tombstone Imports and Jordan Stone.

Her chest tightened as she read over the list.

There was no way she could hide the connection between the troll, the Holbrook Coffee Shop shooter, and Jordan Stone once she created and submitted an official report to Ramsey.

No doubt he would take her off the case as soon as he'd read through the document.

Which means I have less than a week to find the troll.

Deciding she would do all she could in the time she had left, Bailey retrieved the crumpled printout she had been carrying around for two days from her jacket.

It included the names of everyone who'd filed complaints about online death threats from SirGrendel88.

As she scanned the list, her eyes stopped on Rachel Cho's name. Her initial search through the young woman's social media activity hadn't revealed much, since Rachel had deactivated her accounts and gone dark online before her death, likely in an effort to hide from her tormentor.

But perhaps if I widened my search...

Bailey's eyes were starting to droop, and she was thinking of giving up for the night when she found a reference to Rachel Cho on the *Belle Harbor Chronicle* website.

Apparently, the young woman had been an intern and contributing reporter for the local newspaper.

Opening the archive, she found the last article that Rachel had written. Her byline was at the top of a newspaper article titled *Shooting at Summerset Park.*

Bailey was no longer sleepy as she read the article, which was focused on Dolores Santos' abduction by Ronin Godfrey and the death of both the predator and the victim.

Was it the article on Godfrey that drew the troll's attention and ire? Did he target Rachel because she wrote about the killer?

Pondering the question, Bailey checked her direct messages and saw she'd finally received a response from Rachel Cho's parents.

They had responded with one sentence.

Leave us and our daughter's memory alone.

She sighed and shook her head. She couldn't blame the young woman's parents. They'd been through a lot. It was no wonder they wanted to be left alone.

But it meant that she would have to ask Cate to petition Judge Nelson for the exhumation order.

Her eyes fell to the only other message in her inbox, which was from Garth Hamilton.

Sorry to slip into your DMs uninvited, but I've discovered information you might be interested in hearing. There's something about Jordan Stone you should know. I'm staying at an Airbnb on Bellamy Beach if you want to stop by later and discuss.

He had added an address to the bottom of the message. It was a house on North Beach Drive, just off the water.

Glancing at her watch, Bailey sighed and got to her feet, careful not to wake up Ludwig as she left the apartment.

CHAPTER TWENTY-SEVEN

Garth Hamilton checked the big clock over the front door, hoping his carefully calculated offer to provide information about Jordan Stone would entice Bailey Flynn to accept his invitation to join the gathering of friends and neighbors at the big beach house on North Beach Drive.

He was prepared to do Bailey Flynn a favor.

If she was grateful for his help, it would make it much easier for him to ask for a favor in return.

The FBI agent had been involved in several of the serial killer cases he was planning to include in his upcoming book, *Slaughter in Summerset County*, and she would undoubtedly be a valuable source if he could gain her trust.

The night was getting late and he'd just about given up hope when Bailey finally arrived, looking unusually casual in a t-shirt and jeans with her dark blonde hair hanging loose around her shoulders.

Garth decided he'd never seen the agent looking so unarmed as he greeted her and offered her a glass of wine.

"No, thanks," she said. "I've actually already had my share tonight. In fact, I took an Uber over here, just in case I'm near the limit. But I would love a glass of water."

Crossing to the bar, Garth poured cold water into a tumbler and carried it back to Bailey.

He raised an eyebrow as she drained the glass, set the tumbler on a nearby table, and surveyed the room.

"Madeline Mercer told me you canceled your happy hour interview with her," Bailey said. "I assume you decided to throw this little party instead, which must mean that you've already gotten everything you want from her."

Garth raised an eyebrow, surprised by her astute assessment of the situation.

"Someone's not in a very good mood," he said, keeping his voice light. "If you must know, I forgot I'd arranged this little soiree when I asked Madeline to meet up."

But the FBI agent didn't appear to be listening.

"You said you had information on Stone," she said impatiently. "If you were just trying to get me here to-"

"I *do* have information," Garth assured her. "But I wanted you to hear it from the horse's mouth."

He pointed toward the terrace.

"She's out there," he said, gesturing to a woman whose deep tan, along with the sun-bleached highlights in her long brown hair, would fool most people into believing that she spent long hours at the beach or on a boat rather than in a beauty salon.

Leaning forward, he laid a light hand on Bailey's arm.

"Celine's a beauty, isn't she? And a real thoroughbred. The Furst family is one of the oldest in Summerset County."

He lowered his voice to an intimate murmur.

"Unfortunately, she's a total lush. According to my

calculations, that's her third gin and tonic."

Surprise flashed across Bailey's face at the catty comment but was quickly gone.

"You know, Tony Brunner lives only a few houses down the beach," he said, watching her green eyes closely. "And Celine used to be a frequent visitor."

Taking Bailey's arm, he led her onto the terrace before she could protest, liking the way the wind picked up the loose strands of her blond hair and blew them around her face.

"Celine dear, this is Bailey Flynn," he said with a self-satisfied smirk. "She's an FBI agent. Doesn't that sound *exciting*? And Bailey, this is Celine Furst, one of my dearest friends in Summerset County."

"I'm probably your *only* friend in Summerset County," the woman teased. "And even that could be debated."

Garth laughed good-naturedly as he led the two women to the edge of the terrace where the waves would be more likely to drown out their conversation.

"Celine, why don't you tell Agent Flynn what you told me the other day?" he prompted. "I'm sure if you ask nicely she'll keep it off the record."

Bailey raised an eyebrow.

"It doesn't really work like that," she cautioned. "I'm not a reporter who can just-"

"You want me to tell her what I told you about Tony?" Celine asked with a slight slur in her voice.

Garth nodded.

"Yes, what you told me about Tony," he said with an indulgent smile. "You told me you'd been with Tony Brunner the night the police raided the Ashworth Funeral Home. You said he'd gotten a call, right?"

Leaning in toward Bailey, Celine Furst lowered her voice.

"That's right," she said. "I was at Tony's house that night when a woman called. I could only hear his side of the conversation but he got all worked up. He ran out of there as if the house was on fire."

She sighed dramatically.

"He didn't come back for hours. I don't even know how long he was gone because I fell asleep, but the next morning when I woke up, I went out on the balcony upstairs and I could hear him on the terrace below.

"He was talking on the phone to a man he called Stone. Well, I figured he must be talking about *Jordan Stone*. You know that crypto billionaire, don't you?

"I haven't seen the guy in a while, but I've met him several times before. I even made a donation to the Sun Creek Preserve he started before he sold it back to the County.

"And I've been on Jordan Stone's yacht. He threw some fabulous parties. So, I figured when Brunner started talking about this woman named Tamara he had run out on me to go see her.

"Now, I have to admit Tony and I weren't exclusive at the time, and we're not even dating anymore, but I was upset to think that any man would run out on me like that for another woman. Naturally, I was insulted.

"But then I heard Tony say that she'd threatened to go to the police if he didn't help her get out of town. He said he'd given her some cash and put her on a train to Chicago.

"I remember wondering why anyone would want to ride a train all that way when there are airplanes that can get you there in a few hours. And if we're talking about Jordan Stone's girlfriend, why not take a private jet?"

Just then Garth saw Celine's neighbor wave to her from the living room, motioning that she was ready to leave.

"Oh, I need to go say goodbye," Celine said, stumbling slightly as she hurried back inside the house.

Bailey turned to Garth with a frown.

"That's what you wanted to tell me? That Tony Brunner helped Tamara Vincent get on a train up to Chicago the night Emil Lazar was killed?"

She didn't look impressed or even slightly grateful.

"According to the FBI's website, you're looking for Tamara Vincent as well as Jordan Stone," Garth said, suddenly unsure. "I thought it could help with the search."

Bailey's stony expression softened.

"Yeah, I guess it could," she admitted. "But I'm not officially working on that investigation. Of course, I'll pass on the information to the assigned agents. And they may want to speak with Ms. Furst. I can't guarantee Brunner won't hear about it."

Garth shrugged.

"I'm sure Brunner can take care of himself," he said. "And I know Celine can. The woman is like a cat with nine lives."

He produced what he hoped was an ingratiating smile.

"But hopefully you see now that I'm not here to cause any trouble. I just want to help."

Bailey didn't look convinced.

"How is writing a book about serial killers in Summerset County going to help anyone but yourself?" she asked.

Assuming a hurt expression, Garth pulled out the standard answer he always used when asked why he wrote books about murderers and monsters.

"Those who study the criminal mind and how it works are better able to protect themselves in the future," he stated. "The public understands that, which is why most people are eager to learn everything they can about the killers who have targeted their communities."

He cocked his head.

"I'm just trying to give my readers what they want," he continued. "But I do need help and I was hoping you might be willing to share your experiences with-"

"I'm sorry, Mr. Hamilton but-"

"Call me Garth."

Bailey sighed.

"I'm sorry, Garth," she said in a strained voice. "But it's been a long day and I've got a hell of a headache."

Her face did look pale.

"I think I need to...to..."

Suddenly, she swayed on her feet and her knees buckled. Garth reached out just in time to stop her from falling.

"Are you okay?" he asked as he helped her to a lounge chair. "Should I call an ambulance?"

"No, don't," she gasped, lifting a hand to her head. "I just need a minute to rest."

Just then the pocket of her jeans began to buzz.

Reaching down, Bailey managed to pull her phone out of

her pocket before dropping it onto the stone deck.

The name *Dalton West* flashed across the screen as Garth picked up the phone, inadvertently tapping *Accept*.

He heard the faint sound of a man's voice coming from the little speaker and held the phone to his ear.

"Hey there, Dalton?"

There was a moment of silence, and then a man spoke.

"Yes, this is Dalton West. Who are you and why are you answering Bailey's phone? Is she okay? Has something happened to her?'"

"She's okay, I think," Garth said. "She's had a near-fainting spell but doesn't want me to call an ambulance."

He looked over at Bailey, who had her eyes closed and was rubbing the back of her head.

"I'm Garth Hamilton, by the way. I'm having a little get-together at my house with a few friends and Bailey stopped by. I can give her a ride home...although she said she took an Uber here so-"

"I'll send someone to pick her up right away," Dalton said, sounding calm as if he was used to taking charge in stressful situations. "Just send me the address."

Twenty minutes later, Bailey was sitting up and appeared to be feeling better, when the front door swung open and a reporter Garth recognized from Channel 3 News hurried in.

"Where is she? Where's Bailey Flynn?"

CHAPTER TWENTY-EIGHT

Sabrina West made her way through the fashionably dressed crowd in the living room and onto the wide terrace, which was illuminated by several flickering tiki torches. Her blue eyes were as hard as granite as she glared down at the man sitting beside Bailey Flynn.

"What have you done to her?" she demanded as Garth Hamilton stared up at her in shock.

"It's fine," Bailey said, sounding weak but coherent. "I just overdid it today and got a little dizzy. Garth was trying to help me. I'll be fine once I go home and get some sleep."

Studying the agent's pale face, Sabrina nodded stiffly.

"Well, Dalton asked me to come pick you up," she said. "He sounded really worried about you."

She put a hand under Bailey's elbow as the agent got to her feet. When Garth stood and added his support on Bailey's other side, Sabrina didn't object.

Together, they helped Bailey out to Sabrina's news van, which was parked along North Beach Road.

Once she was settled safely into the passenger seat, Sabrina closed the door and turned to Garth.

She was momentarily distracted by his hair, which had

come loose from his ponytail and was whipping wildly around his face in the strong wind off the ocean.

"Thanks for calling my brother," she said. "And sorry for yelling at you like that. I thought you were being a creep."

"That's okay," Garth replied as he tried unsuccessfully to smooth back his hair. "I've got thick skin. It's sort of a prerequisite for being a writer."

Smiling at him despite herself, she circled the van, opened the driver's side door, and then turned back to Garth.

"I've read a few of your books," she said, not ready to admit she'd read them all. "I guess you could say I'm a fan. Or at least, I was, before I heard that you're writing a book about Summerset County."

Garth frowned and cocked his head.

"Why should that bother you? Have you got something to hide?" he teased. "You're not a killer, are you? If you are, I could interview you for my upcoming book. But you'd have to join me for dinner sometime."

"No, I'm not a killer," Sabrina said dryly. "But you should know the last man who took me to dinner ended up dead."

An image of Mario Rocco flashed behind her eyes.

"Good luck with your book."

With a flutter of her hand, she slid behind the wheel and started the engine.

She didn't look back at Garth Hamilton as she turned the news van onto North Beach Drive.

"Thanks for picking me up," Bailey said, once they were on the road heading west toward Sanctuary Street.

She leaned back against the headrest, her eyes closed.

238

"I should have listened to the doctor," she murmured in a low voice. "But I'm sure I'll be fine once I get some sleep."

"You really gave Dalton a scare, you know?" Sabrina said in an accusing tone she didn't bother to temper. "What's he working on anyway?"

When Bailey didn't respond, Sabrina glanced over to make sure she was still breathing, relieved to see that her chest was moving up and down.

"Dalton didn't tell me much about the case he's working on before he left," Sabrina said, turning her eyes back to the road. "He just said he was heading up north and would be gone a few days. Do you know where he went?"

When Bailey still didn't answer Sabrina continued.

"And you never told me what happened to Krystal Devine," she added petulantly. "After I reported the troll and everything, I was told *nothing* after she was killed."

Switching lanes, Sabrina slowed and made a sharp turn into the Sanctuary Apartments, pulling the van into an empty space outside Bailey's building.

"We haven't released an official statement about Krystal Devine, yet," Bailey said as she took off her seatbelt. "We're still investigating and-"

"And you don't want everyone in Belle Harbor to know that we've got an online troll, our very own Grendel, who may have killed one of his victims, is that right?"

She glared over at Bailey.

"I was on that call with you the other day," she reminded Bailey. "I heard you say there were a dozen complaints about SirGrendel88 before mine. That means there's a dozen potential victims out there right now."

Seeing that Bailey had closed her eyes again, Sabrina decided her rant would have to wait for another time.

With a sigh, she got out of the van and helped Bailey to her apartment without another word. As the agent lowered herself onto the sofa, Sabrina took out her phone and called Dalton to report that the mission had been accomplished.

"Your girlfriend is home and sitting here with me," she said after activating the speaker. "She can hear you if there's anything you'd like to say to her before I go."

"What were you doing there?" Dalton asked once Bailey had assured him again that she was fine.

Sabrina held the phone closer to Bailey as she spoke.

"Garth Hamilton sent me a message saying he had information about Jordan Stone. In fact, there was a guest at his party who claimed she overheard Tony Brunner talking to Jordan Stone the night Tamara Vincent left town.

"Apparently, Brunner put Tamara on a train to Chicago that night, although this woman couldn't say what was in Chicago and why Tamara was going there."

Before Dalton could reply, Sabrina pulled the phone back.

"Is that who you're looking for?" she demanded. "You're looking for *Jordan Stone?*"

She was suddenly scared for her brother.

"Are you as crazy as your girlfriend here? Stone and his thugs don't play around. You're going to-"

"Can you put Bailey back on, please?" Dalton cut in, ignoring Sabrina's outburst. "I appreciate your help but right now I just want to make sure Bailey is okay."

With a huff, Sabrina held the phone back toward Bailey.

"Are you sure you should be left alone?" Dalton asked.

"I'm good now," Bailey assured him. "And Cate will be home soon. She'll look after me tonight."

Dalton hesitated.

"Okay, well get some sleep," he finally said. "And check in with me tomorrow. I shouldn't be gone much longer."

"And I'm going to leave Bailey here in peace," Sabrina said, heading toward the door.

Before she could end the call, Dalton asked her to stay on the line. She kept the phone to her ear as she walked back to the news van.

"First of all, thanks again for going to Bailey's rescue like that. I really appreciate you standing in for me when I can't be there. But something's bothering me and I may need your help again.

"You see, what I can't figure out is why Tamara Vincent would run to Chicago if she is working for Stone. And if Stone is there, then I've been looking in the wrong place."

"You shouldn't be looking for Stone at all," Sabrina snapped. "You should let the feds and the police do their jobs. I'm sure there are plenty of missing persons out there for you to be searching for instead."

"Yeah, but it's men like Stone and his gang who are causing a lot of these people to go missing in the first place," Dalton shot back. "If we get to Stone, we get to the source of a very big problem."

His voice darkened.

"And if we don't stop him, more people will end up dead."

* * *

The next morning, Sabrina found herself sitting at a table in the visiting room of the Summerset Detention Center waiting to see Jethro Muldoon.

At Dalton's request, she had agreed to question the former gravedigger, who had worked for Tamara Vincent at the Ashworth Funeral Home before his involvement with Emil Lazar's drug trafficking scheme had been uncovered.

Shifting on the hard wooden bench, she looked up just in time to see Jethro enter the room.

As he walked toward her, she recognized his fleshy face and protruding eyes from the courtroom when she'd reported live outside his unsuccessful bond hearing. His hair, which was a pale, almost colorless blonde, had since been trimmed into a tight crewcut.

"What do you want?" he asked as he sat down. "I'm not interested in being on T.V. so you can-"

"I just want to ask you a few questions about Tamara Vincent," Sabrina said. "Off the record."

The convict frowned as if he wasn't sure what that meant.

"I don't know anything about Tamara," he said. "I haven't seen her since she ran off and left me and Wilmer to get picked up by the cops. Why? What's she done now?"

"She's gone to Chicago," Sabrina said. "I just want to know why. I thought maybe you could tell me."

She forced herself to smile.

"If you do, I'll put a hundred dollars in your commissary account," she added. "And no one will ever know I was here."

Watching Jethro's doughy face closely, she saw his belligerent frown turn into a cunning smile.

"Sure, I know why Tamara went to Chicago," he said. "And it has to do with a lot more money than just a hundred bucks. She went there to make millions."

Sabrina raised an eyebrow.

"How would she make millions?"

"She went up there to get the pills we stashed in Mr. Young's casket," he said. "She probably went to the funeral home and talked them into letting her see the guy before they put him in the ground. On the street, those pills would be worth millions."

He shrugged.

"It's way too late now to stop her though. That would've been months ago. Old Theodore Young is six feet under by now and those pills have been sold on to the buyer."

"And Tamara? What would she do once she had the money?" Sabrina asked. "Where would she go?"

The question seemed to stump Jethro for a minute and then he was smiling again.

"She's a smart lady," he said. "She'd find Sonny's silent partner and give him his cut of the money. She wouldn't want him coming after her."

Sabrina was about to ask him who Sonny was but then it struck her. That had been Emil Lazar's alias when he'd been working undercover prior to his death.

Based on what she'd heard from Dalton and Bailey, she assumed Sonny's silent partner must be Jordan Stone.

"Thank you, Jethro," she said as she stood. "I'll put the

money in your account on the way out. And who knows, I might be back one day soon."

Leaving the detention center, Sabrina called Dalton and told him what Jethro had revealed.

"That's good work."

He sounded impressed.

"And I think it's worth tracking Tamara's activity in Chicago. If she managed to get those pills, she may have delivered Stone's cut of the proceeds personally. She may know where to find him.

"Looks as if the next available flight to Chicago takes off this afternoon and lands around six o'clock at O'Hare," he said. "I'd better go if I'm going to make it on time."

As soon as he ended the call, Sabrina opened her browser. Within minutes, she'd booked her own ticket, figuring her big brother may end up needing her help again.

And if he does, I'm going to be there.

* * *

Sabrina stood by the window, watching as the Boeing 737 pulled up to the gate and the jetway aligned to the exit door.

She was waiting for Dalton when he emerged into the airport carrying a light overnight bag over one shoulder.

"What the hell are you doing here?" he asked as she fell into step beside him. "And how did you get here before me?"

"I'm younger and faster," she said. "And more motivated. I knew if I didn't beat you here you'd leave without me."

Dalton's irritation was short-lived as his focus turned to

finding the fastest mode of transport to the Primrose Park neighborhood. After first heading toward the taxi stand, he allowed Sabrina to pull him toward the train terminal.

"The train will be faster. Especially during rush hour."

An hour later, they were walking into the Primrose Park Funeral Home, which was a small, family-run operation with only one mortician, who quickly identified Tamara Vincent.

He seemed nervous and, in Sabrina's opinion, shifty-eyed.

"Yes, I believe she was here inquiring about Mr. Young," he admitted after glancing at the photo Dalton held. "Said she wasn't going to be able to stay for the viewing the next day and asked for a few minutes alone with the deceased."

He dropped his eyes.

"I couldn't allow that, of course, but I did provide her with a hotel recommendation."

Noticing the nervous tic in the man's left eye, Sabrina was confident the mortician had given Tamara access to the corpse. But she only smiled pleasantly as Dalton asked which hotel the man had recommended.

"Oh, we always recommend the Primrose Park Hotel across the street," he said. "We get a commission on every guest we send over there."

Thanking the mortician for his help, Dalton headed across the street with Sabrina close behind him.

The hotel desk clerk refused to look up Tamara Vincent in their system to confirm she'd been a guest of the hotel but admitted to recognizing her after Dalton pulled out a photo.

"I'm pretty sure she asked about booking the hotel's car service to drive her out of the city but ended up taking a cab," the clerk said. "You could ask the cabbies out there if any of them have seen her. Most of them are regulars who queue along the curb picking up fares from the guests coming out."

With little hope, Sabrina waited in the lobby while Dalton spoke to the drivers of the constant stream of taxis pulling in and out of the hotel.

After he'd been at it for almost an hour with no luck, she walked outside and tapped him on the shoulder.

"You want to get something to eat? I'm kind of hungry."

Dalton gave a dejected shrug and looked around for somewhere close by just as another taxi pulled up to the curb.

He stuck his head in the window.

"You know where we can get a decent slice of pizza?"

The driver climbed out of the cab and circled around to stand next to them on the sidewalk as if eager for an excuse to talk.

His eyes roamed up and down Sabrina's slim figure as he pointed Dalton to a pizza shop around the corner.

He was about to walk away when, almost as an afterthought, Dalton held up the photo of Tamara.

"We're trying to find this woman," he said. "She would have been leaving the hotel a couple of months ago. I know it's a long time to-"

"Yeah, I remember her," the cabbie confirmed. "She was a good-looking woman. I gave her a ride out to Safe Harbor Executive Airport."

Sabrina forced her face to remain calm as Dalton nodded.

"Did you see who she met out there?"

The cabbie frowned and cocked his head, trying to think.

"I can't remember seeing anyone," he admitted. "But I do remember watching her walk out to a plane on the tarmac. Like I said, she was a real looker."

Glancing over at Sabrina, he gave her a little wink.

"The plane was pretty small, maybe a Cessna or something similar. I'm pretty sure it had a yellow stripe down the side. I can take you out there if you want."

It took forty-five minutes in traffic to reach the little airport, and once they arrived, Sabrina soon saw that the only planes with yellow stripes belonged to Flight Ranger Charter Services.

Dalton stopped a man walking out of the charter company's office and confirmed he was a dispatcher.

"Fight plans are submitted for every charter flight going out of the airport, right?" Dalton asked.

The dispatcher nodded.

"Yes, if they're IFR flights it's mandatory," he admitted.

"And the plans are all publicly available?" Dalton asked. "We would just need to know the plane's tail number to access their flight plan?"

Once again, the dispatcher agreed.

"So, I could access the flight plans for all planes in your fleet using tail numbers and filter them by date," Dalton said. "But that would take more time than I want to spend."

He took out a thick roll of cash.

"I'd rather pay someone a good bit of money to give me a list of the planes that were chartered on a certain date and their destinations," he said. "You could be that someone."

Thirty minutes later, he was holding a printout of

chartered flights. There had been only one plane that had filed a last-minute flight plan on the day in question.

The plane, a small Cessna, had carried only a single passenger. It had landed in a private landing strip just south of Wisteria Falls, Virginia.

"I was looking for Stone in the wrong place," Dalton said as he studied the printout. "But I wasn't far off."

CHAPTER TWENTY-NINE

Bailey took a long sip of the warm cappuccino as she leaned back in the patio chair and looked out at her parents' garden, feeling surprisingly well rested. Picking up a piece of wholewheat toast, she spread a generous amount of strawberry jam on top and took a big bite, realizing that, for the first time since she'd woken up in the hospital, her head wasn't hurting.

She glanced warily down at the folded copy of the *Belle Harbor Chronicle* on the table, suddenly reluctant to find out what was happening in the real world.

Although she'd resisted Cate's suggestion that she check herself back into the hospital after her near-fainting spell, Bailey had compromised, agreeing to stay at their parents' house where she could be watched over for any warning signs that her head injury wasn't healing as expected.

And despite her mother's constant hovering over the last two days, she knew it had been a wise decision.

But now that her head had stopped throbbing and she was beginning to feel stronger, she was also starting to feel guilty. It was time to get back to the investigation she was supposed to be working on.

Finishing the toast and jam, Bailey downed the last of her cappuccino and then carried the empty plate and mug into the kitchen where Jackie was stacking dishes into the dishwasher and Ludwig was eating breakfast.

As Bailey headed upstairs, she stopped on the landing to pet Duchess, surprised when the cat accepted the affection with none of her usual disdain.

Her phone was buzzing on the dresser when she entered the bedroom. As she crossed the room to scoop it up from the dresser, she caught a glimpse of her reflection in the mirror, pleased to see that some color had come back into her cheeks.

Looking down at her phone, she hoped to see Dalton's name but instead saw that Luisa Santos had sent her a text.

Her heart dropped as she read the message.

SirGrendel88 sent another DM. I think he's going to kill me.

Bailey stared down at the words, not sure how to reply.

Perhaps, if she spoke to Luisa again, she could convince her to stay offline and behind locked doors, at least for the time being.

But that didn't work for Krystal Devine, did it?

The thought was unsettling.

How had the troll managed to get past Krystal's defenses? The influencer had been alert and ready to call 911 at the slightest sign of trouble. And she'd been ready to fight back.

And yet, Grendel still managed to get to her.

Deciding she would go see Luisa and make sure the woman was okay, Bailey strapped on her holster, slipped in her Glock, and pulled on a jacket.

She went downstairs and stopped in the kitchen doorway.

"I'm going out, Mom. Can you watch Ludwig for me?"

Before her mother could offer a response or a protest, she slipped out the front door and climbed into the Expedition.

When she turned onto Cascadia Drive, she was relieved to see Luisa's dusty white Toyota parked on the driveway.

Dolores' mother opened the door before Bailey had reached the porch. She stepped back to let her inside.

"Is Rodrigo here?" Bailey asked, looking around at the empty room. "Maybe he could stay with you and..."

"He went to work," Luisa said. "He wanted to stay here to watch me but I told him to go. I told him he has to make a living. We can't both hide in here like scared rabbits."

A chime sounded from the coffee table.

Wincing at the sound, Luisa lifted her eyes to Bailey.

With a sigh, she walked over and picked up her phone. A small gasp escaped her as she read the text message and then held the phone out for Bailey to see.

Are you ready to die?

A deep, malicious voice suddenly sounded in Bailey's head, echoing the words on the screen.

Closing her eyes, she willed the voice to go away, but it only got louder, repeating the threat again and again.

"Agent Flynn?"

Luisa laid a tentative hand on her arm.

"Agent Flynn, are you okay?"

Suddenly, the man's voice was gone.

Bailey looked up to find Luisa Santos staring at her.

"I'm sorry," Bailey said. "And I'm fine. You're the one I'm worried about. I want to make sure you're being careful, that you're taking precautions. And you should block calls, messages, and texts from unknown senders and callers. It will be easier that way."

Luisa looked at her with wide, frightened eyes.

"But, if I block his texts and messages, how will I know when he's coming for me?"

* * *

Bailey left the house on Claremont Street early Monday morning, informing her parents that she would be going back to Cate's apartment after work.

"The headaches have stopped and I'm feeling a lot stronger," she assured them when they protested. "It's time to get on with my life now."

She didn't mention the recurrent phantom voice in her head or the flashes of memory that had started to return.

Turning onto Davenport Drive, she parked outside West Security Services and followed Ludwig to the door.

Dalton was back in Belle Harbor and Bailey was eager to see him and get an update on his recent trip to Chicago.

They'd spoken Saturday night after he'd tracked Tamara Vincent to an airfield outside the city, but the only communication she'd received from him Sunday was a text message saying he was flying home late that night and would see her Monday morning.

"So, how was Chicago?" she asked as she pushed through the door to find Dalton at his desk. "Any luck finding Tamara Vincent? Or Jordan Stone for that matter?"

Dalton gave a grim shake of his head.

"No luck yet," he admitted.

Getting to his feet, he walked around the desk and pulled Bailey in for a kiss.

"And I wasn't just in Chicago," he said as he looked down at her. "Yesterday, I flew to Virginia and wasted a day driving around the middle of nowhere."

His jaw tightened in frustration.

"I even organized a drone search of the area around the airfield but couldn't see anything of interest. There aren't even any buildings in the area where Tamara or Stone could be holed up."

Bailey raised her eyebrows.

"A drone?" she said. "Wow, you *are* going all out."

"Well, Giovanni Rocco said to spare no expense," Dalton said. "And I won't argue with him on that. It's his bank account after all. But wasting time? That's another matter. I wasted my day in a Virginia field when I could have spent it here in Belle Harbor with you."

Smiling up at him, Bailey tried to ignore the faint echo in her head and the sound of gunshots ringing in her ears.

"What's wrong?" Dalton asked. "You're as tense as a piano wire. I thought you said you were feeling better."

"I am better," she said. "At least, my head feels as if it's healing. But, as Dr. Pendergrast told me, my memories will likely start coming back over time. And I've been hearing things...voices...gunshots. And having little flashbacks."

He stared down at her in surprise.

"You're starting to regain your memory? But, that's good

news, isn't it? I mean, it's a big step toward catching the shooter. And once you do remember everything, I bet the voices and flashbacks will go away."

Bailey nodded, wishing she could feel as hopeful as he did.

"You should go see that doctor," Dalton said. "What was his name? Dr. Ellis? You should make an appointment and see if there's anything he can do to help you remember."

"What could he do?" she asked. "I mean, I guess he could try to hypnotize me. But, does that really work or is that just something they do in movies and T.V. for dramatic effect?"

She liked the idea of getting her memory back all at once and eliminating the unsettling voices and flashbacks.

But was it really possible?

Deciding there was only one way to find out, she took out her phone and tapped in the psychiatrist's number, startled when he answered on the first ring.

She'd been prepared to leave a voice mail.

"Um, Dr. Ellis? This is Bailey Flynn."

Within minutes, they had scheduled an appointment for that same afternoon. Once she ended the call, she wondered if she'd done the right thing.

Bailey vacillated between hope and doubt all morning, and by the time she walked into Dr. Ellis' office that afternoon and sat down in his session room, she was a nervous wreck.

"I was wondering if hypnosis might work," she said.

"Hypnosis?"

The psychiatrist didn't sound very enthusiastic.

"That's not always an advisable approach when it comes to dealing with trauma," he said, pulling thoughtfully at his beard. "It can sometimes make things worse."

It wasn't the answer Bailey had hoped to hear.

"When the brain disassociates or suppresses traumatic memories, it's an attempt to protect the individual from the distress that comes with the memories. Manipulating a mind into remembering trauma can induce a severe reaction.

"And in the case of a traumatic brain injury, while hypnosis can help improve cognitive function and at times reduce stress, there's no proof that it will *bring back* your memory, so to speak. It can at times even create false memories that replace the actual memories."

Trying to hide her disappointment, Bailey nodded.

"That's okay, I understand. It was just an idea."

"How about I walk you through some visualization exercises?" Dr. Ellis suggested. "That may help your mind and body relax enough for you to feel safe to remember. And if you do these exercises regularly, in time, I'm confident your memories will return."

Bailey reluctantly agreed to the suggestion.

Settling back in a comfortable chair, she closed her eyes and listened to the psychiatrist's soothing voice as he encouraged her to envision herself in calm, peaceful surroundings.

An image of the cozy, aromatic Holbrook Coffee Company automatically came to mind. She could almost smell the freshly baked pastry and just-brewed coffee in the warm, dimly lit building as a strong wind blew outside the window.

Suddenly, the dark figure of a man appeared and a gunshot rang out. Pain exploded through Bailey's head, making her gasp aloud, and bolt upright.

"Oh dear, what just happened?" Dr. Ellis asked as Bailey exhaled out a shaky breath.

"I don't know," she admitted. "When you said to visualize a calm place, my mind went to the coffee shop. The first time I went there, it was so cozy and warm and it smelled so good. I couldn't believe anything bad could ever happen there.

"But just now, I saw a figure..."

She hesitated and swallowed hard, trying to concentrate.

"He was so close. I could almost see him. But then, I heard a gunshot and my head sort of exploded, and...he was gone."

Shaking her head in frustration, she sat up.

"It's okay, Bailey. You have to give yourself time."

But as she booked another appointment for Thursday and walked back out to the parking lot, Bailey thought of Luisa Santos and the others on the list of the troll's victims.

They might not have much time left.

She needed to remember who the shooter was, and she needed to do it soon.

Although Sharma had started contacting and warning all the troll's known targets, he would eventually kill again, just as he'd done with Krystal Devine and Rachel Cho.

At the thought of Rachel Cho, Bailey suddenly remembered what Cate had planned for that morning.

Crossing her fingers, she hoped her sister would have better luck than she'd had last time.

Hopefully, this time, Cate will manage to get Judge Nelson to issue the exhumation order.

CHAPTER THIRTY

Cate Flynn drove toward the Summerset County courthouse, mentally rehearsing the arguments she planned to present to Judge Nelson. Somehow, she had to convince the infuriating man to issue a court order to exhume Rachel Cho's body. But at least this time, she wouldn't be going into his chambers alone.

This time, she had asked Mason Knox to meet her at the courthouse and help her make her case.

She hoped the judge might agree to issue and sign the order if he heard first hand from Summerset County's medical examiner why they needed to exhume Rachel's body.

As she neared downtown, Cate noticed several *Tony Brunner for Judge* yard signs and wrinkled her nose in distaste.

Hopefully, that crook won't win the election.

Not when it was evident to anyone with half a brain that he had engaged in illicit business practices with Jordan Stone for years.

She was still fuming as she parked her Lexus in the garage and walked into the lobby. Her bad mood dissipated when she saw Mason waiting for her by the elevators.

He was wearing an elegantly tailored suit and his dark

curls had been brushed back from his handsome face, which had been freshly shaved.

"You clean up very nicely, Mr. Knox," Cate said as she came up beside him and pushed the elevator call button.

"Thought I'd better do a dry run before the wedding, Ms. Flynn," Mason teased as he gestured for her to enter the elevator in front of him.

When the doors had closed behind them, Cate turned to him for a kiss, inhaling the familiar scent of his cologne.

But once the doors slid open again, revealing the corridor leading to Judge Nelson's chambers, her mood grew somber.

"Okay, let's go get that court order," she said, trying to sound confident. "Just follow my lead."

She was prepared to greet Inez Flores and introduce her to Mason, but the clerk wasn't at her desk.

Deciding she would take a chance and stick her head into Nelson's chamber unannounced, she steeled herself for a cold greeting. But when she approached the door, she heard a woman laughing.

With a frown, she stopped in the doorway and stared in at Mimi Harper, who was standing beside Judge Nelson's desk, showing him something on her phone.

"Come on in, Cate," Mimi called out as she turned to see Cate gaping at her. "I was just showing the judge a video of the bunker shot the mayor took on Friday. He climbed out of there looking as if a sandstorm had hit him. It was hilarious."

"Let's just hope I don't give you something to laugh at when we play on Friday," Judge Nelson said with a good-humored smile.

The smile vanished when he looked over at Cate.

"What is it I can help you with, Ms. Flynn?"

"Oh, don't be such a grump," Mimi said, waving Cate and Mason into the room. "At least give them a chance to have their say before you kick them out."

Moving into the room, Cate cleared her throat.

"This is a petition for an exhumation of a young woman named Rachel Cho. Her death was ruled a suicide three years ago but new evidence has since come to light.

"The M.E. and the BHPD now believe she's the victim of foul play and that her death is connected to a homicide that took place several days ago.

"They want to conduct another autopsy, but they need a court order as soon as possible allowing them to exhume the body. I came by last week and you told me to ask the family for permission.

"So, I tracked down Rachel's parents, who are living in Seoul now, and they've requested to be left alone. I'm hoping you will now issue a court order and I've asked Mason Knox, the Summerset County medical examiner, to come and explain why an exhumation is necessary and what it entails."

Judge Nelson snorted.

"I know exactly what an exhumation entails," he said. "It entails you digging up this poor girl's decomposed remains."

"Exactly," Mason said, stepping forward. "And the longer we wait to dig her up, the less likely it is we will be able to confirm her manner or cause of death. There's also the matter of her death being linked to at least two other deaths in the county. So, time is of the essence here, Judge Nelson."

Before the judge could reply, Mimi spoke up.

"Think carefully, Nelson. If you stop the police from investigating a possible murder, you could be seen as being soft on crime. It could hurt your chances for reelection."

"That's years away," Nelson protested but Cate could see the gears in his mind turning. "Besides, I haven't stopped anyone from investigating the case. There have to be means of investigation other than exhumation."

Mason shook his head.

"I need to examine the bones in Rachel's neck and head before I can overturn the previous ruling of suicide," he explained. "If I can't see her bones, I have no conclusive proof she didn't take her own life. The ruling will stand."

"Sounds as if someone might get away with murder," Mimi said. "And the public wouldn't like that. It certainly wouldn't help your campaign much."

Exhaling loudly, Judge Nelson leaned forward and pushed a button on his desk phone.

"Yes, Judge?"

"Inez, I need you to work up a court order for an exhumation. Ms. Flynn has the necessary petition. Once you have it ready, bring it in here for me to sign."

He punched the button again and glared over at Cate, who acted as if she didn't see the sly wink Mimi sent her way.

"It looks as if we're gonna have an exhumation, after all."

CHAPTER THIRTY-ONE

The sun was setting over Summerset Memorial Park as Mason Knox, Finola Lawson, and the exhumation crew gathered around Rachel Cho's small, untended gravestone. The plot was covered by a layer of thin, rocky soil that had given rise to thick patches of ragweed and crabgrass.

With Finola taking photos and video of the process, Mason stood at the graveside, watching as a small backhoe was used to scoop the top layers of dirt off Rachel Cho's grave and deposit the earth in a growing pile beside it.

The hole in the ground was less than three feet deep when Mason saw the corner of the concrete grave liner.

Calling to the gravediggers that it was time to get their shovels out, he watched as they dug up the rest of the earth, working methodically, taking care not to cause any damage as they exposed the lid of the thick concrete container.

Finally, the men were ready to remove the heavy lid using chains and a specially designed mechanical winch that had been supplied by the cemetery for the purpose.

A solemn silence fell over the group as the lid was raised, revealing the casket within, which appeared to Mason to be in good condition, considering it had been underground for more than three years.

Once he'd confirmed the casket was still sealed and undamaged, Mason motioned for the men to proceed.

They worked quickly, passing lifting straps under the casket and hoisting it up and out of the grave and onto the waiting casket trolley.

Finola took a few final photos and then helped Mason roll the trolley to the waiting medical examiner's van while the exhumation team lowered the lid back into place.

"With any luck, we can have Rachel on the dissecting table this afternoon," Mason said as they drove back toward the M.E.'s office. "Let's hope we find her body as well preserved as her grave."

He knew it was impossible to predict the condition of a dead body that had been in the ground for over three years.

If Rachel Cho's body had been properly embalmed, she may still be almost wholly intact, still dressed in her funeral finery, perhaps with a sprinkling of mold here and there.

Or, if too much moisture had penetrated the grave liner and casket seal, she may be little more than bones covered in grave wax and a skull still sprouting hair.

Either way, he planned to do whatever was necessary to determine if Rachel had taken her own life as Dr. Armbruster had ruled, or if she'd been murdered and hung by the neck in her own attic, possibly by the same sadistic troll who had killed Krystal Devine at the Summerset Pier.

Skipping lunch in favor of getting into the autopsy suite as quickly as possible, Mason was standing beside the remains on the stainless steel metal table just before noon.

To his surprise, Rachel Cho had already decomposed down to little more than bones and dark hair within her casket.

The white cotton dress she had been wearing at burial had all but disintegrated, leaving behind only a nylon waistband and a jade butterfly pendant on a delicate silver chain.

"It looks as if she wasn't embalmed," Mason said, looking up at Bailey Flynn and Jimmy Fraser, who stood at the foot of the table observing as Finola took photos of the remains.

"How can you determine the manner and cause of death now?" Bailey asked from behind her mask.

Bending over the skull, Mason used a gloved hand to gently push aside a lock of dark hair.

"Well, I can tell you one thing," he said, pointing to a deep crack in the skull. "She suffered a significant head injury before she died. Likely sustained from blunt force trauma.

"The injury could have been hidden under her hair during the first autopsy if Armbruster didn't perform a thorough examination of her head and skull."

He moved down to study the cervical vertebrae.

"And I don't see a fracture of the C1 or C2 bones," he said. "Nothing to indicate she dropped from a distance as would have been the case if she had jumped off a ladder under the attic rafter as the scene had been staged to suggest."

There was a moment of silence in the room as Finola snapped several close-up photos of the cervical bones.

"So, you're saying you don't think Rachel committed suicide?" Bailey finally asked.

Mason shook his head.

"I'd say there's clear evidence that she first suffered a

blow to the head, perhaps to render her unconscious, and was then hung from the rafters by the polypropylene rope that was recovered with her body.

"She didn't jump and die from a snap to the neck but instead slowly died by asphyxiation as she hung at the end of the rope. It could have taken anywhere from two to six minutes for her to die."

Mason grimaced at the image of the young woman struggling to breathe as a monster stood below her, watching with demented glee.

He looked up to meet Bailey's eyes.

"I'm officially ruling Rachel Cho's death a homicide by asphyxiation due to hanging."

CHAPTER THIRTY-TWO

Bailey stepped out of the medical examiner's office, keeping her collar up and her head down against the strong, gusty wind blowing in from the east. Sucking in a deep lungful of fresh air, she was relieved to be free from the smell of death and decay inside the building.

Hurrying out to the parking lot, her mind was still full of the disturbing information gleaned from Rachel Cho's second autopsy.

The young woman had been sadistically murdered in her own home. And her grief-stricken parents had been led to believe that their young daughter had been so desperately unhappy that she'd decided to take her own life.

It was unbelievably cruel, which made Bailey even more convinced that the online troll was the person responsible.

As she approached her Expedition, she looked up to see that Sabrina West was waiting for her.

"Who tipped you off about the exhumation?" Bailey asked.

"I have my sources," Sabrina said, sounding unusually somber. "So, what did the M.E. say? Was she murdered?"

Bailey hesitated, knowing she should maintain silence until Rachel Cho's parents were officially notified and a statement about her death had been released.

But Sabrina had been targeted by the troll, as well. Was it really fair for Bailey to keep information from her that might end up saving her life?

"Off the record, I can confirm that both Krystal Devine and Rachel Cho were victims of homicide and that the online troll going by the username SirGrendel88 is our prime suspect. Unfortunately, we still don't know who he is offline."

The reporter received the statement with uncharacteristic gravity. Instead of being pleased about getting a scoop, albeit one that was off the record, she looked grim.

"So, there really is a monster out there calling himself Grendel and destroying people's lives," she said. "That should give Garth Hamilton another chapter in his book."

Shrugging her shoulders, she sighed.

"I might as well give up on the idea of coming out with my own book," she said. "He's bound to come out with a bigger, better book than I could ever write.

"He actually told me this morning when I saw him having breakfast at the Summerset Café that he was on his way to interview Luisa Santos."

She gave an exasperated shake of her head.

"You know how long I've been trying to get that poor woman to give me an interview? But she's always refused."

"Hang on," Bailey said. "Garth Hamilton told you he was going to interview Luisa Santos today?"

Her face creased into a worried frown at the thought of Garth questioning Dolores' grieving mother.

The last time she'd seen Luisa, she'd been stressed and

scared. Certainly in no condition to give an interview.

"I'd better go," Bailey said.

Brushing past Sabrina, she crossed to the Expedition, stopping to look back at the reporter before opening the door.

"Be careful," she said. "Grendel is still out there and you're on the list of his possible targets. We don't know what he might do next."

She left Sabrina staring after her as she pulled out of the parking lot and drove to Cascadia Drive.

But the driveway in front of the Santos house was empty. Neither Luisa's white sedan nor Garth Hamilton's red sportscar were there.

When Bailey knocked on the door, no one answered.

Taking out her phone, she tapped on Luisa's number, but the call rolled to voicemail.

After getting back in the Expedition, she tapped in a text message, hoping Luisa would see it and respond, but the message remained unread.

Glancing at the clock on the dashboard, she was tempted to go pick up Ludwig from Sid Morley's place.

She'd dropped the German shepherd off for a playdate with Amadeus before she'd gone to the medical examiner's office, wanting to spare the dog's highly sensitive nose from the overpowering smells associated with the autopsy of an exhumed body.

But instead of heading toward Mariner Trail, she found herself heading to Garth Hamilton's rented beach house.

As she turned onto North Beach Drive, she saw that his car wasn't out front and there was no sign of Luisa's sedan.

As Bailey sat in the Expedition and stared out at the ocean, she suddenly had a sinking suspicion.

Was Garth really planning to interview Luisa, or was he just messing with Sabrina, trying to rile her up?

Was Luisa really out there somewhere, talking with the writer? Or could she have somehow fallen prey to the troll?

As Bailey tried to think where she should look next, a disturbing question came to mind.

What do I really know about Garth Hamilton anyway?

Taking out her phone, Bailey tapped on Sharma's number.

"Can you do me a favor?" she asked, as soon as the agent picked up. "Can you dig into Garth Hamilton's background?"

"Sure I can, but why? What's going on?"

Bailey hesitated, not wanting to waste Sharma's time.

"Apparently, Garth has plans to interview Luisa Santos this morning but now both of them appear to be missing," she finally said. "I'm going to look around town and see if I can find her. Something doesn't feel right."

"You think Garth could be hiding something?" Sharma asked. "You think *he* could be the troll?"

She sounded doubtful.

"Not really," Bailey admitted. "But he does seem to be overly interested in serial killers and famous murderers. And the woman he was supposed to be interviewing this morning appears to have vanished without a trace."

"Okay, I'll see what I can dig up," Sharma agreed.

After ending the call, Bailey cruised through downtown, becoming more anxious as each minute passed.

When she drove by the courthouse, she saw Tony Brunner

and Mayor Sutherland walking along the sidewalk, deep in conversation.

Impulsively, she pulled up to the curb and climbed out, even as she told herself it wasn't a good idea to confront the men in public. But the voice in her head went unheeded.

Both men were known associates of Jordan Stone, the billionaire who had tried to have her killed. And Brunner had been overheard arranging to help Tamara Vincent leave town in order to escape justice.

Shouldn't I at least ask them if they know where Stone or Tamara are hiding while I have the chance?

Striding over to the men, Bailey cleared her throat.

"How about you tell me where I can find Jordan Stone," she said as the men turned to her in surprise.

Before either could respond, she stepped closer and pointed a finger at Tony Brunner.

"And why don't you tell me where Tamara Vincent is while you're at it?" she added. "Because I know you put her on a train to Chicago the night she left town."

"I don't even know the woman," Brunner sputtered in protest, his face darkening. "And if you and your nosy sister know what's good for you, you'll leave me alone, and you'll forget Tamara Vincent ever existed."

CHAPTER THIRTY-THREE

Tamara Vincent smiled at Jordan Stone, careful not to let him see the hatred that filled her heart as she studied his sharp cheekbones and piercing blue eyes. She watched as he took a long sip of fifty-year-old scotch from his stemless crystal snifter and then lifted her own glass of cabernet, draining it with an audible sigh.

"That is divine," she said, lacing her voice with a tinge of regret. "No wonder they call it the nectar of the gods."

She glanced at the empty bottle on the bar against the wall.

"Too bad all my nectar is gone now," she said, arranging her lips into a flirtatious pout. "I would have enjoyed another glass. Although, I'm not so sure it's a good idea. I'm already feeling a little bit tipsy."

Stretching her long legs out in front of her, she positioned herself against the sofa in a suggestive pose, pleased to see Stone's eyes roaming over her body with obvious interest.

"There are a dozen bottles just like that one in the wine cellar," he said as he shifted closer to her. "I could open one if you'd like. Although, I wouldn't want to pressure you into having another drink if you've already had enough."

He raised a finely shaped eyebrow.

"So, if you don't want it..."

"Oh, I do want it," she said softly.

Before he could move closer, she lifted her glass.

"The wine, that is," she added playfully. "And after that, well, who knows what I'll want."

A flash of impatience crossed Stone's handsome face. But he took the glass from her hand and set it on the table.

"I'll need to go down to the cellar," he said. "Don't you go anywhere while I'm gone."

Tamara waited until he disappeared through the door before jumping to her feet and hurrying into the little bathroom just past the bar.

Opening a small drawer, she took out the crushed pills she'd taken from the pharmacy the day before when she'd told Stone she had a headache and wanted some aspirin.

He'd made the mistake of allowing her several minutes alone in the well-stocked room, which had a large supply of narcotics and sedatives among its vast range of medications.

Grabbing a bottle off the shelf labeled *Benzodiazepines*, she had stuffed it into her pocket before following Stone back to the main living area, where she'd quickly ducked into the bathroom to crush and hide the pills.

Now she carried the powder to the table and sprinkled a generous portion into Stone's scotch, confident he would be unable to smell or taste the sedative.

By the time he returned to the room, Tamara was once again sitting on the sofa, trying to look relaxed despite the frantic beating of her heart against her ribcage.

She had decided that the only way to escape Stone was to

let him think she had come to accept her captivity in the bunker. She would make him think she was even willing to take their relationship to a more intimate level.

Holding up her glass, she waited for him to fill it with the fragrant red wine and then lifted it in a toast.

"Here's to getting to know each other better," she said, clinking her glass against his.

Stone joined her in the toast before throwing back the scotch and setting down his glass.

With a determined gleam in his eye, he reached for her and pulled her toward him, his hands gripping her arms tightly.

"I just need to use the powder room first," Tamara said, pulling back before he could claim her lips with his own. "I'll be right back."

Before he could protest, she slipped into the bathroom and turned on the water, not sure what she was going to do if the sedative didn't work.

There's no way I'll let that animal touch me. I'll use a steak knife to end this first if it comes to that.

Pressing her ear against the door, she listened, expecting to hear Stone calling out for her at any minute.

But there was only silence from the living room.

Slowly, she opened the door and peered out. Her pulse jumped as she saw Stone's long, leanly muscled body slumped back on the sofa with his eyes closed.

Tamara hurried forward and softly called his name.

"Jordan? Are you okay?"

When he didn't respond, she held her hand under his nose and a soft puff of air confirmed he was still breathing.

For one long moment, she considered picking up the pillow on the sofa and holding it over his head, ending everything right then and there.

But she was already wanted for drug trafficking by the feds. There was no need to make things worse by adding murder to her rap sheet.

Besides, if she killed Jordan Stone, she'd be giving up her biggest bargaining chip with the feds. The billionaire could be her get-out-of-jail-free card if she played things right.

Not sure how long he would be out and how much time she would have, Tamara stuck her hand in Stone's pocket and pulled out his phone, which had satellite connectivity.

She used his limp finger to move past the biometric scanning screen before typing in the password she'd seen him use on multiple occasions.

Taking the phone with her to the sumptuous bedroom that had been her prison for the last two months, she pulled on her boots, tucked her own cell phone into her pocket, and made her way to the stairs leading up to the exit door.

When she reached the landing, she opened the app that controlled the bunker's security system and tapped twice on the *Open Outside Door* option.

She held her breath as the door slid smoothly open, revealing a gray, overcast sky overhead.

Stepping out into the fresh air, she felt a moment of exhilaration before she realized that she was still trapped.

The fence around the property was wrapped in barbed wire and she wasn't sure where Stone's security detail was stationed. Would they be notified if she opened the gate?

And she hadn't thought to get the keys for the Land Rover.

Should she go back in and search for them? Should she risk Stone waking up and finding her there?

She looked back at the door, which had already slid shut behind her, and shuddered. There was no way she was going back into the underground bunker ever again.

Backing away from the door, Tamara turned and ran toward the forest, deciding there had to be another way out.

She would find a place on the property to hide. And then she would use the satellite connectivity on Stone's phone to call Giovanni Rocco. With any luck, Mario Rocco's rich father would send someone to help her before it was too late.

CHAPTER THIRTY-FOUR

Dalton West sat by the window in Giovanni Rocco's sumptuous office at Villa Rocco, taking little notice of the breathtaking view of the Atlantic Ocean as he recounted his recent trip to Chicago and Virginia.

"Your source told me that Stone was holed up outside of D.C., but he didn't tell me just how far," Dalton complained. "We now know a charter plane dropped Tamara Vincent at a private airstrip over an hour's drive outside the city."

Before Rocco could reply, his phone vibrated on his desk.

Both men looked down at the screen, which lit up with the words *Unknown Caller* as Rocco reached for the phone.

The older man's eyes widened as a woman's frantic voice sounded in his ear. He quickly activated the speaker to allow Dalton to hear.

"Mr. Rocco? This is Tamara Vincent. Jordan Stone has me trapped and I need your help."

Leaning forward in his chair, Dalton motioned eagerly for Rocco to respond. This could be his first real chance to find the man he'd been searching for.

They couldn't let Tamara end the call without her first telling them where Jordan Stone was hiding.

"Tell me where you are," Rocco said. "I've got someone here who can come get you. But we need to know where."

"I've been held prisoner in Jordan Stone's bunker," Tamara said. "I managed to get outside but there's a fence."

"A bunker?" Rocco asked.

He looked over at Dalton in confusion.

"Like, an underground bunker?"

"Yes, it's some sort of survivalist hideout," she said, sounding panicky. "Stone told me that in the event of an emergency, he can stay holed up here for years without needing anything from the outside."

Her voice broke.

"I need to get out of here. I'm going crazy and-"

"Where's the bunker?" Rocco asked.

Holding his breath, Dalton waited for her reply, ready to spring into action as soon as he knew her location.

"I don't know for sure," she gasped. "Stone arranged to fly me out of Chicago on a private plane. We were in the air for a couple of hours but I don't know where we landed."

Dalton exhaled in disappointment.

"We already know you landed at a private airstrip in Virginia," Rocco said. "But that doesn't give us enough to go on. We need to know a more specific location."

Pulling out his phone, Dalton opened the map app and leaned forward with a frown.

"Can you remember seeing any road signs?" he asked, speaking loudly so that Tamara could hear him.

"There was a sign not far from here," she said after a moment's hesitation. "It said *Welcome to Providence Gap*."

Dalton's eyes scanned the map as she continued.

"I don't know how long we drove after that before we came to a fence with barbed wire and a no trespassing sign," she added. "We drove down a dirt road and then all of a sudden there was this hidden entrance in the side of the hill and a metal door."

Dalton nodded as he saw Providence Gap on the map and noted the remoteness of the location.

"There are a dozen or more old, decommissioned missile silos around the D.C. area," he said. "They were all built in the 1950s during the Cold War if I remember correctly. But they've all been shut down and abandoned for decades. I've heard of people converting them into survival bunkers."

He leaned closer to the phone as he formed a mental picture of the property in his mind.

"Once we get past the fence, how do we find the entrance to the bunker?" he asked. "Is there some sort of landmark? Anything that can help us find the way in?"

"There's a big maple tree near the entrance," Tamara said. "All the leaves have turned bright red. Looks like the damn thing is soaked in blood."

Suddenly, she gasped.

"I have to go," she whispered. "Someone's coming."

"Who's coming?" Rocco asked. "Is Stone there with you?"

But she had already ended the call.

Looking up, Dalton met Rocco's eyes over the phone.

"We'll have to bring out the drone again," he said slowly, starting to formulate a plan. "The camera can take high-definition images of the ground. If we fly the drone over the search area, we could find the bunker entrance."

He got to his feet.

"It'll be expensive to hire a drone pilot on short notice," Dalton added. "Unless you want me to pull in the FBI and see if they can provide a search team?"

Rocco shook his head.

"No, that'll take even longer. And if Stone figures out Tamara called us and told us where he is, he might run. We need to get up there fast."

"We?" Dalton asked. "You don't think that *you're-*"

"Of course, I'm going," Rocco said as he headed toward the door. "It is *my* private jet. Besides, who else is going to fly it at such short notice?"

Before Dalton could ask Rocco if he still had an active pilot's license, the older man threw open the door and called out to the wide-chested security guard who always seemed to be hovering nearby.

"Yuri, you will go with us to Virginia," Rocco said. "We'll leave now for the airfield. Call ahead and make sure the plane is fueled and ready."

Following Rocco out to a metallic grey Range Rover, Dalton climbed in beside him for the ten-minute drive to the small airfield where the retired lawyer kept his private plane, a Cessna Citation that seated up to nine people.

Dalton tried to keep his mind focused on the mission ahead, but the sudden flight on the turbulent plane brought him back to his days as an Army Ranger in the 75th Regiment.

More than once, he'd been flown into a hostile location on

a risky mission to find and retrieve hidden assets.

Only back then, the pilot transporting him to the drop zone wasn't a seventy-year-old civilian with shaky hands.

Relieved when the three-hour, one-thousand-mile flight was over, and they had landed safely at the airfield just south of Wisteria Falls, Dalton emerged from the Cessna to see that the drone pilot he'd met during his prior visit was already waiting for him.

The lanky man wore a sun visor despite the fact that the sun was starting to set, and he introduced himself to Rocco and Yuri simply as Stu.

Leading the men to his big, white van, Stu patiently explained to the men that he was a licensed drone operator and assured them that the drone he would be flying had been duly registered with the FAA.

Once the four men were loaded into the van, they headed south. When they passed a *Welcome to Providence Gap* sign, Dalton motioned for Stu to pull into the next open field.

Bringing the van to a stop, the drone operator jumped out and ran around to the back, opening the double doors to reveal a large backpack and a sleek white drone with a small camera mounted beneath it.

"The battery pack is fully charged," Stu assured them as he opened a small laptop and clicked on an app that displayed a map of the immediate vicinity.

His fingers moved quickly as he established the search grid for the flight mission and set the drone on the ground.

"Okay, step back, we're ready to go."

As Stu tapped on the touchscreen, the drone's propellers

began to spin rapidly, lifting the sleek device off the ground.

Dalton followed its navigation and positioning lights as it rose into the sky, quickly reaching an altitude of a hundred feet over his head.

"The drone will carry out the mission autonomously," Stu explained. "It'll start at the furthest waypoint first and work its way back to us, just in case it runs out of battery."

Dalton looked over the operator's shoulder at the laptop screen, where a red dot followed the progress of the drone, which was flying at a speed of twenty miles an hour while taking images of the ground below.

A stream of images flashed across the screen as Dalton studied them with anxious eyes, hoping to catch sight of the bright red maple tree that would indicate they'd found Jordan Stone's hidden bunker.

The drone had covered over twenty-five acres and the battery pack was growing low when he saw what he was looking for. The maple tree was awash in red leaves just as Tamara had said it would be.

"There it is," he said. "That's Stone's bunker."

Rocco shifted excitedly beside him.

"Let's go get him," he said.

"It's not that easy," Dalton reminded him. "The bunker's been built to withstand all forms of disasters and assaults. It's not as if we can just go up and knock."

He ran a hand through his hair.

"The entry is probably controlled by some sort of biometric entry system managed through an app."

"There's got to be an emergency exit hatch somewhere,"

Rocco said. "If Tamara can find it-"

"We don't even know if Tamara is still alive," Dalton interjected. "We can send her a text message to let her know we're out here just in case, but I think we're going to have to turn this over to the FBI. They must have a way to-"

"Is that the woman you're looking for?" Stu asked.

Dalton and Rocco turned their eyes back to the laptop screen where an image showed a woman with long dark hair running through the forested terrain.

"That's her," Dalton said. "That's Tamara Vincent."

As Stu packed the drone back into the van and climbed behind the wheel, Dalton called 911.

After giving the operator his name and location, Dalton explained that he was a private investigator tracking two individuals wanted by the FBI and local police in South Florida for questioning.

"Fugitives Jordan Stone and Tamara Vincent have been located in an underground bunker in Providence Gap. It may be one of those old missile silos. In any case, they should both be considered armed and dangerous."

Ending the call before the operator could ask more questions, Dalton jumped back into the van, his adrenaline pumping as they headed down a dirt road.

The big van jerked to a stop when they reached the gate of a six-foot chain-link fence topped with barbed wire.

"I need you to back the van up to the fence as close as you can get it," Dalton told Stu. "I'm going to get on top and jump over to the other side."

He just hoped his Ranger training would kick in and he'd

remember how to land properly without twisting an ankle, the way he had when jumping out of an airplane.

The ground was soggy from a recent rainstorm and cushioned in leaves from the shedding trees, and he easily landed on the balls of his feet with his knees bent, finding no need to soften the fall with a forward roll.

His fear now seemed vaguely foolish as he stood on the other side of the fence and looked back at Rocco.

"Just stay here until I get back."

But as he turned toward the forest, Tamara Vincent emerged from the trees, her dark hair wet and straggly around a pale, panicked face.

"Stone's in the bunker," she said as she ran forward and grabbed Dalton's arm. "I've sedated him for now but I don't know how long he'll be out. And he's got security men around here somewhere. They've got guns."

She took a slim black phone out of her pocket and shoved it toward Dalton.

"There's an app on there that opens the gate and the bunker door," she said, reciting the code as she backed away. "I left him on the sofa in the main living area."

Nodding grimly, Dalton lifted the phone, scrolled through the app's menu, and tapped the *Open Front Gate* option.

As the gate swung open, Tamara ran out.

"Keep a close eye on her," Dalton called to Rocco and Yuri. "We don't want to lose her again."

He turned on his heel and ran down the dirt road, keeping his eyes peeled for the red-leafed maple tree.

Within minutes he was standing in front of the metal door,

tapping in a code, his heart racing as he pulled out his Glock and held it out in front of him.

Walking quickly down the stairs, he scanned the large living area where Tamara said she'd left Stone's unconscious body, but the billionaire was nowhere to be seen.

The sound of grating metal led him to what appeared to be a water treatment room containing several tanks for storing purified water and a pump system for removing waste.

Dalton saw right away that an escape hatch in the ceiling had been opened, revealing a metal ladder leading upward and a pair of expensive boots on the bottom rung.

"Stop right there, Stone!" he called out, racing across the room just as the boots disappeared into the tunnel, which Dalton assumed must lead up to the surface. "I'm armed and the police are right outside. You've got nowhere to run."

As he took a quick peek through the escape hatch, a bullet whizzed past his head, narrowly missing him.

Holding his Glock out, Dalton blindly aimed up the tunnel and pulled the trigger, knowing he was almost sure to miss the fleeing billionaire but hoping to give Stone enough of a scare to stop him before he made it to the top.

The plan worked better than he hoped as the bullet ricocheted off the tunnel wall and skimmed Stone's hand, causing the fugitive to release his grip on the ladder and plunge back into the room.

As he hit the floor with a hard thud, the gun in Stone's hand fired, lodging a bullet into the side of a tank, sending water gushing onto the floor.

Jumping on the billionaire before he could catch his

breath, Dalton dug out the zip ties he'd brought with him for just such an opportunity and secured Stone's hands behind his back.

As water gushed over Stone, flattening his hair to his head like a drowned rat, Dalton forced him to his feet and propelled him back into the living area.

"I'll pay you whatever you want if you let me go," Stone said as they neared the exit. "You'll be a rich man."

When Dalton didn't reply, Stone tried a different tactic.

"They'll railroad me and lock me away for good," he said. "And I've never hurt a soul. My hands are clean."

"Maybe so, but you paid others to kill for you," Dalton said. "And I don't want your dirty money."

Using Stone's phone to open the door, he pushed the man outside to find a cruiser from the Wisteria Falls PD waiting.

As two uniformed officers jumped out with guns drawn, a white Interceptor skidded up behind it. A heavyset man with a gray crewcut emerged from the Interceptor, followed by a thin, dark-haired woman with sharp features.

"Mr. Stone? It seems a lot of people have been looking for you," the gray-haired man said as he stepped forward. "I'm Chief Fitzgerald with the Wisteria Falls PD. My officers here will be escorting you to the station just as soon as they read you your rights."

As the officers led Stone to the cruiser, the police chief turned to Dalton.

"We've got Tamara Vincent in the back of a cruiser," he said. "She claims she called you out here and helped you capture Jordan Stone?"

"Ms. Vincent did help me find Stone," he admitted. "But there's an open warrant for her in South Florida on a variety of trafficking charges. The police down there will be relieved she's been apprehended."

Before the chief could respond, a CSI van pulled up.

"I'll need all three of you to provide a statement," he said. "You can follow Detective Kirby back to the station."

As the chief walked over to greet the CSI team, Stone's phone began to buzz and vibrate in Dalton's pocket.

He looked down and saw that a text message had come in from an unknown number.

I've got good news. That little problem that's been bothering you is about to go away for good. She dies tonight.

CHAPTER THIRTY-FIVE

Bailey Flynn stood at the window looking out into the parking lot of the Sanctuary Apartments. She'd spent the afternoon driving around looking for Luisa Santos with no luck. As she crossed to the kitchen, intent on fixing herself a much-needed double espresso, her phone buzzed on the kitchen counter.

She smiled when she saw that Dalton was calling.

"Hey, what's up?" she asked. "Where are you?"

"I've got really good news," he said. "Jordan Stone and Tamara Vincent are in custody. We tracked them down to a survival bunker south of Wisteria Falls, Virginia, and have delivered them both to the local police."

Bailey stared down at the phone, momentarily speechless.

After all this time, the crooked billionaire might finally be held to account for everything he'd done.

"That's incredible," she finally managed to say. "I can't believe Stone's finally behind bars. You're amazing."

"It is a relief," Dalton said. "I wasn't sure we would be able to find him, not with all his money and resources."

Hearing something in his voice that made her uneasy, Bailey frowned.

"Considering what you've accomplished today, you don't sound very happy," she said. "What's wrong?"

Dalton hesitated and then sighed.

"It's just that I saw a message on Stone's phone that's been bothering me," he admitted. "I'm worried he's got someone out there looking for you.

"Promise me you'll be careful until I get home. I'm traveling back on Giovanni Rocco's private jet, so it should only take me a few hours. In fact, I've got to go now."

"I'll be careful," Bailey promised. "Have a safe flight."

As she lowered her phone, it buzzed in her hand.

Looking down, she saw that a response to her barrage of text messages to Luisa Santos had finally come in.

I stopped by the cemetery to visit Dolores. Now my car won't start. Waiting for Rodrigo to get off work. May take a few hours.

Relief flooded through Bailey as she tapped in a response.

I can pick you up now if you want. I'm not far away.

Seconds later, Luisa's reply came through.

That would be great, thanks. You're a lifesaver.

Bailey called to Ludwig and started toward the door just as it opened and Cate walked in.

"You won't believe what's happened," Bailey said as Cate dropped her computer bag on the kitchen counter. "Jordan Stone has been arrested. Dalton tracked him to Virginia where he was hiding in some sort of doomsday bunker and he's been taken into custody."

Looking as stunned as Bailey had felt when she'd heard the news, Cate gave her sister a happy hug.

"I know I should feel a little bit safer now," Bailey said.

"But the troll is still out there. I was actually starting to think he might have gotten hold of Luisa Santos. I've been looking for her all day.

"But luckily, she just texted. Turns out she went to the cemetery to visit Dolores' grave and had car trouble. I'm heading out there now to give her a ride home."

"You should be resting, not driving around town," Cate scolded. "You don't want to overdo it again. How about I go pick her up for you? Or we could call her an Uber?"

"No, I want to talk to her," Bailey said. "She's been getting threats from the troll again. I need to make sure she's okay."

She didn't want to admit she was scared Luisa might end up like Rachel Cho and Krystal Devine. No need to worry her sister. Not after they'd just received such good news.

"Okay, but how about I make dinner while you're gone?" Cate said. "You can come straight back, eat a warm meal, and then get an early night. Now that Stone is in custody, you should be able to sleep easier."

She looked over at Ludwig, who was standing by the door.

"I can walk Ludwig and give him his dinner, too," Cate offered. "But I'm hungry, so don't be gone long."

Promising her sister that she would be back soon, Bailey walked out to the Expedition and headed toward Memorial Parkway.

She tried to call Fraser on the way, wanting to share the news that Jordan Stone had been arrested. When the call rolled to voicemail, she left him a message.

"Not sure if you heard the good news. Jordan Stone and Tamara Vincent are in custody. Call me when you get this."

Dusk was falling by the time Bailey turned into the All Souls Cemetery and drove along the winding road that snaked through the rows of graves.

Stopping behind Luisa's white Toyota, she dropped her phone on the seat beside her and stepped out of the car.

As she passed the sedan, she saw that the car was empty.

Continuing on, she walked down a narrow path toward the grave where Dolores had rested for the last three years.

She gasped as she saw a bloody stain on the gravestone, instantly worried that Luisa had been attacked.

As Bailey bent closer to inspect the blood, a shot rang out.

Instantly, she dived forward and rolled out of the way.

Looking back, she saw a figure darting through the graves.

As more shots rang out, she ran toward the fence that separated the cemetery from the land beyond. Seeing a break in the fence, she ran through the opening just as another bullet skimmed past her.

Her heart sank as she looked around and realized she was standing on wide open ground with no cover in sight.

Not sure what else to do, she headed toward the dilapidated building up ahead, running along rusty tracks until she reached the old Summerset Railroad Depot.

Ducking behind a train car, Bailey reached into her pocket for her phone, wanting to call for backup, planning to request an ambulance for Luisa, just in case.

But her pocket was empty.

She grimaced as she pictured her phone lying on the passenger seat of the car.

Taking her Glock from her holster, she held the gun at the

ready as a familiar voice called out.

Grendel was nearby.

"Are you ready to die, Agent Flynn?"

The words echoed through Bailey's mind, summoning the image of a shadowy figure and a hate-filled face.

Memories of the events in the coffee shop came rushing back. In an instant, Bailey knew who had tried to kill her.

And she knew he was ready to finish the job.

CHAPTER THIRTY-SIX

Jimmy Fraser knocked on Millicent Pruett's office door and pushed it open without waiting for an invitation. He stopped short when he saw Garth Hamilton sitting in a chair across from the police chief, making notes on a yellow legal pad and drinking coffee from a Belle Harbor PD mug.

"Sorry to interrupt," Fraser said. "But I got a message that you wanted to speak to me, Chief?"

Pruett sighed and nodded.

"Yes, I'd better get back to work, Mr. Hamilton, but-"

"Please, call me Garth.

The police chief smiled like a besotted schoolgirl.

"Okay, Garth. Well, it was a pleasure talking to you but I do need to speak to Detective Fraser about an urgent matter."

Turning to leave the office, the writer stopped in front of Fraser and held out a hand.

"I'm Garth Hamilton, by the way. I think we met once before but I didn't get a chance to introduce myself."

With a tight smile, Fraser shook his hand.

"By the way, how did your interview go with Luisa Santos this morning?" Fraser asked.

"Oh, that never ended up happening," Garth said with a

shrug. "We met up at the Summerset Café but then she got a message on her phone and just ran out. She never came back either and I couldn't reach her on her phone."

As the writer left the office, Chief Pruett's simpering smile faded and she waved him toward the chair Garth had vacated.

Fraser closed the door and sat down, still wondering what had spooked Luisa Santos enough to make her run out of the café and never return.

"Sorry for disrupting your meeting," he said. "I didn't realize you had anyone in here."

"Oh, that's okay, Garth was just asking me a few questions pertaining to a book he's writing," Pruett said, sounding smug. "He wanted an expert opinion."

Fraser managed not to roll his eyes as she explained why she had wanted to see him. Apparently, an official complaint had been lodged against Bailey Flynn.

"By Garth Hamilton?" he asked in surprise.

"No, not by Mr. Hamilton," Pruett replied. "Mayor Sutherland called this afternoon. Apparently, Agent Flynn approached him today while he was talking with his lawyer outside the courthouse. He said she was questioning both of them and making all sorts of accusations."

"And he called you for what reason?" Fraser asked. "Does he want us to arrest an FBI agent? Asking questions isn't exactly illegal in Belle Harbor."

"No, but harassment is," Pruett replied.

She lifted a hand to wave away his objection.

"I expect you to have a word with her."

Fraser looked at his watch, knowing he was already going

to be in trouble with Linette if he didn't get home soon.

"Perhaps I'll also have a word with Mayor Sutherland and ask him about his connection to Jordan Stone," Fraser said.

He ignored the indignant look that flashed across Pruett's face as he got to his feet.

"Now, I've got to get going. I was up at dawn to attend Rachel Cho's exhumation and second autopsy and–"

"Oh yes, how did that go?" the chief grudgingly asked, making it clear to Fraser that the dead woman at the pier took a backseat to the mayor's petty grievance. "Did the M.E. rule it a suicide?"

"No," Fraser said. "Mason Knox determined that Rachel Cho's death was definitely a homicide, just like Krystal Devine's. In fact, it looks as if Rachel's death is connected to a series of homicides."

Chief Pruett grimaced, and Fraser assumed she must be thinking of the media attention that always surrounded a serial case.

Of course, if she's willing to give interviews to opportunistic true crime writers like Garth Hamilton, she just might welcome the extra press coverage.

Once he left the chief's office, shutting the door behind him, Fraser listened to Bailey's voicemail, his eyes widening in surprise to hear that Jordan Stone had been arrested.

He tried to call her back when he sat down at his desk, but her phone went straight to voicemail.

Looking over at Geoffrey Gallagher, who was getting ready to go home for the day, Fraser shared the big news about Jordan Stone.

"Wow, that's great," Gallagher said. "I wonder how they found him. You'd think with billions of dollars in the bank, Jordan Stone could buy an island where he could hide."

Fraser wasn't really listening as he tapped on Linette's number. He wanted to tell his wife he'd be home a little late.

"I need to stop by Bailey Flynn's place and check on her," he said, hoping to thaw the icy tone in Linette's voice. "After the shooting and everything, I worry about her. I just want to make sure she's alright."

Once Fraser had ended the call, Gallagher nodded his big head approvingly.

"That's really nice of you, checking on Bailey like that."

"Don't be an idiot," Fraser said. "I'm going by her apartment to see if I can get the details about Stone's arrest."

Looking confused, Gallagher shrugged.

"Okay, I'll go with you."

As they left the station in Fraser's Interceptor, Gallagher turned on the stereo and pressed *Play*.

The last song Fraser had listened to was still queued up and the opening notes of *Runaway Train* filled the vehicle as they drove toward Sanctuary Street.

When they pulled into the apartment complex, Fraser was disappointed not to see Bailey's black Expedition parked in its usual place outside.

As he pulled into a space, he noticed Cate Flynn walking past with Ludwig on a leash.

Stepping out of the SUV, he called to her.

"Evening, Cate. How's it going?"

As Cate approached, Fraser smiled at Ludwig and bent to

scratch the German shepherd behind the ears.

"Is Bailey around?" he asked, looking up at Cate.

"No, she went to give Luisa Santos a ride home."

She checked her watch.

"She's actually been gone a while. Did you need her?"

"Not really," he admitted. "I was just hoping to hear all about Jordan Stone. I know he was arrested."

Cate nodded.

"From what I heard, Dalton West managed to track Jordan Stone and Tamara Vincent up to Virginia. Apparently, they'd been hiding in some sort of survival bunker."

"Stone was holed up in a billionaire bunker?" Gallagher asked as his eyes lit up with interest. "I've heard all about those online. There's a lot of crazy stuff going on out there."

Based on the way Gallagher said it, Fraser suspected his partner considered the *crazy stuff* to be a good thing.

"I'm actually getting worried about Bailey, though," Cate said as she looked up at the darkening sky. "I didn't expect her to be gone so long. Our dinner will be getting cold."

Taking out his phone, Fraser tried calling Bailey again but she still didn't answer.

"Now, *I'm* starting to get worried," he said. "After all, that troll we're looking for already tried to shoot her once before."

Cate stared at him in shock.

"Are you saying the online troll Bailey's looking for is the same guy who shot her at the coffee shop? The one she can't remember?"

Fraser winced, realizing he might have said too much.

"It does look as if the troll who had threatened Rachel Cho

and Krystal Devine also sent a death threat to the owner of the coffee shop the day she was killed," he admitted.

A look of panic flickered in Cate's eyes as she absorbed what Fraser was saying.

She reached into her pocket for her phone, tapped on the screen, and held it to her ear.

"Stupid voicemail," she said under her breath.

After a pause, she left a message.

"Dalton, I'm trying to get in touch with Bailey. She was supposed to give Luisa Santos a ride home from the cemetery and still hasn't come home. I guess the only thing for me to do now is to go out there after her."

Turning to Fraser and Gallagher, she sighed.

"You guys want to go with me?"

"I guess we'd better," Fraser said. "I already told Linette I'd be home late because I was going to check on Bailey. I can't very well show up now and say I didn't even see her."

He climbed into the passenger seat of Cate's Lexus as Gallagher squeezed into the backseat along with Ludwig.

When they pulled into All Souls Cemetery fifteen minutes later, they saw Bailey's Expedition parked behind a white Toyota that Fraser assumed belonged to Luisa Santos.

Both vehicles were empty.

He stood and looked around the dark cemetery, hoping to see Bailey or Luisa walking toward him, but neither woman was there. Then Ludwig barked and ran forward, moving down a narrow path between the gravestones.

Fraser followed after him, managing to grab hold of his leash just as the German shepherd stopped in front of a grave. With a loud bark, he whined and sniffed at the ground.

Spotting the name on the headstone at the same time he saw the bloodstain, Fraser turned to Cate.

"Stay here and call 911. Tell them we need police backup and an ambulance here ASAP."

He turned to Gallagher.

"You and I will take Ludwig and search for Bailey. We need to find her before the troll does."

CHAPTER THIRTY-SEVEN

Grendel scurried through the railroad yard, taking potshots under the train cars and into the boxcars, staying in the shadows, angry at himself for letting Bailey Flynn get away again. How had he missed the shot?

He had known Luisa would act as the perfect bait and Bailey had shown up according to plan. But then she'd had to bend down just as he pulled the trigger.

"You're lucky, you know that, Agent Flynn?" he called out. "That's the second time you escaped my bullet."

"And you're a coward," Bailey shot back. "Too scared to use your real name online. Too scared to show your face in real life."

Anger surged through Grendel as he moved forward, trying to home in on the agent's voice.

Is she inside one of the railroad cars? Or is she on top of one? Or maybe underneath one?

"I know who you are," she called out. "I know you were the courier for Jordan Stone. I know you came to Holbrook's Coffee Company and tried to kill me."

Her voice trembled with emotion. He wasn't sure if the emotion was anger or fear, but he liked it.

"I know it's you, Rodrigo."

The sound of his real name momentarily stopped Rodrigo Santos in his tracks.

"Or would you rather me call you SirGrendel88?"

Shaking off the shock, he started moving again. He needed to find her. He needed to kill her.

"So, you regained your memory, Agent Flynn."

It was a statement, not a question.

"That's good," he said. "Now you'll remember what I said when I shot you at the coffee shop. You'll remember that Mr. Stone wasn't the only one who wanted you dead."

He jerked open the door to a boxcar.

"I've wanted to put a bullet in your head for years. Ever since the day you let my daughter die."

Lunging inside the old metal container, he saw that the boxcar was empty.

"Do you remember? The police called me to the park that day. They told me to ask for you. When you showed me my daughter...when I saw Ronnie lying on the ground? I couldn't believe it.

"I couldn't believe he killed her, or that you'd been stupid enough to shoot him. You didn't even give me a chance to ask the bastard why he'd done it. Or to see his face when I gutted him like the animal that he was."

Rage and hate roared through him for the man who'd been his jail mate and his partner in crime for years.

"Instead of saving my daughter, you allowed her to die next to that God-forsaken pond and..."

Bile rose in his throat at the memory of his daughter's

pink tennis shoe sticking out of the foliage.

"And I swore that one day I would make you pay."

He grinned as he heard movement in the next train car.

"Well, guess what, Agent Flynn? Today's that day."

Racing around the corner of the big, rusty container, he dodged as a bullet skimmed past him.

"I don't want to have to kill you like I killed Godfrey," Bailey called out. "But I will if you force me to."

He could see her shadow. She was standing behind the faded red caboose, waiting for him to make his move.

"I'd rather take you in alive," she called out. "Just like the police up in Virginia took in Jordan Stone alive earlier today. He's probably sitting in a jail cell right now."

"You're lying," Rodrigo said. "You're trying to throw me off. Stone's hiding where nobody can find him. Once I kill you, he's going to-"

"He's not going to do anything for you," Bailey said. "Except put out a hit on you to keep you quiet."

The thought was unsettling.

If Stone thought he might testify against him, he'd put a hit out on him for sure. There would be a price on his head that could be collected whether he was in prison or not.

"Throw down your gun now and I'll let you live," Bailey said. "That's more than you did for Lorraine Holbrook."

Her voice was cold.

"Does your wife know what you are? Does she know what you and Godfrey were? What did you call it? *Partners in crime?* Does she know you were the one who brought that psychopath into your daughter's life?"

"Maybe you can ask her," Rodrigo said. "That is if you can find her. And if she's still alive."

"How did it happen anyway?" Bailey asked. "How did you become such a monster? How did you become Grendel? And how did you manage to find another monster like Godfrey?"

Inching closer, preparing himself to make his move, Rodrigo sneered at the questions.

"I wasn't always a monster," he said.

His jaw tightened at the thought of his miserable childhood.

"I was just a little, wimpy kid like all the others. Just a loser nobody paid any attention to. But then I read about Grendel.

"My moron of an English teacher made us all read that stupid poem Beowulf. Of course, we were supposed to love the hero and hate the monster, but my teacher said one thing that actually made sense.

"He said that without Grendel to conquer, the hero would be useless and the poem would be boring. He told the class that former students always remembered Grendel."

Rodrigo's mouth spread into a nasty smile at the memory.

"That's right. It was the murderous troll and slayer of souls, the monster who terrorized the people around him and ripped off their heads, that was the one they all remembered, not the hero."

"That's when I realized I didn't care if people liked me. I just wanted them to be scared of me. To fear me instead of walking all over me. I wanted to be like Grendel.

"And the first time I was sent to the Summerset Juvenile

Detention Center, I met Ronnie. He was a kindred soul, I guess you could say. We liked the same things. We worked together to take what we wanted from the other inmates. Only Ezra Rosenbaum had to play the tough guy.

"That's why his bones were found there in that caboose. And why his skull was found over there on those tracks. He thought he could beat the monster, but just like Grendel, I took off his head."

Clenching the Beretta in his hand, Rodrigo peered around the corner of the caboose. The agent wasn't there.

"Where are you, Agent Flynn? Don't you want to know why Ronnie killed Dolores? Don't you want to know why he killed my daughter?"

Soft footsteps sounded on the other side of the caboose.

"Ronnie was never able to control his impulses. He was always going in and out of jail. The last time he stopped by my house, I told him not to come by anymore. I didn't want Luisa to see him. I didn't want him to attract the cops' attention. He was pretty mad when he stormed out of there.

"I didn't know Dolores was riding on her skateboard on the sidewalk. I didn't see him take her, but I guess he thought he'd get his revenge for me kicking him out."

Bailey's voice sounded closer than ever when she spoke.

"Why didn't you tell the police that you knew Godfrey?"

"Why should I tell the cops anything? They'd only blame me. Even my own wife would have blamed me if she'd known my old partner killed our daughter.

"Luisa was always threatening to leave me, claiming I was abusive and controlling, telling me to go to therapy for my anger issues. If she'd have known, she'd have left me.

"That's when I decided to start trolling Luisa, too. I figured if she was too scared to leave the house, she'd be too scared to leave me. And once Dolores was gone, Luisa was the only family I had left.

"But, I guess I thought wrong. Turns out Luisa wasn't as scared as I thought. I saw her talking to that writer, Garth Hamilton, this morning. Probably sharing all our secrets and telling him I'm some sort of monster who abused her."

He shook his head in disgust.

"Luisa deserved everything I gave her. She should have kept a better eye on Dolores. She let our daughter be taken and then she expected sympathy and understanding.

"She's no better than the others I killed. The ones who were always trying to get attention or make money off my daughter's death.

"But you, Agent Flynn, were the one I wanted to kill the most. The one who'd let my Dolores die. And when I saw you at that coffee shop, I knew I'd have my chance.

"Not only could I get brownie points with Jordan Stone, but I'd also finally get my revenge. So, you see it really doesn't matter to me if Stone has been captured or not.

"I plan to finish what you started three years ago in Summerset Park. One way or another, it ends tonight."

CHAPTER THIRTY-EIGHT

Bailey listened to Rodrigo's ranting with growing anger as she slowly circled the caboose, biding her time, waiting for the perfect shot. She needed to keep him talking, needed him to reveal what he'd done with his wife.

As she risked another look around the corner of the boxcar, she thought her eyes were playing tricks on her in the dusk, making her see shadowy figures.

Then she realized it wasn't her eyes or some sort of hallucination. Luisa Santos was walking toward her.

The woman's eyes were wide and glassy and blood dripped down her face and onto her blouse.

"I told you to stay in there!" Rodrigo shouted at his wife. "Why can't you ever just listen and do as you're told?"

"I heard you yelling," Luisa answered in a wobbly voice. "I didn't want you to hurt anyone else."

Before Bailey could call to her, Rodrigo lunged out of the shadows. Grabbing his wife by the neck, he held a silver-plated gun to her head and pulled her against him, using her body as a human shield.

Realizing it was the same Berretta she had seen in Rodrigo's hand the morning of the shooting at the Holbrook

Coffee Company, Bailey's heart began to thump in her chest.

Squeezing her eyes shut, she tried to block out the images and sounds that flashed through her mind. The explosion of the gunshot, the moment of impact as she flew backward, the fear and the pain.

She was brought back to the reality of the railroad depot by the sound of Luisa Santos calling her name.

"I'm sorry, Agent Flynn," she gasped. "I never meant to get you involved in all this. He took my phone and sent the text. I tried to stop him. I begged him not to hurt you-"

"Be quiet," Rodrigo ordered his wife. "It's your fault she's here. It's your fault Dolores died. If you'd been watching our daughter properly, none of this would have happened."

His hand tightened around Luisa's throat as he repeated the psalm he'd sent her as SirGrendel88, now changing it to fit with his distorted view of the past.

"For my mother has forsaken me, but the Lord will take me up."

Clenching his teeth, he spoke in his wife's ear.

"You had to go talk to that stupid writer Garth Hamilton, didn't you? He just wants to make money off our tragedy. Like all the others who tried to use Dolores' death for their benefit. That's why I chose them. That's why I killed them."

"What did Rachel Cho ever do to you?" Bailey demanded.

Her outrage grew as she pictured the bones and the jade butterfly necklace in the young student's casket.

"She wrote an article on my daughter's death," Rodrigo said. "She used my family's pain to advance her career."

"And Krystal Devine? What was her crime?"

Rodrigo's face twisted into a grimace.

"She was at my daughter's memorial, shouting into a bullhorn, trying to get attention when she hadn't even known Dolores. She was despicable."

"No, you're the despicable one," Bailey shot back.

Stepping away from the caboose, she aimed her Glock at Rodrigo's head, aiming just between his cold brown eyes.

"You're a psychopath, just like Godfrey. You enjoy torturing and killing people."

"That's right," he said. "And now it's your turn to die."

As his finger tightened on the trigger, Luisa threw her head back, slamming her skull against his nose.

He grunted in pain but kept his hold on the gun, lifting it up and bashing it against his wife's head.

Bailey kept her Glock trained on Rodrigo as Luisa slumped forward, her body now limp as he tried to hold her against him with one arm.

Suddenly, she heard footsteps coming along the tracks behind her. A bark sent adrenaline flooding through her.

Without turning around, she knew that help was coming and that Ludwig was leading the way.

Rodrigo lifted his gun but instead of training it on her, he aimed it at the tracks behind her.

Without hesitation, Bailey took the open shot, knowing she might not get a second chance to stop him from killing someone else. She gasped as the bullet pierced his forehead.

Staggering backward in a spray of blood, he released Luisa, who slumped to the ground.

Bailey turned around just as Ludwig bounded toward her, barking excitedly as Fraser tried to pull him back.

"That dog doesn't listen," Fraser panted as he ran past her with his gun drawn to stand over Rodrigo. "Is that the troll? Is that the guy we've been looking for?"

Looking down at Rodrigo, Bailey nodded wearily.

"I never would have guessed Rodrigo Santos was a killer," Fraser said. "Not to speak ill of the dead, but he always seemed kind of like a wimp."

Footsteps sounded behind them in the dark and the beam of several flashlights announced Gallagher and Cate's arrival.

Fraser knelt beside Luisa, checking her pulse as Cate ran over to Bailey.

"That's the ambulance now," she said as the whine of a siren was heard in the distance.

They both looked over to see flashing lights turn onto the rough gravel road leading up to the decaying depot.

But as the ambulance approached, they saw a black Dodge pickup racing along in front of it.

The truck skidded to a stop and Dalton jumped out.

He ran toward Bailey, keeping his eyes glued to her as if he was trying to convince himself she really was there, and that she really was alright.

As the paramedics jumped out and rushed over to Luisa, Dalton pulled Bailey into his arms, pulling her close as Ludwig barked excitedly beside them.

"I've got you," he said softly. "You're safe now."

CHAPTER THIRTY-NINE

Cate Flynn entered the courthouse and made her way up in the elevator, hoping she wouldn't run into Judge Nelson or anyone else for that matter. She had come on a mission to hunt down Oliver Wen and get information. It had been over a week since Jordan Stone's arrest and she had yet to hear that federal charges had been filed against him.

Stepping off the elevator, Cate followed the signs toward the conference room Oliver had used as a makeshift office in the past but the room was empty.

As she sighed and headed back the way she'd come, she passed the breakroom and caught a glimpse of a tall, thin man with short, dark hair pouring himself a cup of coffee.

When he turned around, she recognized the assistant U.S. attorney for the Southern District of Florida.

"You're just who I was looking for," Cate said. "I understand you're acting as lead prosecutor in the federal case against Jordan Stone."

Oliver gave her a hesitant smile and nodded.

"Yes, that's right."

His dark eyes flicked toward the door as if searching for an escape route past her.

"I'm curious. What charges are you planning to file?" Cate asked. "I know last time we spoke, there wasn't enough evidence to charge him with weapons trafficking and bribery of a public official as I'd recommended."

Oliver cleared his throat.

"Well, fortunately, the situation has changed," he said, shifting his cup of coffee to his other hand. "Several witnesses have come forward and I believe we'll have enough evidence to build a case against Mr. Stone on those charges, as well as conspiracy to commit murder and attempted murder.

"In fact, a search warrant was granted for Jordan Stone's bunker up in Virginia, and evidence of his communications with Rodrigo Santos was found, as was evidence of communications between Mr. Stone and Tony Brunner."

Cate's eyes widened at the news.

"A woman named Tamara Vincent has been talking to my counterpart up in Virginia and says she's ready to testify against Stone and his associates in exchange for an immunity deal and placement in the witness protection program."

The federal prosecutor checked his watch.

"Based on the evidence found in the bunker and Ms. Vincent's sworn statement, a federal warrant for Tony Brunner's arrest is being issued as we speak."

Unable to hide her smile, Cate nodded happily.

"That's good news," she said. "I imagine Mayor Sutherland will be retracting his endorsement of Mr. Brunner shortly thereafter. I can't imagine Brunner will continue his campaign for a seat on the Summerset County bench in any case."

"Whatever happened to *your* campaign?" Oliver asked with

a sudden frown. "I thought you had thrown your hat into the ring a few months ago."

Shrugging her shoulders, Cate smiled.

"I decided to wait for a more opportune time," she said.

As she left the breakroom and headed toward the elevator, she was filled with sudden relief. No doubt Brunner would have to drop out of the race now. His campaign was finished.

She was still smiling when she stepped out of the elevator into the courthouse lobby to see her mother and Mimi Harper.

"We're going to lunch to celebrate," Jackie said. "I'm sure you've heard the news about Tony Brunner's arrest?"

"Yes, I have. And I guess congratulations are in order, *Judge Harper*," Cate said, shooting Mimi a wink. "Looks as if you are the last candidate standing."

Jackie beamed at her friend and then at her daughter.

"And it'll be your turn soon enough, Cate," she teased, ignoring Mimi's sudden look of warning. "You'll give Judge Nelson a run for his money when he's up for re-election in two years' time. The old curmudgeon will-"

She faltered as she caught sight of Judge Nelson standing beside her. Gaping at him in surprise, Jackie began to stammer out an apology but he was already moving toward the exit.

"You don't think he heard me, do you?" she asked as she turned to Cate. "And even if he did, it was just a little joke."

"I'm sure he'll get over it," Cate said, shrugging off Mimi's invitation to join them for lunch. "I'd better go. I have some important errands to run."

Hurrying out to her Lexus, she sped toward the medical examiner's office, eager to see Mason and give him the news about Tony Brunner before he heard it from anyone else.

And if she had time afterward, she might even stop by the Belle Harbor Bridal Boutique. It was about time she decided on a wedding dress.

But all thoughts of weddings and celebrations left her mind as she walked into the lobby of the medical examiner's office to see a small woman with steel gray hair quietly sobbing in one of the red vinyl chairs against the wall.

Before Cate could ask if she was okay, the door to the back opened and Mason walked out, looking somber and holding a clipboard and pen.

"Mrs. Rosenbaum, I'm sorry to have kept you waiting," he said. "I just need you to sign this one form and then we'll get your son's remains over to the funeral home."

Sitting next to her, he waited as she carefully added her signature to the bottom of the form.

"He'll be laid to rest in Summerset Memorial Park," the woman said, looking over at Cate with tears in her eyes.

"That's a very good choice," Mason said. "I'll just get you a copy of this form and you'll be ready to go."

As he disappeared into the back, the woman sniffed and opened her purse, pulling out an empty tissue package.

"Oh, let me get you one," Cate said.

Plucking a tissue out of a nearby box, she held it out to the woman with a sympathetic smile.

"I hear Summerset Memorial Park is a very peaceful place," she said. "I'm so sorry for your loss."

The woman took the tissue and wiped under her eyes.

"My Ezra was such a sweet child," she said quietly. "He got

into some trouble when he was a teenager. But he was a good boy, really. I never did stop wondering where he was and if he was okay."

She smiled as she dabbed away more tears.

"I'll have a place to go visit him now," she said. "It'll be nice to go to bed at night knowing where he is and that he's finally at rest."

As Cate stood beside Mason and watched Ezra Rosenbaum's mother leave, a fresh burst of anger surged through her.

"Rodrigo Santos and Ronin Godfrey caused so much grief to so many people," she said, shaking her head. "I just don't understand why some people enjoy causing others pain."

Pulling Cate toward him, Mason wrapped his arms around her and sighed.

"I've come to believe that some people are just born evil," he said softly. "They only know hate. They don't know what it is to love. Not like we do."

Cate lifted her bright green eyes to his.

"I think you're right," she said. "And I think I'm really glad that Rodrigo Santos can never hurt anyone else again."

CHAPTER FORTY

Bailey followed Dr. Ellis into the session room and sat in the chair across from him with a nervous smile. She hadn't seen the psychiatrist since their last session when she'd suffered a traumatic flashback to the day of the Holbrook Coffee Company shooting. He looked almost as nervous as she felt as he studied her across the room.

"I wasn't sure you'd be back after the last session," Dr. Ellis said. "But I'm glad you've decided to continue with your treatment. How have things been going?"

"Things are actually going better," Bailey said. "My memory of the events leading to my head injury returned a few weeks ago, and while it was upsetting at first, the voices and flashbacks are gone now, as are the headaches, but..."

She hesitated.

"Is there something else that's bothering you?" Dr. Ellis asked. "Something you'd like to discuss?"

Bailey nodded.

"Well, I've been having nightmares and trouble sleeping for years," she said, suddenly feeling self-conscious. "I thought maybe if I tried to figure out why, I could get rid of them like I got rid of the voices and flashbacks."

Shifting in her seat, she shrugged.

"I thought maybe you could help me."

The psychiatrist smiled.

"I can certainly try," he agreed. "Psychotherapy can help you deal with past traumatic experiences that could be at the root of your nightmares. It could help with your sleep and moods. It may even help you be a better agent."

Lifting a hand to tug on his beard, he cocked his head.

"How about we have one session a week to begin? Depending on how it goes, we can adjust the schedule."

"That sounds good to me," Bailey said. "And I'm sure Ford Ramsey will be happy to hear it."

She didn't add that Ramsey's happiness would only apply if she still had a job. And she wouldn't know about that until she met with the SAC later that afternoon.

Once the session was over, Bailey drove over to the FBI's Miami field office, arriving just in time for her scheduled meeting with Ford Ramsey.

As she took the elevator to her usual floor, she wasn't sure what to expect. Not only had she been involved in another fatal shooting, but the man she had killed was the very same man who had shot her in the coffee shop.

The man also happened to work for Jordan Stone, who had ordered the hit, and who was now in federal custody.

Would Ramsey suspect the shooting had been personally motivated? And what was he thinking about her prior connection to Rodrigo Santos, now that it had been revealed that the man had been the reason the undercover operation had been compromised in the first place?

Would she be blamed and summarily fired? Would her career in the Bureau be over? If so, what would she do?

Of course, her mother would love it if she went back to law school, but the thought of it made Bailey cringe.

Maybe Dalton will let me work with him. I would make a good private investigator, wouldn't I?

As she walked down the hall, Bailey saw that the door to Ramsey's office was open and that Aisha Sharma and Will Griffin were sitting at a small conference table by the window.

Sharma offered Bailey a bright smile as she entered the room, and even Will Griffin seemed happy to see her.

"Congratulations," Griff said. "You got the bastard."

Not sure if the agent was talking about Rodrigo Santos or Jordan Stone, Bailey just nodded and took a seat across from Ramsey, who had remained seated at his desk.

"Yes, it seems that congratulations are in order," the SAC said. "Our internal investigations into the Holbrook Coffee Company shooting and the fatal shooting at the Summerset Railroad Depot have been completed."

He smiled.

"You have been cleared to return to work."

Relief flooded through Bailey.

"You mean, I'm not being fired?"

Ramsey shook his head.

"No, you've actually officially been assigned to the Miami office, at least for the time being," he informed her. "In fact, Sharma and Griff have started up a new investigation and I'd like you to join them."

"Is it that money laundering investigation Sharma was

working on?" she asked.

Leaning forward in her chair, she tried to look interested.

"Actually, no," Ramsey said. "This investigation is a little more complicated than that. And it requires complete discretion. If news gets out..."

He lowered his voice.

"Well, let's just say it could get very dangerous, very fast."

Bailey smiled.

"Sounds like my type of assignment."

* * *

On the way home from work, Bailey made a detour to Cascadia Drive, wanting to check on Luisa Santos, who was out of the hospital and back at home.

As she pulled onto the driveway, she saw that the marigolds were back in the window boxes. And when she walked up to the porch, she looked up to see that the security camera was gone.

Perhaps Luisa wanted to remove all signs of Rodrigo.

Bailey knew that the Santos house had been searched from top to bottom after his death and that an old train chisel had been found in the utility room.

DNA from dried blood in the cracks of the handle had been matched to the DNA from Ezra Rosenbaum's bones.

Knocking on the door, Bailey held her breath, wondering if Luisa would be willing to see the woman who had killed her husband.

And perhaps she also blames me for Dolores' death.

But when Luisa opened the door, she greeted Bailey warmly and led her inside, offering her a cup of tea and asking how she was feeling.

"I'm fine," Bailey said, meaning it for the first time in a long time. "I was just worried about you."

"Don't worry, I'm fine, too," Luisa said. "In fact, I just authorized the M.E.'s office to donate Rodrigo's remains to the medical school for research. Maybe someone can figure out what made that man the way he was. I never could."

She sighed and shook her head.

"Rodrigo was always controlling and abusive," she admitted. "And I guess I just learned to live with it. But after Dolores died, he got much worse. He kept his past and his work a secret. I never knew he worked for Jordan Stone. And I never knew he was the troll sending me those messages.

"But I know now that he wanted to keep me scared and hiding. And I know that I'm no longer a prisoner in my own home. I don't have to be afraid anymore."

Bailey drove away from Cascadia Drive feeling hopeful.

Stopping by Morley's house to pick up Ludwig, she was startled to see Garth Hamilton's sportscar parked in the driveway between Sabrina's news van and Dalton's Dodge.

"Are you guys having a party without me?" she asked as Ludwig and Amadeus ran out to greet her, barking happily.

"I guess you could say that," Morley said as he waved to her from a chair beside his grill, tending to what appeared to be vegetable kabobs. "I invited Dalton over and he brought his sister with him. I guess the writer came along as a plus one."

Sabrina rolled her eyes from her position next to Garth on a wooden loveseat.

"We're collaborating on a project. Garth will write and publish his book and I'll produce a special true crime documentary to go with it."

"But, I thought you were writing your own book," Bailey said. "Why give that up?"

Lowering her voice, Sabrina sighed.

"To be honest, I hadn't even started writing Chapter One yet," she admitted. "I guess I'm a reporter at heart. I'm not cut out to be a writer."

"I think we'll make a good team," Garth said. "I just hope there won't be another murder around here before *Slaughter in Summerset County* hits the stores. Otherwise, I'll have to release a revised edition, and that's always a pain."

Leaving Sabrina and Garth to their work, Bailey crossed to the back fence, where Dalton was watching a hefty gopher tortoise munching on dandelions and clover.

"I haven't been fired," she said. "In fact, I've been officially assigned to the Miami field office."

"So, you're staying in South Florida permanently?"

Dalton sounded hopeful.

"Well, nothing in this world is permanent," Bailey said with a wistful smile. "Working as an agent has certainly taught me that. But I'll be staying for the foreseeable future."

"I'll take whatever time I can get," Dalton said, pulling her in for a kiss. "Here's to hoping it's forever."

The End

In the mood for your next thriller series?
Try Melinda Woodhall's
**Lessons in Evil: A Bridget Bishop FBI Mystery Thriller**.
In the first book of the series, criminal psychologist and
FBI Profiler Bridget Bishop tackles a chilling string of
homicides that bear a startling resemblance to a series of
murders committed by a man since convicted and executed
for the crimes.
Read on for an excerpt of Lessons in Evil!

LESSONS IN EVIL

A Bridget Bishop Thriller: Book One

CHAPTER ONE

The needle on the gas gauge hovered on empty as Libby Palmer steered her mother's old Buick down the Wisteria Falls exit ramp. The heavy traffic on the interstate had added an extra hour to her drive back from D.C., and Libby had just decided she was going to run out of gas when the Gas & Go sign came into view.

Eyeing the gas station with relief, Libby turned into the parking lot, brought the car to a jerking halt beside an available pump, and shut off the engine with a resigned sigh.

Her trip into D.C. certainly hadn't turned out the way she'd hoped when she'd left home that morning. Despite her new clothes and valiant efforts to impress the hiring manager at the Smithsonian, she was still woefully unemployed.

So much for showing Mom once and for all that majoring in art history wasn't a colossal mistake.

A fat drop of rain plunked onto the windshield and slid down the glass as Libby opened the door and stepped out into the dusky twilight, credit card in hand.

A hand-written note had been taped over the card reader.

Machine broken. Pay inside.

Looking up at the darkening sky in irritation, Libby pulled the hood of her jacket over her dark curls and hurried toward the store. She hesitated as she saw the missing person flyer taped to the glass door.

It was the third time that day she'd seen one of the flyers with a picture of the pretty blonde girl who'd gone missing from her apartment near Dupont Circle the week before.

Brooke Nelson hadn't been seen since; foul play was suspected. The FBI had been asking anyone with information to call a dedicated tip line, and a slew of the flyers had been posted around Washington D.C. and the surrounding area.

"You going in or not?"

A man in a black jacket and faded jeans held the door open, waiting for Libby to pass through.

"Uh...yeah, sorry about that," she said, ducking her head as she stepped into the brightly lit building.

Wrinkling her nose against the pungent scent of stale coffee which hung in the air, Libby made her way to the counter and presented her credit card to the clerk.

"Twenty dollars on pump one," she said, hoping her card wasn't maxed out. "And can I get the key to the restroom?"

The clerk looked her up and down, taking in her disheveled curls and rain-spattered jacket as he handed her a receipt and a silver key on a red plastic keyring.

His eyes held a suspicious gleam.

"Restrooms are outside to the left." He held up her credit card. "You'll get this back when you return the key."

Libby nodded and stepped back, bumping into the solid figure of a man in line behind her.

"Sorry," she murmured, avoiding eye contact as she turned and headed outside.

Keeping her head down against the spitting rain, she hurried around the little building to the restroom, stuck the metal key in the lock, and found the tiny, tiled room surprisingly clean.

She stopped in front of the chipped mirror over the sink, wiping at the mascara smudged under her disappointed brown eyes.

"You didn't want to work at that stupid museum anyway, did you?" she asked her reflection. "I mean, who'd want to live in boring old Washington D.C. when they could live in exciting Wisteria Falls?"

Rain was falling in a steady downpour by the time Libby had returned the key to the clerk, retrieved her credit card, and pumped twenty dollars' worth of gas into the Buick's big tank.

Dropping back into the driver's seat, she started the engine and pulled back onto the highway, lowering the volume on the radio as she picked up speed, uninterested in the local weather and traffic report.

As she drove over Landsend Bridge, she glanced down toward the Shenandoah River but could see nothing of the dark water churning below the metal and concrete structure.

Always fearful the ancient truss bridge might suddenly give way beneath her, Libby drove cautiously, holding her breath until the Buick's wheels were back on solid ground before pressing her foot toward the floor, eager to get home.

She didn't see the girl standing on the side of the road until she rounded the sharp curve just past Beaufort Hollow.

Stomping on the brakes as the Buick's headlights lit up a pale face framed by sodden blonde hair, Libby brought the car to a sudden stop in the middle of the empty road.

Worried another car may round the curve behind her and plow into her rear bumper, she steered the Buick onto the shoulder and shut off the engine.

With a quick glance in the rearview mirror, she climbed out into the rain and ran toward the girl, who stood beside a black sedan. The car's trunk was wide open, and the emergency lights were blinking.

"Are you okay?" Libby called as she approached the car.

The girl's face was hidden in shadow, no longer illuminated by the Buick's headlights, but the jarring blink, blink, blink of the sedan's emergency lights revealed the outline of her bowed head and thin shoulders.

"Did your car break down?"

Libby's question was met with silence. She wondered if the girl had been in an accident. Perhaps a tire had blown.

Maybe she hit her head on the dashboard. Or maybe she...

The thought was interrupted by the girl's raspy whisper, but Libby couldn't make out what she was saying.

Stepping close enough to put her hand on the girl's thin shoulder, she inhaled sharply.

"You're trembling," Libby said, impulsively pulling off her jacket and draping it over the girl's shoulders. "You must be hurt. Come with me to my car and..."

"Help...me."

As the girl lifted her head, the emergency blinkers lit up a heart-shaped face, which looked strangely familiar.

Libby stared into the girl's tormented blue eyes, her pulse quickening as she pictured the missing person flyer on the door at Gas & Go.

"You're that girl, aren't you? You're Brooke Nelson."

"I'm...sorry," the girl croaked and swayed on her feet as if she no longer had the strength to stand. "I'm so sorry."

The crack of a branch behind Libby sent her spinning around just as a dark figure loomed up in front of her.

A scream froze in her throat as she stared up, gaping in terror. The man's face was half-hidden by the hood of his jacket, but she recognized his cold stare.

Adrenaline shot through her as she saw the knife in his hand. Lunging toward the road in a desperate bid to get back to the safety of the old Buick, she slipped and fell to her knees.

An iron fist reached out and grabbed a handful of her hair.

Snapping her head back, the man pulled her to her feet and wrapped his free arm around her neck.

He tightened his hold until Libby could no longer breathe.

"Brooke and I were...waiting for you," he hissed, his breath coming in excited gasps. "The time...of reckoning is...here."

Waves of dizziness washed over Libby as she scratched and pried at the unyielding arm around her throat, and hot tears blurred the flashing lights around her.

"Stay still...or I'll break your neck."

His breath was hot in her ear as he dragged her toward the open trunk of the sedan, then forced her inside.

She opened her mouth to scream as she looked back and met Brook Nelson's anguished eyes but could only manage a raspy cry before the trunk slammed shut, throwing her into darkness.

* * *

Water trickled somewhere nearby as Libby struggled to open her eyes. Her throat burned, and it was hard to swallow as she blinked around the dimly lit room.

Where am I? What is this place?

Rough walls and a cracked wooden floor held a small metal-framed bed and a straight-backed chair. Rickety stairs led up to a small landing and a narrow door.

"You awake?"

She jumped at the man's voice.

"I thought maybe I'd squeezed too hard."

A dark figure stepped into view. The man who'd forced her into the trunk of his car stared down at her.

"It'd be a shame to go through all that trouble to snatch you only to kill you off so soon."

Studying her face, he reached out a hand to tuck a still soggy curl behind her ear.

Libby cringed in terror but found she couldn't pull away. Her hands were bound to the chair with bright blue duct tape, as were her ankles.

"Where am I?" she croaked, wincing at the pain in her throat. "Why are you doing this?"

He appeared not to have heard her questions as he moved toward the stairs. Propping a booted foot on the bottom step, he stopped and cocked his head as if listening.

"I know what to do," he finally said, giving a resolute nod. "I've read the handbook. I won't take any chances."

Libby looked around the room, confused.

Who's he talking to?

She suddenly remembered Brook Nelson's terrified eyes. The poor girl must have been abducted, too. Was she being held in the same place?

"Where's Brooke?" Libby wheezed out, ignoring the stabbing pain in her throat. "What have you done to her?"

Turning to face her, the man frowned.

"You're not gonna try anything stupid, are you?" he asked, shifting his weight on the creaking wooden floor. "My mentor warned me you'd cause trouble. He told me not to be fooled."

"Who warned you?" she asked, looking up the stairs toward the door. "Is someone else here?"

The man cocked his head.

"I guess you could say that. Now stop asking so many questions. I've got important work to do."

"Please," Libby called out as he turned away. "Tell me what you did to Brooke. Tell me where she is."

Looking over his shoulder, the man shrugged.

"She's served her purpose," he said softly. "As will you."

ACKNOWLEDGEMENTS

I AM IMMENSELY GRATEFUL TO HAVE been given the time, space, and support I needed to write this book by my wonderful husband, Giles, and my five amazing children, Michael, Joey, Linda, Owen, and Juliet.

The ongoing encouragement of my extended family, including Melissa Romero, Leopoldo Romero, David Woodhall, and Tessa Woodhall, keeps me motivated, as do the memories of my mother and sister, who are always with me as I write.

ABOUT THE AUTHOR

Melinda Woodhall is the author of heart-pounding, emotional thrillers with a twist, including the *Mercy Harbor Thriller Series*, the *Veronica Lee Thriller Series*, the *Detective Nessa Ainsley Novella Series*, and the *Bridget Bishop FBI Mystery Thriller Series*.

When she's not writing, Melinda can be found reading, gardening, and playing in the back garden with her tortoise. Melinda is a native Floridian and the proud mother of five children. She lives with her family in Orlando.

Visit Melinda's website at www.melindawoodhall.com.

Other Books by Melinda Woodhall

FORSAKEN SOULS

Her Last Summer
Her Final Fall
Her Winter of Darkness
Her Silent Spring
Her Day to Die
Her Darkest Night
Her Fatal Hour
Her Bitter End
The River Girls
Girl Eight
Catch the Girl
Girls Who Lie
Steal Her Breath
Take Her Life
Make Her Pay
Break Her Heart
Lessons in Evil
Taken By Evil
Where Evil Hides
Road to Evil
Valley of Evil
Save Her from Evil
Betrayed by Evil
His Soul to Keep
His Heart of Darkness
Vanishing Angels
Gathering Bones
Chasing Monsters
Forgotten Remains
Dreading Darkness

Made in the USA
Monee, IL
30 June 2025

20302269R00192